Visit us at www.boldstrokesbooks.com

By the Author

Love On The Red Rocks

The Butterfly Whisperer

Picture Perfect

PICTURE PERFECT

by
Lisa Moreau

2017

PICTURE PERFECT

ISBN 13: 978-1-62639-975-4

This Trade Paperback Original Is Published By
Bold Strokes Books, Inc.
P.O. Box 249
Valley Falls, NY 12185

First Edition: November 2017

CREDITS
Editor: Shelley Thrasher
Production Design: Susan Ramundo
Cover Design By Melody Pond

Acknowledgments

This book wouldn't exist without the hard work of so many people at Bold Strokes Books: Radclyffe, Sandy Lowe, Cindy Cresap, and so many more. A big thank you to my editor, Shelley Thrasher, for your invaluable input, suggestions, patience, and superb copy editing. Also, thanks to Carsen Taite for the awesome marketing job you do for BSB.

This is the first book in which I used beta readers. Ana B. Good and Dena Blake (aka Blondie), your feedback was invaluable. You're both writers with busy schedules so I'm appreciative of the time and effort you took to make this an improved story. You're both super cool chicks.

Speaking of cool chicks, thanks to my BSB writer friends who have given me so much support, advice, and laughs: Kris, Holly, Kim, Jeanie, MJ, Laydin, and so many more.

Judi, I saved the best for last...in more ways than one. You're the most thoughtful, romantic woman I've ever known. Thank you for your support in regards to my writing. It takes away from my time with you so I appreciate your understanding and encouragement. And most of all, thank you for the sweetness and joy you bring into my life. My heart is yours.

Dedication

For Sasha

My niece, most favorite person in the universe, and someone who has taken her fair share of awkward photographs.

Thanks for unintentionally giving me the idea of writing a book about photographers.

CHAPTER ONE

MAMMA PACELLI'S PIZZA

The pungent scent of scorched tomato sauce and blackened peperoni assaulted Gabby Pacelli's nostrils and made her stomach roll. "Did Kevin burn another one?" she asked Tony, who had just opened her office door.

"More like caught it on fire."

Gabby groaned. Maybe hiring the "interloper"—as her mamma called Kevin since he wasn't Italian—had been a mistake after all. He'd worked at Pizza Planet for five years, but they didn't make authentic Italian cuisine, not like Mamma Pacelli's Pizza.

"Give him time. He'll learn," Gabby said, hoping that was true.

"Aren't you supposed to be on a boat right now?" Tony glanced at the pizza-shaped clock above her desk, which had sausages in the place of numbers.

"I missed the boat. Story of my life." Gabby chuckled. "I'll grab the one tomorrow."

"Gina will blow a gasket if you're late."

Why mild-mannered Tony was marrying her Tyrannosaurs Rex of a sister was beyond Gabby. Third born of the six Pacelli sisters, Gina was the most difficult of them all—aside from their mamma, of course. As much as Gabby wanted to go Judas on Gina and tell Tony to catch the next bus to Escapesville, she resisted. The Pacellis were a quarrelsome lot, but they never backstabbed. Families are supposed to protect and care for each other, no matter what.

"I don't know why you're going to Catalina Island so early," Tony said. "The wedding's still a month away."

"Mamma's got it in her head that we need bonding time. Like we don't see each other enough already. Plus, she wants to take pre-wedding photos to give the false impression that we're having a blast and all love each other."

Tony chuckled. "Good thing I love the Pacellis, because when you marry one, you marry them all."

Personally, Gabby was going to Catalina for one reason only, and it had nothing to do with Gina's wedding. If all went as planned, she wouldn't be coming back to Mamma Pacelli's Pizza ever again. Gabby pushed down the guilt that bubbled in the pit of her stomach. If her mamma knew what she was planning, she'd be hotter than the 450-degree oven in the kitchen, and her papa would rise from the grave and bop her over the head with a rolling pin.

Gabby popped an antacid into her mouth and eyed the Pacelli family motto framed on her desk: YOU CAN'T MAKE EVERYONE HAPPY. YOU'RE NOT PIZZA. To them, pizza was a demigod and the sole source of their livelihood. To Gabby...well, she was lactose intolerant, which was equivalent to having the plague. An Italian who couldn't stomach mozzarella was a disgrace. Despite Mamma Pacelli's novenas to, maybe the saint of cheese—Lord knows there's a saint for everything—nothing helped. Finally, Gabby's parents accepted the fact that their youngest child was defective, the first of many of her flaws.

"Will you and Dante be okay covering here until mid-February?" Gabby asked.

Tony scrunched his eyebrows together into a uni-brow, his ebony eyes filled with concern. "That's a month and a half away. You're not coming back after the wedding?"

"We talked about this. I'm staying in Catalina through Valentine's Day. You're handling things before the ceremony, and Dante will take over when you leave for the honeymoon."

"I can do it, but...Dante..."

As though on cue, her eldest sister's husband, who wasn't the sharpest tack in the box, entered the office.

"Oh good, you're still here," Dante said, looking relieved. "Where did you say we keep the time cards?"

Seriously? Was the man blind? They were next to the humongous time clock, where they'd been for umpteen years. If her lazy, loser brother-in-law couldn't handle things while she was gone, then that wasn't her problem. Well, actually it was. When her papa passed away a year ago, Gabby had taken over as general manager. According to the family, she was the only reasonable choice since all her sisters, except Gina, were married with kids. Plus, Gabby had worked at the pizza parlor since she was sixteen and was the only one who'd gone to college, a fact that her mamma frequently reminded her about, along with how expensive it'd been. So, she reluctantly accepted the position, not out of desire, but out of familial duty…and maybe a little guilt.

"Tony, can you show him where the time cards are?" Gabby said. "And remember. You need to collect them on Friday to run the payroll."

The place would probably burn down without her, but Gabby wasn't changing her plans. She took a deep breath and eyed a photograph hanging across from her desk. It was a picture of a hummingbird she'd taken years ago. What she wouldn't give to be that buzzing little bird right now. Free to go anywhere she pleased, no responsibilities, nothing holding her back.

"Oh, I forgot to give you this." Tony handed her a package.

Gabby beamed when she saw the label. It had arrived just in time for her trip. Without thinking, she ripped open the box and pulled out a brand-new Nikon DSLR camera.

"Whoa, that's some fancy equipment. That must have set you back at least a thousand," Tony said.

Gabby stuffed the camera back into the box. "It wasn't that much." Actually, it was more like two grand, but Tony didn't need to know that.

"I thought you said you were giving up photography," Dante said.

"I figured I'd take some pictures on the island."

Tony raised an eyebrow. "That's a professional-looking camera for snapshots."

Gabby shrugged, looked at the caller ID when the phone rang, and groaned. Normally, she wouldn't have answered, but maybe it'd stop Tony from asking any more questions. Reluctantly, she picked up the receiver.

"Where are you?" Gina asked before Gabby could even say hello.

"Uhh, you called the office, sooo take a wild guess."

"You're not on the boat?!"

"Again...office." Gabby looked at Tony and whispered, "It's your blushing bride." He flashed a starry-eyed, lovesick grin. Poor sap. He didn't know what he was in for.

"You're supposed to be here. We're having breakfast with the photographer tomorrow, and the first photo shoot is in the afternoon." Gina huffed and puffed, which probably meant she was walking at warp speed. Gabby could picture people and dogs scattering left and right to clear a path for the tornado.

Gabby heard a commotion of voices in the background, which she recognized all too well as her sisters deliberating at fast-talking, ear-splitting volumes. Gabby hadn't realized how quiet it'd been the past twenty-four hours without her family around.

"Gabriella Maria, where are you?" Ugh. Gina must have given the phone to her mamma.

"At the office. Where I always am."

"Did you miss the boat?"

Gabby sighed. "Yes, but I'll be there tomorrow. Jesus Christ. Can't you'll leave me alone for even one day?"

"Watch your language, young lady! When was the last time you went to confession?"

Gabby rolled her eyes. "I gotta go. Bye." She hung up the phone while her mamma was still yapping. She'd pay for that later, but right now all Gabby wanted to do was get as far away from the stench of burning pizza as she could. Without another word to Tony and Dante, Gabby grabbed her new, professional camera and headed out the door...not looking back.

CHAPTER TWO

SAY CHEEZE

The last thing Olive Hayes wanted to see was Mr. Sanchez in a Speedo. He was a super nice guy who frequently gave her extra relish at his boardwalk hot-dog stand, but that didn't mean she wanted to take a gander at his almost three-hundred-pound physique stuffed into an itty bitty piece of cloth.

"What was that?" Olive hoped—no, prayed—she'd heard incorrectly since Mr. Sanchez's English left a lot to be desired.

"How you say…bar-door?"

"Do you mean boudoir? As in…um…sexy bedroom photos?"

Mr. Sanchez nodded enthusiastically. *Damn.*

Olive sat back in her chair at Say Cheeze photography studio on Catalina Island and inwardly sighed. Mr. Finkelmeier, Olive's boss, cleared his throat and pointed at a sign: THE CUSTOMER IS NEVER WRONG. He thought it was a cute play on words from *the customer is always right*. It wasn't. Mr. Finkelmeier sneered at Olive and disappeared into his office, leaving her alone with the Spanish Casanova.

"Of course, we'd be happy to do that." Olive said "we" knowing it'd be her, not that she'd ever complain.

Mr. Finkelmeier wasn't a horrible boss, except that he consistently stuck her with the undesirable photo shoots while he took the good ones. Even so, Olive was thankful for her job, especially since it was the only photography position on the island.

She could've struck out on her own, but Avalon—the minuscule town on Catalina—didn't need more than one portrait studio. And anyway, inside work wasn't really her thing. She loved photographing landscapes, trees, sunsets, anything nature-related.

"Sooo, when would you like to do the shoot?" Olive opened the appointment book and scanned available dates.

"Before Valentine's Day," Mr. Sanchez said, still smiling and nodding.

Oh, that was kinda sweet. It must be a present for his wife. Not many men would have the nerve to do a sexy photo shoot. Mr. Sanchez had balls—and hopefully ones Olive wouldn't see up close and personal. Yep, he was pretty cool, but that still didn't mean she wanted to see him in a Speedo.

With Mr. Sanchez's photo shoot scheduled and him back to serving hot dogs, Olive reclined in her chair and admired the walls. She'd convinced Mr. Finkelmeier to let her paint the place yellow to brighten things up. Olive often felt claustrophobic in the small office. It consisted of two rooms in a red and white building sandwiched between an ice cream parlor and souvenir shop on Crescent Avenue, the busiest street on the island. One room was Mr. Finkelmeier's office, and the other housed Olive's desk and an array of cameras, tripods, lights, and various backdrops. Now if Olive could just convince Mr. Finkelmeier to change his cheesy—no pun intended—sign, the place wouldn't look half bad. Why he insisted on having a mouse cut-out sitting on the C of SAY CHEEZE, Olive would never understand. This wasn't the Mickey Mouse Club. Mice had nothing to do with serious photography.

Olive looked at her watch. Since she had thirty minutes to kill before lunch, she thumbed through a Catalina Island continuing-education flyer. There were classes in basket weaving, yoga, first-aid training. Last year, she took a course in how to perform the Heimlich maneuver to save a choking victim but luckily hadn't had to use that skill yet.

As Olive flipped through the pages, she halted on the MAKE YOUR PHOBIA YOUR FRIEND seminar. Now that was a class she could use. She stared into space and visualized the scene. Her nerves vibrated like the tail of an angry rattlesnake as she sat on a hard, yellow plastic chair. On wobbly legs she stood and said, "Hello, my name is Olive, and I'm a lily-liver scaredy cat." Or maybe, "Hello, my name is Olive, and I'm a yellow-bellied chicken."

Screw it. No one likes a wuss. Olive tossed the flyer into the trash and grabbed the newest copy of her favorite travel magazine, *Journeys*. Her heart leapt as she turned the pages, completely absorbed in vibrant, crisp photos of the Taj Mahal, Hawaiian volcanoes, the Venice Grand Canal, all places she dreamed about seeing in person. Most of the photos were taken by her favorite photographer, Robert Klein. Olive would love to live his life for just one day. She gazed at a photo of Niagara Falls and lightly ran a finger down the plunging waterfall. She closed her eyes and could practically feel the cool rush of water spray on her skin. Catalina was beautiful, but let's face it. Anyone would get tired of photographing the same scenery over and over. She'd give anything to pack up her camera and travel the world. Well, almost anything.

Olive sighed, closed the magazine, and stuffed it into a drawer. *Maybe someday.* She sat upright and attempted a smile. The last thing she needed to do was to get depressed before having lunch with Nicki. She was an incessantly cheerful person who wasn't satisfied unless Olive sported a ginormous, happy clown face. Speaking of faces, Olive took off her red glasses and slathered SPF 70 sunscreen over her pale complexion. Without it, she'd get redder than a genetically modified tomato, not to mention freckled. Olive hated freckles. They were cute on seven-year-olds but not a woman in her late twenties.

When Olive reached Tito's Taco Stand, Nicki was already seated. She was wearing an ever-present Dodgers baseball cap, Nike tank top, and had a bigger-than-normal smile plastered across her face. They'd met several years ago when Nicki moved to Avalon to start a snorkeling business and had actually gone out on three dates, which in retrospect was hilarious. They fit together girlfriend-wise about as well as Superglue and fingers. Nicki was an over-the-top, obsessive sports fanatic...and that was putting it nicely. Olive, on the other hand, didn't know a field goal from a homerun.

Their first date had consisted of a twenty-mile mountain-bike ride followed by a four-mile hike. Olive was so sore the next day she could barely lift a finger to press the shutter button. Date number two was less physical but no less sporty. They'd had lunch at Frank's Sports Bar, where Olive had spent the entire night staring at Nicki's profile since she couldn't keep her eyes off the LA Lakers' basketball game on the big screen. She'd had high hopes for their third date when Nicki invited her to dinner at her apartment. Her optimism plummeted, though, when she opened the door. Nicki had donned a gold and purple jersey with a number-one foam finger perched on her hand. The real kicker, though, was the "LA" tattooed on one cheek, "Lakers" on the other, and about ten purple stars scattered on her forehead. That might be fine for a stadium getup but not in one's living room. They'd agreed that night, while watching the NBA playoffs, to just be friends and had been ever since. Too bad they hadn't hit it off romantically, since Nicki was the only woman Olive dated who'd stayed on the island.

Olive sat across from Nicki and said, "I'm starving, so don't look at me weird when I order ten fish tacos."

"Guess what I just found out!" Nicki's eyes lit up like two fireflies as she bounced in her chair.

Olive grunted. She hated the guessing game. "That's impossible to know. How am I supposed to—"

"I know you said you weren't entering the Catalina photography contest this year, but when you find out the grand prize and who's sponsoring it, you'll just die. Just *die*!"

This was coming from a woman who screamed uncontrollably at winning five dollars on a scratch-off lotto ticket. Olive wasn't falling for it. So what if they upped the prize from one thousand dollars to two? Or even three? Olive seriously doubted she'd keel over with excitement. And anyway, she was done with that competition.

"The Italian Stallion wins every year by seducing the judges, so what's the point? I'm skipping it this year. Now where's our waitress?" Olive glanced around the restaurant.

"You won last year!"

"That was by default because she got disqualified." In fact, Olive was the one who'd reported the Highness of Hotness when she saw the judge slip into her hotel room at two a.m. Contestants were dissuaded from speaking with the judges, much less giving them orgasms. Not that Olive knew there'd been orgasms, but in her private tell-no-one fantasies, the Italian Stallion *always* produced mind-numbing, ecstasy-rippled, euphoric releases.

"She *is* sexy." Nicki sighed and stared dreamily into space.

Actually, the woman was beyond sexy. Like sexy to the millionth power. Olive would trade her Nikon for even a fraction of charisma the Italian Stallion oozed. She could cast a spell over lesbians and straight women alike with just one wink. Admittedly, Olive had done her fair share of swooning when they'd first met, but that was before she found out what a deceiving, do-anything-to-win woman she was.

Olive snapped her fingers in front of Nicki's face. "Focus, please. Other than last year, I've come in second three years in a row to the She-Devil Temptress." Even though Olive could pick the woman out of a lineup, she preferred to block out her real name and refer to her in creatively invented nicknames.

"She-Devil? That's a new one." Nicki chuckled.

"Just popped into my head. Now where's our freakin' waitress?"

"I never took you for a quitter." Nicki's smile dropped and she shook her head, which made Olive feel slightly ashamed, but not enough to change her mind. "Don't you at least want to know about the contest?"

"Fine. What's the theme this year?" Olive faked interest, hoping it'd take the focus off her being a defeatist.

"The Isle of Love." Nicki swept her arms out in a grand gesture. "The contest takes place on Valentine's Day."

"How original," Olive said sarcastically.

Nicki playfully slapped her arm. "All the entries have to reflect the romance of the island."

"Great. Hundreds of photos with couples holding hands gazing at a sunset."

"You can be more creative than that."

Could she be? The Italian Stallion was creative. In fact, she was known as an unconventional, badass, avant-garde photographer. No one would ever refer to Olive as cutting edge. Olive didn't know why the woman resorted to flirting with the female judges when her work was so good. She didn't need to cheat to win.

Nicki bounced in her seat, so much so that Olive almost looked down to see if she was sitting on a basketball.

"All right, let's have it," Olive said. "What's the grand prize this year?"

Nicki removed her baseball cap and carefully placed it on the table. A shiver ran down Olive's spine. Maybe this was big after all. Nicki had only done that move once. Years ago, Olive had told Nicki about a life-altering event she rarely shared with anyone. At the time, they were in Olive's condo, and Nicki had taken off her cap and placed it on the coffee table. Other than that, Nicki was never seen without a Dodgers hat. Olive wondered if she even slept with it.

"The sponsor is…" Nicki pulled out a flyer and held it against her chest so Olive couldn't see. Talk about overly dramatic. "*Journeys* magazine!"

An electrical impulse sparked in Olive's brain.

"And the winner will be offered a position as staff travel photographer!"

A trillion volts shot through Olive, from head to toe.

Had she heard correctly? Nicki slapped the flyer down on the table. With mouth agape, Olive scanned the text. Slowly, she lifted her head and silently mouthed, "Wow."

"You bet your ass, wow!" Nicki shoved a piece of paper into Olive's hand. "Here's the entry form. The deadline is tomorrow. This is your opportunity to be a real photographer, just like that Klein guy you love so much, and travel the world like you've always dreamed. And with your favorite magazine, no less!"

Olive nodded, her heart pounding wildly. Nicki was right. This was the chance of a lifetime.

"You can get off this island once and for all."

Olive stopped nodding. Oh, right. She'd have to actually leave Catalina, wouldn't she? Her pulse raced, but for a different reason than before. Olive folded the papers and stuffed them into her bag. "I'll...uhh...think about it."

Nicki gawked at her like she'd just said, "Thanks, but no thanks" to Ed McMahon standing in the doorway with a giant multi-million-dollar check. "What's there to think about?" When Olive didn't respond, Nicki's eyes softened and she laid a hand on her arm. "You can do this, Ollie. I know you can. Remember that workshop you dragged me to? What was that woman's name? Happy Sunspot?"

Olive rolled her eyes. "Harmony Moondrop." Okay, so that was a totally made-up, airy-fairy name, but her books and seminars were insightful and enlightening. They'd gotten Olive through several difficult times, but this...this was seemingly insurmountable. Even Harmony hadn't been able to help.

"Right. And remember what she said? 'What you're most afraid of doing is what will set you free.' You even made it into a plaque and hung it on your wall."

"I know...but—"

"No buts. Now let's see that smile I love so much."

Olive attempted a grin, which probably resembled an evil killer clown.

I can do this...I can get off the island...I can...except for the fact that I'm a lily-livered scaredy cat.

CHAPTER THREE

THE ITALIAN INVASION

Mr. Finkelmeier burst into the office like his pants were on fire. He stood in front of Olive's desk practically shaking, whether in excitement or fear she wasn't sure. His pasty, albino complexion was brick red, and the fuzz on his head was standing upright like he'd just been electrocuted. Before Olive could ask if he was okay, he tore into a breathless rampage.

"I just had breakfast with a celebrity who hired us to photograph her daughter's wedding. I'm beside myself." Mr. Finkelmeier paced back and forth. "Do you know what this means?" He stopped and faced Olive, who absentmindedly shook her head. "This could be the beginning of a whole new breed of clientele."

Olive was all for that. They needed some new blood. "Who's the celebrity?"

"Brace yourself."

Instinctively, Olive gripped the arm of her chair.

Mr. Finkelmeier took a deep breath and said, "Mamma Pacelli!"

Who? The name sounded vaguely familiar, but...who?

When Olive undoubtedly looked mystified, he continued. "Of Mamma Pacelli's Pizza. The chain of famous West Coast restaurants. You know, from the commercials." Mr. Finkelmeier attempted to sing a sad rendition of their jingle. "Don't be a clown, for the best pizza in town, it's Mamma Pacelli's..."

That's a celebrity? Olive was thinking more like Angelina Jolie. Now there was a boudoir session she wouldn't mind doing.

"Oh, right. I know who you're talking about." And she did know, because the large Italian screaming through the TV always made her want to change the channel. Mamma Pacelli wasn't exactly the warm, cozy type. "So I'll get to photograph her daughter's wedding?" Tingles rippled down Olive's spine. Maybe she'd have a chance to do real photography for a change.

"I'll be doing that, of course." Mr. Finkelmeier said it in a way that made Olive feel stupid for even asking.

"Of course." She sank into her chair.

"But you'll be in charge of the pre-wedding events for Mamma Pacelli and her daughters."

Olive raised an eyebrow. "What exactly does that entail?"

"You'll capture whatever they want. And I do mean *whatever*." Mr. Finkelmeier leaned over the desk, nose-to-nose with Olive, so close she knew he'd had garlic for breakfast. "It's imperative that Mamma Pacelli be happy, Olive. The future of the company is counting on you."

Olive felt like she were about to go into battle to save the world from alien forces. "I'll do my best," she said and resisted the urge to salute.

"No. You'll do better than that." Mr. Finkelmeier's beady eyes glared.

"Right. You can count on me."

"Good. Mamma Pacelli and her daughters will be here any minute to go over the schedule." Mr. Finkelmeier broke out in a wide smile and skipped into his office, giddy as a schoolgirl.

Olive was about to Google the new clients when she heard voices. Loud voices. And lots of them. The door swung open, and a barrage of hair, legs, and boobs piled in. The pack was ushered by Mamma Pacelli, who looked exactly like she did on TV: two hundred pounds of feisty, pure Italian pride packed into a five-foot frame. Following close behind were five identical women, who were probably her daughters, although that was difficult to fathom considering they looked like super models. They wore clinging black shirts that accentuated their upper assets, and snug black miniskirts that accentuated their lower assets, along with wide, looping silver belts. They had dark-brown eyes, long, shiny, voluminous hair, unblemished olive complexions, and each stood over six feet tall in heels. Even their stance was identical, with one hand on a jutted right hip. Sex appeal radiated off them like steam from a hot iron.

Suddenly, everyone stopped yapping when Olive stood, and six pairs of dark eyes appraised her critically, like she'd just intruded on a personal conversation. Tentatively, Olive steadied herself with a hand on her desk, glad to have a shield between her and the gang.

"Who are you?" Mamma Pacelli asked in a thick Italian accent.

"I'm Olive. Your…uhh…photographer."

Mamma Pacelli's eyes narrowed. "*Sei troppo giovane.*"

"Excuse me?"

"She said you're too young," one of the goddesses said and smacked her gum.

Mr. Finkelmeier came out of his office and practically bowed at Mamma Pacelli's feet like she was the pope or something. "Welcome! These must be your beautiful daughters."

"Bianca Adele, Gina Luciana, Rose Marie, Isabella Elena, Bella Francesca. And this is Nonna." Mamma Pacelli frantically scanned the office. "Where's Nonna?"

A shriveled-up raisin of a woman peeked from behind a pair of legs. She had sunken eyes, hair as white and fluffy as a cloud, and protectively clutched an over-sized shiny black purse like it was the Hope Diamond.

"Ah, that is Nonna, Mamma to my dearly departed Alberto." Mamma Pacelli made the sign of the cross and nudged the woman next to her, which prompted everyone to cross themselves at warp speed.

Mr. Finkelmeier bowed down to be eye level with the elderly woman. "How are you today?"

"She no speak." Mamma Pacelli waved her hand.

Mr. Finkelmeier straightened and looked the herd over. "Are we missing someone? I thought you had six daughters."

Six!? Five wasn't enough? As it was, Olive would never remember all those names.

Mamma Pacelli turned to one of the women. "Gina, did you call her again?"

Suddenly, the woman burst into tears...except there were no actual tears, just a lot of wailing, contorted expressions, and shoulder-shaking. "Gabby is going to ruin my wedding! She's late for everything and refuses to wear a dress."

The supermodels circled the fake crier, hugging her like she'd just been crowned Ms. America. Only one of the sisters stood aside and dramatically rolled her eyes.

Gina, the distressed bride-to-be, pulled out a phone, punched in a number, and said through a sob, "Mamma wants to talk to you."

Mamma Pacelli grabbed the phone. "Gabriella Maria, *vieni immediatamente!*" Pause. "Don't oh-Mamma me." An even longer pause. "*Vieni qui!*" Mamma Pacelli jabbed the phone at the eye-roller. "Isabella, talk some sense into your sister. You're the only one she listens to."

Isabella scurried into a corner and spoke in hushed tones.

"*Scusi.* My youngest daughter, Gabriella, can be...difficult."

Mr. Finkelmeier nodded like he understood what it was like to have a problem child, even though he was childless.

Gabriella Pacelli. Something about that name sounded familiar, something that sent a shiver down Olive's spine. Where had she heard the name Pacelli before, aside from the pizza commercials?

❖

Gabby considered throwing her phone into the ocean. She saw her mamma and sisters every single day. Couldn't they leave her alone for even an hour? She loved her family, but they were downright smothering sometimes...all right, all the time. Gabby held her cell away from her ear as her mamma screamed something in Italian. She stayed in that position for several long seconds until she heard Isabella's voice. Out of all her sisters, Gabby was closest to Isabella, probably because they were only a year apart. They told each other everything.

"Izzy, is that you?"

"Mamma told me to talk some sense into you. Like that's possible." Isabella snorted. "You better get here soon before Gina has a meltdown."

Gabby growled. "I told her I was on my way."

"As a little incentive to get here faster, our photographer is adorable. Just your type."

Gabby perked up. "Oh yeah? Does she play for my team?"

"Not sure, but when has that stopped you?"

"True. What's the name of this place again?"

"Say Cheeze."

"Say what?"

"Cheeze, as in...you know...cheese."

Gabby knew cheese. She was surrounded by it every single day, along with tomato sauce, onions, anchovies, spices, and on and on.

"Gina had us all dress alike in black skirts and shirts. We look like gothic quintuplets. She has your outfit here."

"I'm *not* wearing a skirt."

Gabby was not looking forward to the inevitable fights in the coming weeks over her attire, particularly the bridesmaid dress. No way in hell was she wearing that God-awful hot-pink, chiffon nightmare. Gabby didn't do dresses and she didn't do hideous.

"What's all that noise? Where are you?" Isabella asked.

"I'm on a boat in the middle of the Pacific Ocean." Gabby sat upright and craned her neck. "I can see the island so I'm not too far away. Probably fifteen minutes or so, but I have to go to the Chamber of Commerce to register for the photography contest. The deadline is today."

"I don't know why you'd want to enter, after what happened last year."

Heat rose to Gabby's cheeks. She'd never been so humiliated. She'd love to get her hands on the person who turned her in for fraternizing with a judge. *Probably a jealous, third-rate photographer.*

"When are you going to tell Mamma?" Isabella asked. "You promised to give up photography."

"I know. I'll figure that out later if I win."

"You'll win."

Gabby grinned. Isabella had always been her biggest supporter. At least her only supporter when it came to family.

"I'll get there as soon as I can, and don't breathe a word about the competition."

"I know. Listen. I gotta go. Mamma's giving the photographer a hard time."

"Okay. Go protect my future girlfriend."

Isabella chuckled, probably at Gabby's choice of words. Gabby didn't have girlfriends. She had flings, lovers, affairs, one-night stands, but never girlfriends.

Gabby's heart pounded when her eye caught a pod of dolphins jumping and swimming through the water like a torpedo, as though they were racing the boat. She grabbed her Nikon and snapped photos. There had to be at least twenty-five of them. Their contagious energy and joy made Gabby's lips curl into a smile. This was why she loved photographing wild creatures. They were so free, uninhibited. Gabby lowered her camera as the dolphins increased speed and whizzed past the boat. She watched until they disappeared into the horizon. Why couldn't the Catalina contest be called Isle of Wildlife instead of Isle of Love? She didn't know much about that particular emotion.

Gabby stretched out her legs and raised her face to the sun. This was the perfect place to be, with the wind in her hair, a cool mist of salt water on her skin, and as far away from work as possible. Maybe the boat would speed past Catalina and go all the way to Hawaii. She could live out her days in a secluded hut, making love to hula girls and taking photographs. She'd never have to look at another pizza again. Or better yet, Gabby could take the grand prize and travel the world as *Journeys'* top photographer. Even though she'd said "if I win" to Isabella, Gabby knew she was a shoo-in.

Her stomach soured as the exhilaration quickly turned to panic. When Gabby's papa died, she'd promised to give up her "silly" (as her mamma put it) dream of being a photographer and take over the family business. She'd regretted the promise the moment it was out of her mouth. At the time, though, her mamma had been hysterical about losing her husband and the possibility of their livelihood going down the drain. Gabby had not only picked up where her papa left off, but had made Mamma Pacelli's Pizza even more of a success than he had. How could she tell them she was quitting? How could she disappoint her mamma, Nonna, her sisters, and, most of all, her papa?

Gabby pulled a tin can of Spezzatina out of her bag and squinted as the sun glared off the box. She opened it, grabbed a miniature black licorice, tossed it high into the air, and caught it in her mouth.

"Impressive."

Gabby looked up to find a towering, gorgeous woman standing beside her. She had long blond hair, eyes the color of the Pacific Ocean, and shapely tan legs. Just the type of woman Gabby would date, if she actually dated, so more like the type she'd sleep with.

"Quite a talented mouth you have." The woman cocked her head and smirked.

Gabby lowered her voice an octave and flashed a sexy grin. "You don't know the half of it."

"Maybe you can show me sometime." The woman sat beside Gabby, so close that a sliver of paper wouldn't have fit between them. "When we're alone, that is."

This woman was definitely flirting, which happened often with Gabby, but not quite so overtly.

"Do you plan to get me alone?"

"If I'm lucky." The woman crossed her legs, Gabby's eyes glued to smooth, toned thighs.

"Oh, I think you could get lucky." Gabby held out her hand. "Hi, I'm Gabby."

The woman pumped her arm twice in a firm handshake. Even though the flirty woman was dressed casually, she carried a briefcase and computer bag, and exuded the self-assurance of a highly paid executive.

When the woman didn't respond, Gabby asked, "And you are?"

"Do we really need names?"

"I suppose not, but I usually don't allow anyone to get me alone unless I at least know her name first."

The woman stared into space until she finally said, "You can call me Carmen."

Was that her real name? It sounded made-up in an opera sort of way. But then again, did it really matter?

The woman leaned closer and inhaled deeply. "Is that oregano and...maybe red pepper?"

Gabby inwardly groaned. One of the many drawbacks of working in a pizza joint was consistently reeking of spices. "Yeah. I manage a chain of pizza restaurants. What do you do for a living?"

"That's not important, is it?"

"No, I suppose not, but why so secretive?"

"I like to keep things simple. I find that the less that's shared the better."

Gabby couldn't have agreed more. It made it so much easier to part ways in the end...and there was always an end.

Carmen smiled and placed a hand on Gabby's leg. "Trust me. I won't hold back on the important things."

Sex. The woman was most certainly referring to sex.

"What's that?" Carmen motioned toward the tin can in Gabby's hand.

"Spezzatina. Would you like one?" Gabby popped open the lid.

"I believe I've had those in Italy. Are you Italian?"

"One-hundred percent."

"So is it true what they say? Are Italians passionate between the sheets?"

Gabby smirked. "I can't speak for everyone, but I've never had any complaints."

"I bet you haven't." Carmen laid an arm across the back of Gabby's chair. "How long will you be in Catalina?"

"A month." Carmen didn't need to know about her sister's wedding, the photography contest, or anything else. Like she'd said, keep it simple.

"Perfect. We should get together. What's your number?" As Gabby rattled off her cell, Carmen entered it into her contacts.

Maybe this trip wouldn't be so bad after all. Gabby had no trouble getting hot women, but they usually didn't fall out of the sky and land in her lap. This was almost too good to be true.

❖

With the missing sixth Pacelli, the photo shoot was delayed a day, which was fine by Olive. It'd give her some time to look over Mamma Pacelli's elaborate schedule. Olive glanced at the clock when her stomach grumbled. She hadn't eaten in almost six hours.

She stuck her head in Mr. Finkelmeier's office. "I'm off to lunch."

He peered over his spectacles. "Be back by two. Remember you have a PSP."

"PSP?" Olive wracked her brain trying to remember what that stood for. Mr. Finkelmeier's insistence on speaking in acronyms annoyed the hell out of her.

"Photoshoot with pets."

Ugh. She'd mentally blocked the Johnson's appointment. Photographing rambunctious kids was bad enough, but toss in a dog or cat, and that spelled chaos. Once, she'd spent an hour attempting to take a reasonably good shot of a boy and his German shepherd. That pooch wouldn't sit still for anything, not to mention the issue of his weak bladder.

When Olive returned from lunch, she wondered if she'd walked into Say Cheeze or a zoo. It took a moment to comprehend what she was seeing. A boy held a leash with a large, angry-looking iguana on the other end, a parakeet continuously squawking "you suck" as he sat on another boy's shoulder, and…Olive did a double take…a monkey was sitting in her chair. A real-life, living, breathing primate, which for a second, she thought was funny since she'd often said that a monkey could do her job. Apparently, the Johnson kids were too exotic for a dog.

"Oh, good. You're here." Mr. Finkelmeier grabbed Olive's arm and pulled her into the office. She gazed from the monkey to the iguana to Mr. Finkelmeier's bald head as he retreated into his office and slammed the door.

"Uh, hi?" Olive said to Mrs. Johnson, but she kept the monkey in her peripheral vision when he jumped on her desk and scratched his belly. He looked like he could pounce on her at any moment.

"I believe our appointment was for two." Mrs. Johnson tapped her watch.

"Sorry I'm a little late." Olive flinched when the iguana hissed. Just how sturdy was that leash? Seems like the kid could have a better hold on the thing. Did iguanas have sharp teeth? Olive really should have paid more attention when they covered reptiles in school.

"Wow, so these are some interesting pets," Olive said.

"We like to encourage our kids to be unique." Mrs. Johnson puffed out her chest.

No kidding.

Olive approached the boy and parakeet, since they seemed the most harmless, and guided them in front of the forest backdrop.

"Fat-ass," the parakeet screeched as the kid giggled. Olive shot the bird a dirty look and resisted the urge to spout a retort. She was far too mature to argue with a winged creature.

Olive positioned the boy and iguana—making sure to stay clear of the reptilian creature—next to the foul-mouthed parakeet. Now for the monkey. Olive glanced around, but he was nowhere in sight. She looked at Mrs. Johnson, who pointed upward. The damn ape was sitting by the mouse on the Say Cheeze sign. Great. How in the world was she supposed to coax a monkey down? This was worse than trying to get a cat out of a tree.

Olive looked at Mrs. Johnson and sighed. "Guess you don't have a banana on you?"

The woman leered, her mouth set in a hard, thin line. She'd be no help.

"Here, monkey," Olive said as she repeatedly snapped her fingers.

"Dingbat," the ornery parakeet squawked.

"Birdbrain!" Okay, maybe she wasn't so mature after all, but that blooming bird wasn't helping an already tense situation.

"The monkey's name is Chuckles," one boy said. "Hold out your arms and he'll jump down."

That sounded like it could be painful...for Olive. But since the finger-snapping was going nowhere, she did as suggested. The beast immediately leapt off the sign, wrapped his prickly, hairy arms around Olive's neck, and yelped in her ear. She really needed to ask for a raise.

After an hour of fighting with the monkey, dodging iguana bites, and having her self-esteem bashed by a parakeet, Olive collapsed into her chair.

Mr. Finkelmeier peeked his head out of the office. "Are they gone?"

"Yes. It's safe to come out now." *You deadbeat sloth.* But Olive didn't say that. Instead, she bit her tongue, as always.

Mr. Finkelmeier strolled out of his office. "I have to take off early today, so be sure and lock up when you leave." He slammed the door on his way out.

Olive propped her feet on the desk and rubbed her tired, itchy eyes. That was one photo shoot that would go down in the books, and unfortunately, she'd done many others like it. Olive couldn't believe she'd been at Say Cheeze for ten years. Ten years of snapping photos that took little to no creativity, ten years of doing Mr. Finkelmeier's dirty work, ten years of daydreaming about being a travel photographer. She was twenty-eight, for Christ's sake. Would she still be here when she was thirty? Forty?

Olive grabbed the Catalina Isle of Love entry form and began filling it out. It was time. Past time. She was determined to win the contest, and nothing would stand in her way. Not her job. Not the Italian Stallion. And not even the fact that she'd never been off the island...ever.

CHAPTER FOUR

THE SIXTH SISTER

When the clock struck six, Olive grabbed her camera, locked up Say Cheeze, and headed to the marina. She didn't lead the most exciting life, but there was something to be said for routine. She got up at seven, went to work, and took random photos until quitting time, when she'd hang out by the beach until the sun set. She found comfort and safety in knowing what to expect in a day. Not that she was a control freak, but surprises weren't high on her list. She'd had enough of those from ex-girlfriends. Just when she'd get close to someone they'd suddenly announce that they were moving. They'd all recite the same customary speech: we'll keep in touch, long-distance relationships work, I'll visit, blah, blah…none of which would ever happen. How would she ever have a meaningful, long-term relationship like that?

Olive stepped onto the cobblestone street and lifted her face to the sun. Catalina was a picture-postcard island in the Pacific Ocean twenty-six miles from Southern California. The only way to reach it was by boat or helicopter. It consisted of rugged hills, a craggy coastline, brightly painted quaint shops, and crystal-clear waters. It was considered one of the top ten romantic islands in the world. It did, though, have a few peculiarities. The post office didn't deliver, but the grocery store did, and everyone drove golf carts instead of cars. Considering the small size of Avalon, it was easier to maneuver and park on the narrow streets in miniature transportation. But Olive lived in a condo in the hills. As her golf cart trudged up the steep incline, she always felt like the little engine who could, often reciting to herself, "I think I can, I think I can."

Olive smiled when she approached Mr. Piccolo's SnoCone Zone. She'd known him since she was a kid, and he always reminded her of the scarecrow from the Wizard of Oz: tall, lanky, and gangly armed. Once, when she was six, she'd asked him if he had a brain, which had provoked a boisterous belly laugh. He was one of the nicest residents on the island and someone Olive owed a heck of a lot to.

"Hey, Mr. P. How's business?" Olive stepped up to the rainbow-colored kiosk and rested her elbows on the bar.

"Olive! So good to see you. It's chillin', but I expect things to pick up soon." Mr. Piccolo winked and vigorously shook a pink, syrupy concoction in a clear jug. "I could still use some help if you're interested."

For years, he'd tried to convince Olive to ditch her job and work for him. Although he was much nicer than her current boss, frozen fun wasn't exactly her passion. There was a travel photography job with her name on it. Somewhere. Someday.

"I formulated a new flavor. Here. Take a taste." Mr. Piccolo handed Olive a shot glass of shaved ice. "You can help me come up with a name."

As Olive chugged down the snow cone, her lips immediately puckered, and the glands in her neck twisted like a pretzel. Could it have been any tarter?

"What do you think?" Mr. Piccolo asked, seeming anxious.

"Well," Olive said, not wanting to hurt his feelings. "It has a hint of apple, so maybe you could call it apple pie or…sour apple or…I've got it! Tongue twister." That was exactly what had happened when she'd tasted the bitter concoction.

"That's it! Olive, you're a genius."

"Glad I could help, but I better get going. Tell the missus hi for me."

Olive waved as she walked away. She was thankful for the few long-standing Avalon citizens, since the island could be a revolving door. Just when she'd get to know someone they'd move to the mainland. That went for friends as well as lovers.

Olive gazed at hundreds of sailboats in the sparkling turquoise water. She took out her camera and snapped a few photos. Olive loved photography more than anything. When she was eight, her parents had given her a camera for Christmas, and she was instantly hooked. One of the first photos she took was of her grandmother hand-stitching a shirt while sitting on a worn-out green couch. The elderly woman was gazing over bifocals with a slight grin on her tired, weathered face. Not three hours after the photo was taken, Olive's grandmother had a stroke and died. Olive had stared at the picture for days afterward, marveling at the power one image could hold. That photograph was the only tangible icon of her grandmother. In a constantly moving, revolving world, a picture was permanent. It didn't change and it never disappeared.

As dusk set, the sky streaked in vibrant red and orange. Olive took images of the ocean, sailboats, and the setting sun. Every shot looked amazing. Some of these might even be good enough for the Isle of Love contest. But then again, she needed something more original than a sunset to win.

Lost in a world of brilliant colors, Olive flinched when she heard a loud voice. It sounded like someone said "turn around." She kept snapping pictures, sure the comment wasn't directed at her. Suddenly, a pair of big brown eyes filled Olive's camera lens, causing her to stumble backward. A woman had stepped right in front of her.

"Turn around," the voice repeated.

Olive lowered the camera and fumbled it in her hands. If it hadn't been hanging from her neck it surely would've crashed to the ground. Olive stared at the woman and blinked several times. It wasn't just any woman. It was the Italian Stallion! Olive had never been this close to her, at least not enough to see her reflection in quite possibly the most beautiful eyes ever. They were the color of toffee with swirls of chocolate and tiny mahogany flecks. No, maybe more like honey sprinkled with cinnamon. What was Olive thinking? They were just eyes, an apparatus used to utilize the sense of sight. She'd never put this much thought into the color of someone's eyes before...chocolate, honey...she must be hungry. It was almost dinnertime.

Olive took a gigantic step backward, the Italian Stallion's face coming into full view. Could her bone structure be any more perfect? And her skin looked so soft and smooth, Olive was tempted to stroke her cheek. Luckily, though, she had the sense to know that would be highly inappropriate, not to mention embarrassing.

"Sorry. I didn't mean to scare you," the Italian Stallion said.

Surprisingly, her voice was soft, almost musical. Olive waited for her to say something else, sure that the sound of her first words was just a fluke.

"If you don't hurry, you're going to miss it."

Nope. Not a fluke. Her tone was as refreshing as a tall, cold glass of sweet tea in the middle of a sweltering July. Apparently, Olive was not only hungry but thirsty, too.

The Italian Stallion raised a perfectly manicured eyebrow and gawked at Olive. On a scale of one to ten, her irritation looked close to a nine, and understandably so, since it'd been several seconds, or maybe even minutes, and Olive still hadn't uttered a word.

Finally, sounds tumbled out of her mouth. "Umm...miss what?" It wasn't the most eloquent response, but at least it was something.

"The ultimate photo op."

Olive wrinkled her brow. "Aren't you pointing in the wrong direction? The sunset is over there. Not behind me." *Was the woman blind?*

The Italian Stallion sighed dramatically, grabbed Olive's shoulders, and whirled her around. Just as Olive was about to protest at being manhandled, she was struck by a breathtaking sight. The lighting couldn't have been more perfect. Everything was illuminated in a warm pink glow, the brightly colored buildings more vibrant than she'd ever seen. Even the touristy T-shirt shops took on an iridescent, otherworldly feel. None of that, though, compared to the people. Many had stopped on Crescent Avenue to admire the sunset, the look of awe on their faces priceless.

"This light isn't going to last forever," the woman warned her.

Even though Olive was irked that she'd been right, she snapped several photographs anyway. The scene was too good to pass up.

Olive peered at the Italian Stallion out of the corner of her eye. Catalina wasn't the only thing that looked beautiful in the lighting. The woman's toffee, chocolaty, cinnamon eyes sparkled, and her complexion glowed in the soft rays. She looked so breathtaking Olive was tempted to take a picture. Instead, she mentally conked herself over the head. What was she thinking? This was the Italian Stallion she was swooning over. Beauty did not trump honorability. Not in Olive's world, anyway.

"Never forget what's behind you," the Italian Stallion said. "Most people only look at the obvious, which is usually what's in front of them."

"Right. Got it." Olive didn't particularly want a speech, so she squatted and began packing up her camera.

"Also, when taking a sunset, the key is to slightly underexpose by using a fast shutter speed. That makes the colors look more rich and defined."

What was this? Photography 101? Olive lived on an island. If anyone knew how to photograph a sunset, it was her. In fact, she'd taught a continuing-education class on that one topic alone.

"Got it," Olive said sternly.

"Just trying to give you some tips to be a better photographer."

Olive stood and stared the Italian Stallion dead in the eye... well, almost in the eye since the goddess was a few inches taller, not to mention built like an Olympic swimmer. "What makes you think I'm not already a good photographer? Or for that matter a fabulous one?"

The Italian Stallion held up her hands in defense. "Don't get your feathers ruffled. Just trying to help."

Olive slung her camera bag over her shoulder. "I gotta get going."

"What's your rush? You live around here?"

"Not interested, thanks."

Olive started to walk away, but the Italian Stallion grabbed her arm. "Hey, that wasn't a come-on. Although, if you want to get together we could..." The way her voice trailed off was probably due to Olive's no-way-in-hell expression. "Actually, I was asking because I wondered if you knew where the photography studio Say Cheeze is located."

Olive eyed her suspiciously. Why would she want to know that? "It's a few blocks down this street, but they're closed."

The Italian Stallion looked at her watch and mumbled something about being late. She grinned, held out her hand, and said, "I'm Gabby Pacelli, by the way."

Olive's heart skipped a beat. Pacelli. She was the missing sister from the photo shoot! Olive limply shook her hand.

Gabby squinted, studied Olive closely, and wagged a finger. "Hey, don't I know you? And that's not a come-on, either. You look familiar."

Seriously? She doesn't recognize me? We've been in the same photography contest the last three years. Obviously, Gabby didn't notice anything more than her winning trophy and wad of cash.

"Don't think so," Olive said.

"I'm sure I've seen you before."

"Yeah. Well. I have to get going. See ya around." Olive practically sprinted away. The quicker she got away from those beautiful brown eyes the better.

Olive trudged up the mountain in her little red golf cart to her condo, cursing her unbelievable luck. Out of all the people in the world, why would the Italian Stallion have to be the sixth Pacelli sister?

The front door had barely closed when Olive stripped down, looking forward to pouring herself into a comfy pair of gray sweats. She paused before unhooking her bra, possible errands running through her mind. Did she need groceries? No. Should she work out? Yes, but no. Olive unhooked. Once the bra was off, she was in for the night. After changing and nuking some dinner, she sat on her balcony with a glass of red wine and mac and cheese. Olive stared at the sparkling lights of Avalon below as she ate. It was beautiful, but even more so in the daylight, when she had a glorious view of turquoise water as far as she could see and green, rolling hills.

The single life wasn't so bad. If she had a girlfriend she'd probably be in a loud restaurant right now, wearing that prickly knit shirt, which was itchy as hell but complemented her shape, while enduring mind-numbingly boring conversation. Olive hadn't met anyone who captured her attention in…well, ever. Granted, it was slim lesbian pickings on the island, but it wasn't like she didn't date. Maybe she was just meant to be alone, which, at twenty-eight, was terribly depressing. Olive made a mental note to reread Harmony Moondrop's latest book: *Expect Love in Unexpected Places*. She needed to get out of this negative thinking. As Harmony said, "We often find love with the most unexpected person and at the most unexpected time."

Olive grabbed her cell phone as it rang. "Hey, Nic. What's up?"

"Where are you?"

"On my balcony. Where are you? What's all that noise?"

"I'm at Frank's. You were supposed to meet me here."

"Oh, my gosh, I'm so sorry. I completely forgot." Actually, she'd probably blocked it out since the sports bar wasn't her scene. With some coaxing, though, she had promised Nicki that she'd accompany her on occasion.

"It's not too late. Bra, off or on?"

"Off."

Nicki growled. "You need to get out more, Ollie. How are you going to ever meet anyone?"

"I don't think my future girlfriend would be at a sports bar. No offense."

"None taken. I know it's not your thing."

"Besides, there aren't even any lesbians there."

"Uhhh…I'm looking at three right now."

"They're probably here on vacation and will be gone in a few days."

Nicki sighed loudly. "I know you want forever, but you have to actually take a chance on someone first for that to happen."

"You of all people know how many girlfriends I've had that moved back to the mainland. No one stays on Catalina."

"All right. Whatever you say. I'll let you get back to your mac and cheese." Nicki knew her so well.

"Wait. I was going to call you later. Guess who I just ran into."

"I thought you hated the guessing game."

"That's when *I* have to guess, not you. Never mind. It was the one and only…Italian Stallion!"

"Seriously!? You met her?"

"I saw her tonight while I was taking sunset photos. She was giving me photography tips, like I need it." Olive snorted and left the part out about Gabby being right. "Not only that, but her mother hired us to take photos of her sister's wedding, so I'll be seeing a lot of her in the coming weeks."

"Did she look hot?"

Not just hot, but more like sizzling. Undoubtedly, Nicki wanted details, but Olive had no desire to outwardly lust over a gigolo. Inwardly was another story.

"Yes, and she knows it, too. And get this, she didn't even recognize me!" Olive was still appalled and a little insulted by that one.

"If she's in town, I wonder if that means she's entering in the contest this year?"

"If so, there goes my chance of winning."

"Don't shortchange yourself. You're an amazing photographer."

"Thanks." Olive winced from rambunctious, ear-splitting yelps in the background. "Sounds like someone just hit a homerun."

"Actually, it was a touchdown. It's not baseball season."

"Right. Okay. I'll let you go. Talk to you later."

Olive gathered her dishes and headed back into her condo. She settled on the couch and grabbed her camera, intending to review the sunset photos. She didn't get very far, though, when she stalled on an extreme close-up of Gabby's striking eyes. Olive must've pressed the shutter button right when Gabby stepped in front of her. Ignoring her better judgement, Olive focused on the screen far longer than she should have, sucked into the spellbinding kaleidoscope of colors.

Chapter Five

Bridezilla and Her Sisters

Gabby blinked her eyes open, rolled over in bed, and nearly had a heart attack. Three of her sisters were towering over her, looking none too pleased. They fired questions faster than a machine gun, their voices irritatingly shrill so early in the morning. Where were you, why were you late, you made Gina cry, and on and on. Luckily, Mamma Pacelli burst into the room and shooed them away. She sat on the edge of Gabby's bed, leaned over, and kissed her on the cheek.

Gabby sat upright and said hoarsely, "Mornin', Mamma."

"What time did you get in?"

"Late. I had to wrap things up at the restaurant. I'll be gone a month, you know." That wasn't a complete lie, but she did leave the part out about registering for the contest and scoping out the Catalina night scene, which happily was quite lively.

Mamma Pacelli attempted to fix Gabby's chaotic hair. "What am I going to do with you? *Sei il mia bambina.*"

"I'm not a baby anymore."

"You will always be mia bambina," Mamma Pacelli said sternly and lightly tapped a finger on Gabby's nose. "You were your papa's favorite, you know." Mamma Pacelli made the sign of the cross at the mention of Alberto, which prompted Gabby to do the same. "He'd be so proud of you for taking over the family business. He always said you were the only one he trusted."

"Don't cry." Gabby's heart clinched as fat teardrops rolled down her mamma's cheeks.

Everyone missed Papa, but no one more than her mamma. They'd been high school sweethearts. Gabby couldn't imagine how painful it'd be to lose a spouse of over forty years. Hell, she couldn't even imagine being with anyone for four months. If Gabby remembered one thing about her childhood, it was the deep love her parents had shared. When she was little she adored wiggling between them on the couch. The affection and tenderness she felt was palpable. Their bright eyes shone with affection for each other…and for her. Yes, she'd heard lots of yelling, mostly from Mamma, but it was mostly a household filled with love.

Mamma Pacelli grabbed a tissue from the nightstand and blew her nose. "Your papa and I…we worried about you."

"What do you mean?" Gabby sat up straighter in bed.

"We wanted you to settle down, get married, have kids. Like your sisters. Who's going to take care of you? I'm not going to live forever, you know."

Gabby laid her palm over Mamma's pudgy hand. "I can take care of myself. Marriage, and all that, it's just not for me. And it doesn't have anything to do with being gay. I don't want to be tied down or feel trapped, you know? I want my freedom."

"Life is about love, it's about family!" Mamma Pacelli threw her hands up in the air.

Gabby lowered her gaze. Her mamma was wrong. Life was about making your own choices and living your dreams. If Gabby didn't look so much like her sisters, she'd wonder if she was adopted. She was the only Pacelli who wanted to break free from the family. She really needed to grow some balls and just do it. And she needed to fess up about entering the contest and what that would mean when she won.

Gabby cleared her throat. "Umm…Mamma, I need to tell you something."

Mamma Pacelli tucked a strand of hair behind Gabby's ear. "What is it, mia bambina?"

Gabby gazed at her mamma's tear-stained face, eyes puffy and bloodshot. Maybe now wasn't the time to come clean. Not when she was already so sad.

"Nothing. It can wait."

"Are you hungry? I'll fix you something to eat."

"No. I'm fine."

"I made biscotti. You'll have that."

Mamma Pacelli hoisted her large body from the bed and kissed the top of Gabby's head. "You better get moving. Don't be late for your sister's photo shoot."

Gabby lay in bed and stared at the ceiling, her mamma's words echoing in her ears. "Your papa would be proud of you..." Gabby's blood ran cold, guilt flooding her. She doubted he'd be proud of her abandoning the family. Despite being twenty-eight, Gabby still felt like a kid sometimes. She didn't want to disappoint or hurt the people she loved, but more than anything, she wanted to live her own life. And that's exactly what she intended to do.

By the time Gabby got up, everyone had already left. They'd rented a house on the island. After the wedding in a few weeks, Gabby, Mamma Pacelli, and Nonna would stay on Catalina several weeks longer while everyone else headed back to LA. The timing was perfect for the photography contest. Gabby would have plenty of time to take photos on the island before and after the nuptials.

Gabby took a shower, got dressed, and hurried out the door. After getting a big-gulp-sized coffee, she headed to the photography studio. She smiled to herself as she passed the marina and recalled the strawberry-blonde from the day before. The girl had been a little testy but cute...really cute, in a girl-next-door, American-pie sort of way with light freckles, red glasses, and a dimple in her right cheek when she pursed her lips together in a frown. And Gabby would have to be blind not to notice the woman's slightly swaying full hips as she'd stomped away. It was a tempting view that she'd replayed as she fell asleep. The woman had a delightfully soft form, which Gabby wouldn't mind embracing. It bugged her, though, as to where she'd seen her before. She seemed so familiar.

Gabby shook off the odd sensation when she spotted the Say Cheeze sign. She stood outside the red door and looked at her watch. She was early, which was unusual for her. She eyed the surroundings but nothing looked inviting, so she entered the studio. Had it not been for who she saw sitting behind the desk, Gabby would have balked at the tacky Say Cheeze sign and brightly colored walls.

"Well, hello. If it isn't Sunset Girl." Gabby flashed a ginormous smile.

The woman was sitting at a desk with her head down and writing something in a book. She glanced up and down so quickly that if Gabby had blinked she'd have missed it. "Oh, hi."

"So we meet again." No response. "Do you remember me?"

"Yes." The girl pushed up her glasses and flipped through several pages. She didn't seem surprised to see Gabby, or very happy about it either.

She looked even prettier today, hair pulled back in a ponytail and big green eyes that sparkled under the fluorescent lights. If you looked up *bedroom eyes* in a colloquial dictionary it'd refer to this woman. How had Gabby missed those beautiful eyes yesterday? She must have been preoccupied appreciating everything else.

"So, you're the receptionist here?"

The girl stilled, gaped at Gabby, and pressed her lips together so tight that an inch-deep dimple appeared. "I'm a photographer."

"*Really?*" Gabby hadn't meant to sound surprised, but from the fire in the woman's eyes, her question must have come across that way. "I mean, that's great. So, what's your name?"

The woman paused, looked downward, and said, "Olive."

Cute name. Gabby resisted the urge to make a Popeye and Olive Oyl joke. She didn't think it'd go over well.

"I'm supposed to meet my family here for a photo shoot."

Olive silently nodded as she frantically turned pages. Gabby might have to downgrade her from testy to rude. The woman was definitely not in a good mood. Gabby shrugged and wandered around the office. When she glanced over her shoulder, Olive was staring right at her. She cleared her throat and quickly averted her gaze. Gabby approached a camera perched on a tripod, looked through the viewfinder, and fiddled with the dials.

"Don't touch that," Olive said.

"If you're taking portrait photos then you really should be using f/2. You need a wide aperture so the background is blurred. The f/5.6 setting you have now isn't wide enough."

Olive bolted out of her chair, went to the camera, and changed the setting back. A fierce, go-to-hell glower caused Gabby to take a step back. Olive had some fire in her. Good thing Gabby liked feisty women. This could be fun.

"I'd appreciate you not messing with anything in the studio."

"I probably should have mentioned that I'm a photographer, so I do know a thing or two about cameras." When that information didn't seem to appease Olive, Gabby retreated. "But you're right. I apologize."

Olive paused for a few seconds before she sat back at her desk. Gabby followed and peered over her shoulder at the computer screen.

"Is that one of the sunset photos you took last night? Can I see them?"

"I'd rather you..."

Gabby pressed an arrow key, which displayed the next photo. "Wow, that looks great. Maybe you were right to choose the sunset after all." The next photo had been taken when Olive turned around as Gabby had suggested. "Oh no, never mind. This is so much better."

Gabby cocked her head at the next picture. "Is that me?" It was an extreme close-up of two, big brown eyes.

Olive squirmed in her chair. "I must have snapped the picture right when you stepped in front of the camera."

"Oh yeah. Sorry about that." Gabby chuckled. "I figured you would have deleted it."

Olive's cheeks flushed rosy pink. She stared at the screen for several seconds before she pressed the delete button. They both looked up when a short, plump man barreled out of a closed door. He stopped when he saw Gabby.

"Mr. Finkelmeier, this is Gabby Pacelli."

"Oh yes, the youngest daughter." The man bounded toward Gabby and shook her hand. "It's so nice to meet you."

"Sorry I didn't make it yesterday, but I had some things to wrap up."

"Your mother told me you're the general manager of Pacelli's Pizza. We do love your family's cuisine. Don't we, Olive?"

Olive momentarily looked confused before profusely shaking her head. She'd probably never even had a slice, not that Gabby could blame her.

"I thought you were a photographer," Olive said.

"That's a hobby." Okay, so she'd lied, but Gabby didn't want anyone mentioning anything about photography in front of her family. In fact, she should have never mentioned it to Olive. Stupidly, she was trying to impress her, which didn't seem to have any effect whatsoever. Gabby would tell her family about her dreams and plans in due time, like maybe after the contest when she was already in Tahiti far away from her mamma's wrath.

Mr. Finkelmeier wagged a finger at Olive. "Don't forget about Mr. Sanchez's BPS at eleven. Mrs. Johnson was none too happy you were late the other day."

"About that," Olive said. "Considering the...nature of the shoot...perhaps you could, you know..."

"What?" Mr. Finkelmeier blankly stared.

Olive glanced at Gabby, who was looking right at her. "Maybe you could take care of Mr. Sanchez's request...since it's a...you know..."

"What's BPS?" Gabby asked.

"A...uhh...boudoir photo shoot," Olive said.

Mr. Finkelmeier's eyebrows shot up. "Are you suggesting I do your job?"

"No, of course not. But I do seem to get all the more...difficult cases. Mrs. Johnson's zootopia shoot was a nightmare, as one example of many."

"I know at least a dozen people who would love to have your job, Olive. If you can't handle it, then maybe I should—"

"No, sir. It's not that. Never mind. You're right. I won't be late for Mr. Sanchez." Olive sulked in her chair.

"That's better." Mr. Finkelmeier smiled brightly at Gabby and disappeared into his office.

Gabby sat on the corner of Olive's desk. "You shouldn't let him order you around like that."

"He's the boss."

"So?"

"Sooo, he owns the joint. He could fire me."

"That doesn't mean he can treat you like a slave."

"He doesn't treat me like a slave. You don't know what you're talking about." Olive swiveled her chair and stared at her computer screen, her back to Gabby.

"Let me take a wild guess. He gives you all the crap jobs while he sits in his office twiddling his thumbs." Olive's shoulders stiffened. "You have to photograph half-naked guys, and I don't even want to guess what the zootopia shoot entailed. Hopefully, monkeys weren't hanging from the rafters." Gabby chuckled.

Surprise filled Olive's eyes when she glanced over her shoulder. "He's letting me photograph your family."

"Obviously, you don't know my family. Monkeys would be a picnic in the park compared to us."

The corners of Olive's mouth quirked up. Technically, it wasn't an actual smile, but Gabby would take what she could get. When Gabby stood and leaned across the desk with both hands, Olive's eyes went directly to her cleavage, which showed nicely in the low-cut shirt.

"So," Gabby said. "How about you showing me around the island sometime?"

"I...uh...what?"

Gabby grinned wickedly. "See something you like?"

Olive's eyes shot up, her face redder than the sunset last night. "I was *not* looking at your breasts. You have a tattoo." Olive pointed.

Gabby lowered her collar to fully reveal the symbol.

"What is it?" Olive leaned a little closer.

"It's a bird."

Gabby straightened her shirt and stood upright before Olive could ask any questions. "So how about dinner, a stroll along the beach, and then...who knows what." Gabby winked and displayed the sexiest grin she could muster.

"No thanks."

It took Gabby a moment to comprehend what Olive had said. The wink-and-grin combo were rejection-less. Maybe she'd misunderstood.

"We could grab something at that Greek place on the corner."

"I said no thanks."

"Italian, then?"

"Do you have a hearing problem?" Olive asked, incredulous.

Apparently, she wasn't biting. That was a first.

❖

Olive had to admit she took immense satisfaction in turning the Italian Stallion's advances down. From the look on her face, she'd probably never heard "no" before. Normally, Olive would have been googly-eyed over Gabby's obviously practiced come-hither grin, but she wasn't attracted to players. Well, she could be *attracted* to them, but only on a physical level, which wasn't enough to sustain a meaningful, long-lasting relationship.

After a lengthy, uncomfortable pause, Gabby looked like she might take another stab at asking Olive out again when her family came bursting through the door. The Pacellis were loud people, the kind of loud that made you want to wear ear muffs in ninety-degree weather. The supermodels were wearing the same outfits as yesterday: black mini-skirts, black fitted shirts, and silver belts. Even though they were all talking at once—at earsplitting, fast-forward speed—the loudest conversation was between Mamma Pacelli and Bridezilla.

"This is my wedding, Mamma," Gina said. "Gabby has to—"

"Gina Luciana, you are going to send me to an early grave."

"She ruins everything always having to be different!" Gina stomped one foot. She certainly had the ten-year-old temper-tantrum thing down.

"Alberto, how could you leave me with these girls?" Mamma Pacelli raised her arms to the ceiling before making the sign of the cross.

Gabby leaned close to Olive and whispered, "I told you monkeys would be a breeze compared to us."

As the shouting continued, Gabby approached Nonna. The woman pulled Gabby down, planted a kiss on each cheek, and whispered something in her ear, which was weird since Mamma Pacelli had said she didn't speak. Gabby smiled, took the elderly woman's hand, and lightly patted it, which was actually kind of sweet.

Olive stood and cleared her throat, a sad attempt at getting everyone's attention. She clapped a few times, but booming voices drowned out the sound. Gabby crossed her arms and sneered smugly at Olive's efforts.

"Excuse me. Uhh…everyone. Can I have your attention?" Olive could have been a wax figurine for all they cared. Gabby raised an eyebrow, just daring her to try again.

Olive stepped from behind her desk and stood a few feet from the raging Italians. "Hello? Maybe we should get started." Olive ducked when Mamma Pacelli's arms flailed wildly. She could knock someone's eye out.

Seemingly taking pity on her, Gabby put two fingers in her mouth and whistled loud enough for Olive's eardrums to vibrate. Everyone immediately quietened.

"I believe our photographer is trying to get our attention," Gabby said with a self-satisfied grin. All eyes turned to Olive.

Olive glanced at Gabby and nodded once. She had helped, after all. "According to the schedule, we have a studio shoot this morning, so we should probably get started."

"Gabby has to change." Gina smacked her gum and put her hands on her hips. "Into a *skirt*. We're all supposed to be dressed alike."

Gabby rolled her eyes. Olive hoped Gina's future husband had a high tolerance for bitchiness. Otherwise the marriage wouldn't last very long.

"Mamma?" Gina whined.

Mamma Pacelli put her hands on Gabby's shoulders and looked directly into her eyes. Olive would have shaken like an earthquake under such a stern gaze. "This is your sister's wedding. We'll do what she wants."

"I'm not wearing a skirt," Gabby said adamantly.

Mamma Pacelli held up a hand before Gina could protest. "You can wear black shorts. And that's the last I want to hear of it." She shot them both a murderous glare.

Gina huffed and whispered, "She's wearing the bridesmaid dress."

Mamma Pacelli handed Gabby her outfit and pointed to the bathroom.

Gabby sighed and muttered, "This is so lame. We're on a tropical island. Why does she want to take photos in front of a fake ocean when the real thing is right outside the door?"

Olive agreed but wasn't about to cross Bridezilla. With her temper and well-defined arms, she could probably uproot a redwood tree with her bare hands.

While Gabby changed, Olive arranged the five sisters in front of the backdrop. They did a hair flip in unison and struck matching poses, right hand on jutted hip and chest out. Olive stepped back and assessed the arrangement. She took another step and almost knocked over Nonna.

"Oh my gosh, I'm so sorry." Olive grabbed the woman's bony arm so she wouldn't topple to the floor. Once Nonna was steady on her feet, Olive asked, "How are you today?" Nonna stared straight ahead and didn't even flinch. "Are you enjoying the island?" No response.

"She no speak," Mamma Pacelli said.

Olive was about to ask if that meant she didn't speak English, but was momentarily struck dumb when Gabby walked out of the bathroom. The Italian Stallion certainly lived up to her sexy reputation in short shorts, looking like the spiciest thing this side of the Mexican border. Olive's eyes immediately went to Gabby's breasts—not her tattoo this time—but her absolutely flawless-looking breasts, yet it wasn't her fault. Ninety-nine percent of all lesbians would have done the same thing. The beauties were buoyant and perfectly rounded, and the way her shirt stretched out would've made anyone feel a little frisky. Olive imagined stroking the smooth fabric, causing Gabby's nipples to harden and become erect. For a moment, Olive almost forgave the judge last year for abandoning all ethics and sleeping with Gabby. Almost.

"Where do you want me?" Gabby asked.

That question ignited a whole host of other thoughts, like maybe attached to Olive's lips, or on her knees, or lying on top of her? Olive shook her head and forced her eyes upward. Hopefully, Gabby's arrogant grin didn't mean she'd read Olive's mind.

Olive reached for Gabby's arm but then retreated. Skin contact probably wasn't a good idea when her body was buzzing like a hummingbird. Instead, she pointed and said, "There." That's all she could muster with her mouth suddenly dry. She needed a drink, a very tall, preferably strong, alcoholic drink.

Gabby stood in front of her sisters, since she was the shortest with everyone wearing five-inch heels and her in sandals.

"I just want it to go on record that I wouldn't be caught dead in a silver belt. This isn't 1974," Gabby said. "And who'd wear those shoes to—"

Mamma Pacelli held up a hand from the sidelines, immediately silencing Gabby. Obviously, that move carried a lot of weight.

Olive stood behind the camera and looked through the viewfinder, suddenly struck by how different Gabby seemed from her sisters. They were all gorgeous and had attitudes the size of Texas, but Gabby was the only one with short hair, little makeup (which she didn't need), no ring on her left hand, and didn't seem to get along with anyone except Nonna and Isabella. She was like the smallest nesting doll trapped inside five larger ones. Maybe being a lesbian made her an outcast. Olive gritted her teeth. No one deserved that.

Suddenly feeling a desire to defend Gabby, Olive said, "Duly noted about the belt. This isn't a cover shoot for *Tiger Beat*." She was risking the wrath of Bridezilla but was glad she'd walked the plank when Gabby flashed a smile. They held eye contact for several heartbeats, until Gabby spoke and ruined their little bonding moment.

"What setting do you have on the camera? Are you using f/2? Also, we should be angled more."

"Gabriella Maria, shush. Leave the photography to the professional," Mamma Pacelli said.

Gabby winced like she'd just been slapped across the face.

The professional? Gabby *was* the professional. Not that Olive wanted her help, but didn't they know Gabby was a photographer? Great. Now Olive felt the need to defend her again.

"Actually, she's right," Olive said. "About the positioning, *not* the aperture. Could everyone turn a slight bit to the left? Perfect." Olive twisted the lens until it was focused and placed her finger on the shutter button. "Now, say cheese." Totally corny phrase, but it was one of Mr. Finkelmeier's rules so she had no choice.

After twenty minutes of taking photos in various poses, Mr. Finkelmeier came out of his office. It figured he'd make an appearance after all the work was done.

"I hope Olive took good care of you." Mr. Finkelmeier gave Olive the evil eye, like she was a screw-up.

"*Sì, sì.*" Mamma Pacelli waved her hand and focused on several of her daughters who were having a heated debate. "What's the commotion about?"

"We paid to use the beach volleyball court, but now Bianca doesn't want to go. It was supposed to be a foursome," maybe Isabella said. Olive would never remember all their names.

"So the three of you go." Mamma Pacelli pointed to Gabby, Gina, and probably Isabella.

"We can't have three against one," Gina whined.

Mr. Finkelmeier chimed in. "Olive can be the fourth."

"What? No! I mean, I have to work. Remember, Mr. Sanchez?" Olive wasn't sure if she'd rather do a bedroom shoot or play a sport she despised. Neither one sounded appealing.

"What time is your game?" Mr. Finkelmeier asked.

"Not until two, and I believe you said that Mr. Sanchez is at eleven." Gabby beamed, seemingly much too excited about the prospect of Olive joining.

"I don't have any casual clothes with me," Olive said, hoping the desperation didn't show on her face.

"You can go home at lunch and change." Mr. Finkelmeier shot Olive a stern look.

"Perfect," Gabby said. "It'll be me and Isabella against Olive and Gina."

Great. Stick me with Bridezilla.

Isabella leaned over and whispered to Gabby loud enough for everyone to hear. "I knew you'd have a thing for the photographer."

Mamma Pacelli looked back and forth between Olive and Gabby. "You like my daughter?"

Olive wasn't sure what was happening, but she had the sinking feeling she was about to be set up. "Um, well, no...I mean, yes, of course...but..."

Mamma Pacelli smiled widely. "*Stupendoa!* You come to dinner Sunday. Your boss, Mr..." Mamma wagged a finger at Mr. Finkelmeier since she didn't seem to be able to pronounce his name. "He come, too."

Mr. Finkelmeier squealed, Gabby beamed, and Olive wanted to jump in a very deep well.

❖

"There's two types of scoring: rally and side out. Side out is where a team wins a point only if they serve the ball. But they'll probably use rally, which is when teams score points on every rally, regardless of which team serves. Play is to twenty-five points, and a team must win a set by two points. There's no ceiling, so a set continues until one of the teams gains a two-point advantage."

Olive gaped at Nicki and blinked rapidly. She'd considered Googling "volleyball for dummies" but figured she had her own personal sports authority, so she'd asked Nicki to meet her at the court before the Italians arrived.

"Now, a team can touch the ball three times on its side of the net. The usual pattern is a dig, a set, and a spike. The ball is—"

"Wait! I'm so not comprehending any of this." Olive glanced around the beach. "They'll be here any minute. Just tell me something quick so I won't look like a moron."

Nicki paused, adjusted her Dodgers cap, and said, "Just don't hit the ball twice in a row and don't let it fall in the sand."

Olive wiped a bead of sweat from her forehead, the sun beating down. This day really sucked. She'd spent over an hour on Mr. Sanchez's photo shoot. Considering their language barrier, she had to physically pose him in sexy positions, which meant lots of skin contact, plus up-close views of things she'd rather not see. And even worse than that, it'd be at least a year before she could make eye contact with the man without picturing him half-naked, which meant his hot-dog stand named Who Let the Dogs Out—her favorite hangout—was off limits. And now this. Olive was about as athletic as a tortoise. The last thing she wanted to do was embarrass herself in front of Gabby.

Nicki grabbed her shoulders. "You'll be fine. Just relax."

"What were you saying about rally and sideline?"

"Side out. It's simple. A rally is the time between the serve and the end of the play. A side out is when the receiving team wins the rally. The receiving team then rotates positions, and they're the serving team."

Olive closed her eyes. "I'm so fucked."

"How'd you get roped into this, anyway?"

"Mr. Finkelmeier."

"What a douche bag. He probably didn't even ask, did he?"

Olive spotted the three sisters trudging through the sand. "Oh, God. Here they come."

"Bow chicka wow wow." Nicki practically growled.

"I know. All six of 'em look like they just stepped off a Paris runway," Olive murmured. "Be cool." Easier said than done when Gabby was wearing nothing but a bikini top and cut-off blue-jean shorts. Gawking at her toned abs probably wasn't the definition of cool.

Gabby eyed Nicki suspiciously as they approached. Gina and Isabella stood under a palm tree and looked like they were about to keel over from heat stroke. Maybe this would be a short game after all.

"Hey." Gabby bobbed her head once, never taking her eyes off Nicki, which Olive didn't mind since it gave her a chance to ogle those amazing abs unnoticed.

"This is Nicki. Nicki, this is Gabby."

"Nice to meet you," Nicki said.

"Likewise." Gabby finally turned to Olive. "You ready for some v-ball?" She twirled the volleyball on a finger like a Harlem Globetrotter.

"Sure." *Did that sound convincing?*

"Let's see what you've got." Gabby walked across the sand and tugged on the net, maybe to check the tension.

"Man...she is...man...oh, like...yeah..." Even though that made no sense whatsoever, Olive knew what Nicki meant.

"Any last words of wisdom?"

Nicki forced her eyes from Gabby's rear end. "Put your game face on, baby. You're gonna need it."

Olive stared blankly. *There was a game face?*

"Go get 'em, killer." Nicki slapped Olive's ass and pushed her onto the court.

Mr. Finkelmeier was dead meat. This was so not in her job description.

Gabby repeatedly tossed the ball in the air and yelled to her sisters, "You girls wanna play or stand in the shade all day painting your fingernails?"

Gina sneered and stomped through the sand. Isabella approached Gabby and gave her a high-five. Gabby reached into her back pocket and pulled out what looked like a tin can. She opened it, grabbed something, threw it high into the air, and caught it in her mouth. What a showoff.

Gina joined Olive on their side of the court and asked, "You do know how to play volleyball, right? I don't like to lose."

Olive briefly considered spouting off about rallies and side outs but didn't think that'd impress her much. Instead, she gulped and nodded.

"We'll serve first," Gabby said.

"Wait a second. Why do you get to decide?" Gina yelled across the court.

Gabby sighed and put a hand on her hip. Those sisters did like that hip stance. "Good God, Gina. This is just a friendly game. What does it matter?"

Except it wasn't so friendly after Gabby forcefully served the ball directly at Gina's face, which had her diving into the sand to save her life. These girls played rough. They were more competitive than Olympians. Luckily, Gina was a control freak, which meant Olive didn't have to participate much. She managed to hit the ball a few times, but mostly Gina pushed her out of the way so she could take a crack at it. After an hour of rigorous play, they were all dirty, sweaty, and exhausted. Gabby and Isabella won by a long shot, which Gina blamed on her novice teammate, of course. Olive could have cared less, though. She was just glad it was over.

Gabby and Olive collapsed under a palm tree, while the other two headed back to the house.

Gabby took a swig of water. "So, is Nicki your girlfriend?"

"No. We're just friends."

"But she's a lesbian, right?"

"Yes, but why does that matter?"

"Just wondering if you are as well." Gabby took another drink and peered at Olive out of the corner of her eye.

"What does your gaydar say?"

Gabby removed her sunglasses and studied Olive for several long, uncomfortable moments. Olive glanced down, wanting to escape the mesmerizing honey-colored eyes just inches away.

"What makes you think I have a gaydar?" Gabby asked.

"I believe you were rather persistent in asking me out on a date."

"I don't date."

Olive's eyes narrowed. "I just imagined that you asked me out?"

"No, but I never called it a date. Why can't it just be two people having fun? Why does everyone feel the need to label everything? Are you?"

Olive reclined against the palm tree. "Am I what?"

"Are you a lesbian?" Gabby raised her voice and sighed dramatically.

Olive took a long swig of water, purposefully prolonging her answer. She liked seeing the normally cool woman flustered. "Yes," she finally said.

"Excellent," Gabby whispered.

"But my answer is still no."

Gabby's smile dropped. "Why?"

"I have my reasons." Olive wasn't sure why she hadn't revealed who she was. Maybe it was because she actually enjoyed the flirting, even though it was coming from the Italian Stallion, someone she'd never date. It was an ego booster, and she was pretty sure it'd cease the moment Gabby found out they were contest rivals.

"Women," Gabby mumbled and ran a hand through her hair.

The woman even had sexy hair. It was short in the back but lengthy on top, with bangs that fell across her forehead in an alluring way. She must request extra texturing when getting it cut because it was separated, in a messy kind of way that was probably meant to be on purpose. She undoubtedly got highlights, too, considering red and gold strands shimmered in the sunlight. The Pacelli sisters definitely had good genes, which made Olive wonder what Gabby's father looked like since their mother wasn't much of a looker.

Gabby lay on the ground with her hands behind her head. "You haven't played volleyball much, have you?" Gabby asked.

Olive cringed. "Did it show? I'm not exactly the athletic type."

"You did all right."

"Thanks. You and your sisters are awfully competitive."

"It's in our blood. I'll do anything to win. Anything."

Just when Olive was halfway starting to like Gabby, she had to remind her of the cheating scoundrel that she was.

CHAPTER SIX

ANATOMY OF AN ITALIAN MEAL

A s Olive drove to the Pacellis', she fantasized about ways to kill Mr. Finkelmeier. She could push him off a cliff—if he ever got out of his chair—or maybe feed him to Mrs. Johnson's iguana. Not only had he roped her into Sunday dinner, but he'd canceled a few hours ago, saying he needed to tend to his sick cat. *Sick cat, my ass. He probably doesn't even have one.*

Olive parked her golf cart in the driveway and stared up at the humongous two-story house painted blue and white. She'd driven by many times but had never been inside. She eyed the bottle of red wine in the passenger seat, tempted to pop the cork and take a few swigs. The last thing she wanted to do on her night off was spend it with clients.

Olive walked to the door and rang the bell. No answer. She pressed it again. Maybe she had the wrong day, hopefully. One more attempt and she was out of there. When no one opened the door, Olive grinned widely and practically skipped down the sidewalk. Before she reached her golf cart, someone stepped right in front of her.

I'd know those big brown eyes anywhere.

"Where'd you come from?" Olive stumbled backward.

"Through the gate." Gabby pointed to an open door in the towering redwood fence that surrounded the house. "We're in the backyard."

Olive couldn't help but notice how cute Gabby looked in blue-jean shorts, despite the fact that her shirt was a color Olive absolutely despised. When she was ten she'd thrown away every white piece of clothing and object she owned. It was difficult to look at Gabby's shirt and not remember what had provoked her to do so.

Gabby giggled when she eyed Olive's vehicle. "Is that yours? It's smaller than a Smart Car."

"Yes," Olive said defensively. "If you haven't noticed, everyone drives golf carts around here. What do you have? A Hummer?"

"Hey, I didn't mean anything...it's...cute."

Olive felt a little bad about snapping at Gabby, but the woman was frustrating, always one-upping her.

"Here." Olive jabbed the bottle of wine at Gabby, who studied the label.

"Nice choice. Thanks. I hope you're hungry. Mamma tends to overdo Sunday dinner."

"Actually, I'm famished." Olive hadn't eaten anything all day, dreading a night at the Pacellis'.

"Follow me." Gabby held out her hand. Olive paused and stared at it, unsure what to do. She wasn't accustomed to holding hands with strangers. This certainly wasn't a date, and it wasn't like they were friends. It could just be an innocent gesture, though, considering the Pacellis were the touchy-feely sort. On the other hand, she didn't want to give Gabby the wrong idea. After too long of a delay, Olive decided it'd be rude to slap her hand away. Their fingers automatically laced, like they'd been holding hands forever. Olive suppressed a sigh at the feel of soft, smooth skin. It'd been a while since she'd held hands with a woman, or anyone for that matter. This wasn't so bad after all. In fact, it was kind of nice...in a non-dating sort of way, of course.

Gabby led them to the backyard, which looked like the Garden of Eden. Fragrant lemon trees, green grass, and a cute gazebo stood in the corner, surrounded with overhanging vines. In the middle of the yard, the Pacelli sisters sat at a long picnic table. Nonna was in a porch swing dozing off, and Mamma Pacelli was nowhere in sight.

Isabella approached with a curious look at their clasped hands. Olive shook free and crossed her arms.

"I'm so glad you could make it." Isabella slipped an arm around Olive's waist and guided her to the others. Yes, they were definitely the touchy-feely type, which probably meant Gabby's hand-holding had been completely innocent. Strangely, that probability was a little disappointing.

The sisters were having a loud discussion, about what Olive wasn't sure, since she couldn't make out one word with everyone talking at once. It was almost like they were trying to see who could yell the loudest.

Gabby put her fingers in her mouth and whistled. "Shush! Everyone, Olive is here."

The yard grew eerily silent as four pairs of eyes stared at Olive, like she was the one who'd interrupted them.

"Um, hi. It's nice to see you all again. Excuse me if I don't remember your names, aside from Gina, since she's the bride and all."

Gina sat upright and puffed out her voluptuous chest.

"I'm Bianca Adele."

"Rose Marie."

"Bella Francesca."

"And I'm Isabella Elena."

Why did they have to use middle names? That was like trying to remember eight instead of four.

Olive patted Isabella on the back. "Yes. I remember you since you whipped our butts at volleyball."

"We should have won," Gina murmured and looked at Olive like she'd cost them the gold medal.

"Where's your mom?" Olive asked, ignoring Gina's comment.

"Inside cooking," Isabella said. "She doesn't let anyone in her kitchen."

Olive nodded and scanned the yard. "It's beautiful here. How long do you have this place?"

"About a month," Gabby said. "Most everyone will head back to LA after the wedding in a few weeks."

Olive looked at Gabby. "What about you? Are you sticking around?"

The twinkle in Gabby's eye probably meant she thought Olive was flirting, when that was the farthest thing from the truth. She was angling to see if Gabby had entered the contest this year.

"Actually, I am. I'll be here through Valentine's Day." Olive had her answer, which wasn't the one she wanted to hear. "Have you changed your mind about having dinner with me?"

"No. I have not."

"Wait a minute," one of the sisters said. "You mean our baby sister got *rejected?*"

"Ooohhh," the Pacelli sisters said in unison, followed by rambunctious laughter.

"That's a first," Gina said, slapping her thigh. She pointed at Olive. "I like you after all."

What? She didn't like me before?

Another sister stood and ruffled Gabby's hair, which, oddly, made it look even better. "Finally, a woman who said no to our little Casanova."

Gabby rolled her eyes at her sister's teasing, but from her flushed face and stiff posture it must have bothered her. "If you'll excuse me, I'm going to check on Nonna."

Olive watched Gabby walk across the yard and sit in the swing next to her grandmother. The elderly woman's eyes fluttered open. She looked at Gabby with a tired smile and rested her head on Gabby's shoulder. Gabby gently propelled the swing, lulling Nonna to sleep. A hard lump formed in Olive's throat as she recalled the photo she'd taken of her grandmother right before she died. She'd give anything to snuggle with her on a porch swing right now.

"Are you okay?" Isabella touched Olive's arm.

Olive blinked back tears. "Yeah. It's just…I guess I miss having family around. You all seem so close."

"We do butt heads, but yeah, we're a pretty tight bunch."

"So, what's the deal with your grandmother? I mean, your mom said she doesn't speak, but I've seen her whisper to Gabby."

Isabella chuckled. "Nonna is a bit superstitious. When our father died, the last words he spoke were to Gabby. So, she insists on doing the same. Otherwise she thinks it's bad luck. According to Nonna, a person's final words are more important than anything they've ever spoken their entire life."

"Oh, my. She isn't sick, is she?" Olive put a hand over her heart. The elderly woman was probably about to croak if she didn't want to risk speaking to anyone else.

"No. She's fine."

"What does your grandmother say to Gabby?"

"No one knows. Gabby can't tell us until after Nonna departs this life."

Olive knew some people were superstitious, but this was by far the weirdest thing she'd ever heard.

As though reading her mind, Isabella put her arm around Olive's shoulder and said, "Welcome to our dysfunctional family."

Mamma Pacelli swooshed open the patio doors and yelled, "*Andiamo! È ora di mangiare!*" which caused everyone to spring into action. A couple of women laid out a tablecloth, while others disappeared into the house and came out carrying plates, glasses, silverware, and platters of food. Gabby helped Nonna take a seat at the head of the picnic table. Olive felt in the way, not sure where to stand or what to do. After things settled down and most of the sisters were seated, Mamma Pacelli bustled out with yet another dish and put it on the table.

"Olive, you sit next to Gabby," Mamma Pacelli ordered. "Rose Marie, *alzarsi*."

The woman huffed and moved to the next chair. Gabby sat next to Nonna, with Olive beside her. Mamma Pacelli, who was at the head of the table, poured herself a glass of wine and passed the bottle around.

"Everything looks amazing," Olive said.

Gabby leaned over and whispered, "This is just the *antipasti*, the starter."

Olive gaped. All the platters of meat, cheese, bread, and a bunch of other unidentifiable items looked like a main course to her. Everyone grabbed a dish, filled their plates, and passed it around the table.

"You don't like cheese?" Olive asked Gabby when she waved off that particular item.

"I can't eat dairy."

"Gabby is the only Italian we know who is lactose intolerant," one of the sisters said, like it was a sin or something.

"Oh, so you probably don't even eat your family's pizza then, huh?" Olive asked.

"No, but that's not the only reason," Gabby whispered. "I'm a little pizzaed out. It's kind of a big deal with us." Gabby handed Olive a tray of sliced meat. "This is *Mortadella di Bologna*."

"Oh, you mean baloney?"

It was as though someone had pressed the pause button on a remote control. Everyone stilled, all eyes on Olive. She'd never seen them so quiet before. Nonna shook her head in seeming disgust, the sisters looked like they'd been zapped with a hundred volts of electricity, but the worse reaction of all was Mamma Pacelli, whose nostrils flared like an angry bull.

"Did I say something wrong?" Olive said, suddenly fearful.

"Mamma, forgive her. Not everyone is Italian," Gabby said.

Olive looked back and forth between the hissing bull and Gabby. "What's going on?" Olive whispered to Gabby.

"Mortadella di Bologna is made from finely ground pork with a blend of salt, white pepper, coriander, anise, pieces of pistachio, and wine. The mixture is stuffed into a casing and cooked. When it's sliced, it does look like supermarket baloney, but it's not." Gabby looked at Mamma Pacelli. "And most Italians take offense to the comparison."

"I'm so sorry. I didn't know."

All eyes darted to Mamma Pacelli, as though she were a Supreme Court judge about to announce Olive's sentencing.

"Mamma, it was an honest mistake," Gabby said.

Everyone was motionless until Mamma Pacelli threw her hands into the air and yelled, "*Mangiare! Mangiare!*"

"She's telling everyone to eat." Gabby gently squeezed Olive's knee. It hadn't felt like a flirty, lecherous move, but more for reassurance. Olive released a sigh, thankful that she wasn't going to the guillotine.

Everyone ate in silence until Mamma Pacelli bolted upright, which prompted everyone but Nonna to do the same.

"It's time for the *primi piatti*," Gabby told Olive. "You sit here and we'll bring it out."

With everyone in the house, Olive glanced at Nonna and smiled. "How are you today?"

Real bright, Olive. Ask a question to someone who doesn't speak.

"Umm...the food is scrumptious." Olive stared at the table cloth, trying to think of something else to say. "You must be excited about your granddaughter's wedding. I'm sure it'll be beautiful."

Nonna stared at Olive like she hadn't understood one word she'd said. An awkward silence settled between them until everyone arrived with more food. After all the women were seated again, they passed around plates.

"This is gnocchi," Gabby said. It looked like dumplings, but Olive wasn't about to make that mistake again. "And risotto."

This must be the carb portion of the meal, with all the pasta and rice dishes. How did all the sisters stay so trim with all this scrumptious, rich food?

"Olive, tell us about your family," Mamma Pacelli said before shoving a fork full of pasta into her mouth.

Olive swallowed, sipped wine, and cleared her throat. "Not much to tell. I'm an only child. My parents live in Wisconsin. They own a tax-consulting business. I have a few aunts, uncles, and cousins spread around."

"An only child?!" Mamma Pacelli shook her head and mumbled something in Italian.

"Where were you born?" Isabella asked.

"Here on the island. My parents moved away years ago. My mom wanted to be closer to one of her sisters."

"Why didn't you go with them?" Mamma Pacelli asked. "Families should stay together."

"My job and life are here."

Mamma Pacelli shook her head and made some "tsk, tsk" sounds. Olive was batting a thousand. First the baloney and now this. It couldn't get much worse.

"What other places have you lived?" Gabby asked.

Okay, maybe it could get worse.

"Nowhere. Just here."

Gabby put her fork down and faced Olive. "You've never lived anywhere other than Avalon?"

Olive took a bite and shook her head.

"You must travel a lot then, right?"

Olive took a drink of wine, a futile attempt to delay the inevitable. "Not really."

"You mean...not a lot? Where have you been?"

Olive took another bite and chewed about a thousand times, hoping Gabby would forget the question she'd just asked. No such luck when Gabby stared right at her, patiently waiting for Olive to swallow. "Actually, nowhere."

"What a second. You've *never* been off the island?" Gabby gawked at Olive like she was a bearded lady in the circus.

"I love it here. Why would I leave?"

"It's beautiful, but it's so small. I can't believe you've never been anywhere else. Not even to California? It's only twenty-six miles away."

"Nope. No desire to do so." That was a lie, but no one needed to know that.

Gabby sat back in her chair. "Wow."

"Why is that so strange? I'm sure lots of people have never left their hometown."

"I suppose, but Catalina is so isolated."

Olive shrugged and stuffed her mouth with more pasta, hoping Gabby would drop the subject.

"I love it here," Isabella said. "I wouldn't want to leave either."

Isabella was now Olive's favorite Pacelli.

"But...there's a whole world out there," Gabby muttered, more to herself than anyone.

Mamma Pacelli stood, and everyone but Olive and Nonna disappeared into the house again. Apparently, it was time for the next course. Olive sat back in her chair and fumed. It wasn't anyone's business where she chose to live. All right, if she were being completely honest, she'd love to travel, and she would when she won the *Journeys* contest. Olive could do it, she *would* do it. Gabby was good, but so was she.

Olive glanced at Nonna, who was staring at her and looked like she actually wanted to speak. Instead, she pointed to Olive with a shaky finger and then at the house.

"Are you trying to tell me something?"

Nonna pointed again but this time ended with crossed arms over her chest, the sign language for love.

"Are you asking if Gabby and I are together?"

Nonna nodded.

"Oh no, not that way. I mean, not romantically. No."

Nonna nodded resolutely and crossed her arms again. Olive was about to protest, but everyone was already seated and filling their plates with meatballs and veggies. Luckily, they ate in silence, with no more personal questions.

After ingesting way more than she should have, Olive reclined in her chair, patted her stomach, and groaned. "That was sooo good. You're an amazing cook, Mrs. Pacelli."

"Please, call me Mamma."

Olive smiled, not completely sure she'd ever feel comfortable doing so. "I'm stuffed. I couldn't eat another bite."

"*Dolce!*" Mamma Pacelli popped out of her chair, disappeared into the house, and returned with a cake.

Oh my God, more food?

Gabby leaned close to Olive. "Tiramisu. Mamma's specialty."

"It looks incredible, but I couldn't."

"That's not an option." Gabby's full lips curled upward.

She sure is pretty when she smiles. And doesn't smile. And frowns. And...

Olive peeled her gaze away from Gabby, glanced down as her protruding stomach, and groaned. Mamma Pacelli placed a large piece of tiramisu in front of Olive and said, "Mangiare," which she'd quickly learned meant "eat."

Olive took a small bite of the cool, refreshing treat and groaned again, but for an entirely different reason than before. It was maybe the best thing she'd ever tasted. She took another bite, bigger this time.

"You know what tiramisu means?" Mamma Pacelli asked. Olive shook her head, unable to speak with a mouth full. "It means *cheer me up.*"

Olive wasn't sure if it was the caffeine kick from the coffee-soaked dessert or the company, but she certainly felt joyful. She scanned the boisterous women at the table, laughing, talking, and eating. No doubt they were a passionate family who argued a lot, but they also obviously loved each other as well. Olive had often heard the cliché "close-knit family" but never really knew what it meant until tonight.

"Olive, would you like to get married some day and have kids?" Mamma Pacelli asked between bites.

"Actually, I would, but I've never met the woman I'd want to settle down with."

"Gabriella is quite the cook, you know. And very handy around the house."

"Mamma, you promised to be good." Gabby shot her a threatening glance.

"What? I'm just getting to know our guest a little better." Mamma Pacelli innocently batted her eyelashes. "She has a very good job, too. General manager for our pizza restaurants."

Gabby turned to Olive, her cheeks flushed. "Sorry."

Olive smiled, enjoying Gabby's embarrassment. "That sounds like a lot of responsibility. When do you have time for your photography?"

"Pshaw." Mamma Pacelli waved her fork in the air. "Gabriella doesn't have time for silly hobbies."

Gabby stiffened and studied the napkin in her lap.

"But she's so talented." From the sour look on Mamma Pacelli's face, Olive probably should have kept her mouth shut.

"How would you know that?" Gabby peered at Olive.

"Because you always win the…" Olive bit her tongue. Now was obviously not the time to bring up the photography competition.

Gabby cocked her head and squinted at Olive for several long moments before her eyes widened. She opened her mouth, like she was about to speak, but then snapped it shut. Gabby had finally recognized her. Olive was certain of it.

CHAPTER SEVEN

THE GODFATHER SPEAKS

Gabby was often accused of being hot-headed and impetuous, although she preferred to think of herself as enthusiastic. She *was* Italian, after all. She stood outside the red Say Cheeze door and took a deep breath, attempting to tame her temper. Olive knew they'd been competitors but hadn't said anything. What a sneaky move. Was she trying to get inside info on Gabby's photography entry this year? It wasn't surprising that Gabby hadn't immediately recognized Olive. In fact, when they'd competed, Gabby had purposefully avoided her biggest rival. She hadn't wanted to know Olive's name, much less what she looked like.

Gabby swung the door open and glanced around the empty office. Mr. Finkelmeier's light was on so she stuck her head in. He was reclining in his chair with his feet propped on the desk watching *Charlie's Angels* on his computer and drooling. What a lazy sleaze. When Gabby cleared her throat, he quickly pressed Pause and jumped up.

"Gabby, what can I do for you?"

"I was looking for Olive."

"This is her day off. Do you need something? I can call her."

"No. That's fine. I just wanted to speak to her about something."

"Let me give you her address. I'm sure she wouldn't mind."

Mr. Finkelmeier grabbed a yellow sticky note, jotted something down, and handed it to Gabby.

"I don't want to bother her."

"It's no problem. Anything for a Pacelli." The corners of Mr. Finkelmeier's eyes crinkled with a smile.

"Thanks." Gabby nodded and left.

She leaned outside the doorframe and read the paper: Island Shores Condominiums, along with an address and phone number. Normally she wouldn't barge in unexpectedly, but she didn't want to wait until tomorrow and sort of liked the idea of surprising Olive. Gabby paused for a few moments before she walked half a block and rented an electric golf cart.

Gabby wasn't the squeamish type, but she couldn't help but cringe as she drove precariously close to the edge of a winding, narrow mountain road. One wrong move and she'd tumble thousands of feet down a canyon. Despite the heart-pounding trek, the scenery was gorgeous. She stopped several times along the way to marvel at the ocean views. At one point, she was so high up that Avalon looked like a miniature town made out of Legos. After a twenty-minute drive, Gabby pulled into the complex and knocked on Olive's door. No answer. She was about to ring the bell when she saw a familiar figure walking down the sidewalk. The woman approached, clearly shocked to see Gabby.

"Aren't you Nicki? Olive's friend?"

"Yeah. Aren't you the Italian Stallion?" Nicki gasped and put a hand over her mouth, her face bright crimson.

"Excuse me? The what?"

"I didn't mean…I…Christ…Olive is gonna kill me."

The Italian Stallion? Sounds like a nickname. My *nickname.* This really cinched it. Not only did Olive know who she was, but she'd obviously gossiped to her friend.

"Do you live here?" Gabby pointed to Olive's door.

Nicki rubbed her forehead, still apparently shaken by her slip. "No. I live in an apartment a couple of blocks down."

"Do you know where Olive is? She isn't answering."

"Yeah. She's at the pool. Is she expecting you?"

Gabby ignored the question. "Is it this way?" Gabby pointed in the direction the woman had come from. Considering her hair was drenched and she was wearing a bikini top, she must have been with Olive.

"Yeah, but—"

"Thanks. You've been a wealth of information." Gabby walked away, leaving Nicki standing on the sidewalk.

Once Gabby rounded the corner, the sparkling, sapphire pool was easy to spot. It looked like something at a fancy Vegas hotel, with waterfalls and Jacuzzis, and surrounded by palm trees. Even though it was crowded, Gabby spotted Olive within seconds. Her hair pulled back, she looked amazing lounging in a chair wearing oversized, dark sunglasses, like Carole Lombard on the cover of a vintage movie magazine. Her one-piece emerald bathing suit revealed an abundance of glowing, pale skin. Gabby walked in a wide circle and crept up behind Olive. She breathed in the intoxicating scent of piña colada as her gaze traveled down shapely legs. From this vantage point, Gabby had a sizzling view of milky, ample cleavage. She inwardly sighed and licked her lips. What she wouldn't give to...Gabby's carnal musings were interrupted when she saw the *Journeys* magazine in Olive's hand, reminding her that they were competitors. Too bad. They could have had a lot of fun together.

Gabby reached over Olive's head and snatched the magazine out of her hand.

"Hey!" Olive protested but didn't turn around. "Very funny, Nicki. I thought you were going home."

"It's not Nicki."

Olive twisted around so fast it was surprising she didn't get whiplash. "What the...what are you doing here?" She grabbed a towel and clutched it to her chest.

"Don't cover up on my account. I was just enjoying the view."

"How in the world did you find me?"

"Mr. Finkelmeier."

Olive's face twisted. "Do you need something?"

"No." Gabby flipped through the magazine.

After a few moments, Olive asked, "Sooo, why are you here?"

Gabby settled her gaze on Olive. "I see you're a fan of *Journeys.*"

Olive turned scarlet, which probably wasn't a result of the sun. She swung her legs around and stood up. "All right. I know you recognized me last night and realized I knew who you were."

Gabby tossed the magazine on the lounger. "Why didn't you say anything? Were you trying to see if you could infiltrate the competition?"

"Of course not."

"So you did enter the contest this year?"

"Yes. But I didn't mean to be sneaky about it." Olive sighed and stared up at the clouds. When she whipped off her sunglasses, Gabby was awestruck by how green her eyes were. Maybe it was the lighting or the reflection from her swimsuit, but they sparkled like an emerald. "Look. I guess I was a little miffed that you didn't know who I was. I mean, we've been in the same competition for the past three years. How could you not recognize me?" Olive's eyes clouded in a surprising sadness.

"When I'm competing, I have a one-track mind. If you'd said who you were, I'm sure I would have put two-and-two together. I knew you looked familiar."

"I guess I should've been upfront with you, Gabby."

"Don't you mean the Italian Stallion?" Olive's mouth fell open, but no words came out. "I ran into Nicki and she let it slip." Olive closed her eyes and shook her head. "That was Rocky Balboa's nickname. I'm not a boxer."

Olive opened her eyes and looked like she wanted to dive into the pool and never resurface. "We sorta came up with it the first year you won. I guess because you're so competitive. It's a compliment."

"Do you have any other nicknames for me?" Olive paused, her eyes shifting. "Oh my God, you do. What are they?"

"Nothing...too bad."

"Yeah, right," Gabby said, sarcastically.

"Sorry?" That came out more as a question than a statement.

"It doesn't matter." But it sort of did. Gabby didn't like that Olive had a negative opinion of her.

"Can I get you something to eat or drink? We could go back to my condo."

Olive was probably trying to smooth things over, but hanging out with the cute Say Cheeze photographer wasn't an option.

"That's probably not the best idea, considering we're competitors and all."

"Ah, so no more dinner invitations, I gather?" Olive actually looked disappointed.

"That's right. Put your game face on, baby!"

Olive sighed. "You're the second person who's said that to me the past few days. I have absolutely no idea what that means."

Gabby narrowed her eyes, scrunched her face, and flashed the best Don Vito Corleone expression she could muster.

Olive stuck her tongue in her cheek, possibly to suppress a laugh. "*That's* your game face?"

"It's my Marlon Brando impression. You know, from *The Godfather*." Gabby rubbed a hand over her chin and said in a gruff, baritone voice, "Revenge is a dish best served cold."

"I have no idea what that means."

Gabby relaxed her expression. "You've obviously never seen *The Godfather*."

"True. So that face..." Olive waved her hand toward Gabby. "It was supposed to intimidate me?"

"It's more to put me in the right mindset to win. And I *will* win."

Olive raised an eyebrow. "Is that right? Just make sure you do it fair and square."

"What's that supposed to mean?"

"It's no secret what happened last year."

Gabby's heart pounded as adrenaline coursed through her body. "For your information, nothing happened. I was falsely accused of sleeping with a judge."

"Is that right?" Olive smirked in a way that clearly said Gabby was full of crap.

"And if you really want to know the truth, you owe me a thousand dollars!"

Olive laughed aloud, which ignited Gabby's anger even more. "What in the world are you talking about?"

"The judge I so-called slept with came clean after I was disqualified and you were already announced as the winner. They were going to renounce your prize and crown me instead but... well...I told them to let it go."

"You're insane. There's no way you'd pass up a thousand dollars and a chance to vindicate yourself. That so did not happen." Olive rolled her eyes and grabbed her beach towel, folding it into a neat, perfect square.

"Yes, it did! And I'd love to get my hands on the person who turned me in."

Olive stiffened, her expression stern as a bull.

"Excellent game face," Gabby said. "Keep it. You'll need it." She turned to walk away but stopped, which was too bad because that would've made an excellent exit. Instead, she said, "I need you to do me a favor."

"I'm not giving you a thousand dollars. I deserved to win."

"Not that. Don't mention anything about the contest to my family."

"Okay. But—"

"Good."

"They don't know you entered?"

Gabby ignored the question and walked away. Olive didn't need to know her personal business. It's not like they were going to be friends and definitely not lovers now.

When Gabby was coasting back down the mountain, her cell phone rang. It was a number she didn't recognize, but she answered anyway, thinking it might be work-related.

"This is Gabby Pacelli. How can I help you?"

"Oh my, so formal. Do you always answer the phone that way?" The woman's voice was deep and sultry, with a hint of playfulness.

"Who am I speaking with?"

"This is Carmen." Gabby was fairly certain she didn't know a Carmen. When she didn't respond, the woman said, "We met the other day on the boat to Catalina."

That Carmen. Gabby definitely remembered her. Blond hair, blue eyes, and sexy curves.

"Of course. I'm so sorry. I didn't recognize the number and thought it was someone from work. How are you?"

"I'm great. I thought we could meet for a drink later."

"Sure. How about Frank's Sports Bar?"

"Sports bar?"

"Or anywhere you'd like."

"No, no, that sounds fine. Say sevenish?"

"Perfect. I'll see you then. Oh, and Carmen, I'm really glad you called."

So things hadn't worked out with Olive. Carmen was more Gabby's type anyway. Olive probably wanted happily-ever-after, and Gabby had no intention of shacking up with anyone. She didn't want anything impeding her freedom or holding her back from her dreams.

CHAPTER EIGHT

ZOMBIE FLESH EATERS

Gabby sat on a stool at Frank's and glanced between a basketball game on the big screen and the front door. Once Carmen arrived maybe they could find a more intimate setting, considering the bar was loud and crowded. Too bad they weren't in LA, where they could go to Gabby's apartment. If things went as expected, she'd be whipping up an omelet for Carmen in the morning. Gabby's heart raced when Olive strolled in with Nicki. It was bad enough to be bombarded with the woman's cuteness in broad daylight; she didn't particularly want to see how beautiful Olive looked in a dim setting. Gabby had to keep her head in the game, stay focused, if she was going to win. And being attracted to Olive wasn't part of the plan.

Before Gabby could turn away, their eyes met. Olive paused for several seconds, probably debating whether to acknowledge or ignore Gabby. Unfortunately, she decided to play nice and approached, with Nicki tentatively following. Olive was wearing light-gray jeans and a red shirt that revealed the enticing cleavage Gabby had drooled over earlier. Her normally pale complexion was tinged pink, probably from an overexposure of sun, and the freckles across her nose were more pronounced, which made her look even cuter. Olive stood directly in front of Gabby, her gorgeous green eyes filled with trepidation. She pushed up her red glasses, which

Gabby figured had little to do with adjusting her specs and more about being nervous.

"Hey," Olive said.

"Hey. You two basketball fans?" Gabby briefly glanced at Nicki, who was hiding behind Olive, probably still embarrassed about her *Italian Stallion* blunder.

"Nicki is." Olive cocked her head toward her friend. "I'm just here for a drink. What brings you out tonight?"

"I'm meeting someone."

"Someone?" Olive raised an eyebrow.

"A woman."

"Wow, you work fast. You just got into town."

Gabby shrugged. "We're having a drink together."

"In a non-dating sort of way, of course, since you don't date."

Nicki popped her head over Olive's shoulder. "You don't date?"

"She probably doesn't believe in long-term relationships or marriage," Olive said, smugly.

"I don't like labels. And if you must know, I'm not the marrying kind. I don't want anything tying me down." Olive squinted and regarded Gabby critically for several moments. "What's that look mean?"

Olive slightly shook her head. "Nothing. It's just your family is so close, I figured you'd want to find the love of your life and commit like your sisters have."

"I've always been a bit of a rebel."

Olive chuckled. "I'm sure that goes over well with your mother."

"What about you? I bet you want a fairy-tale relationship, princess on a horse, white picket fence, the works."

"I don't know about all that, but I do want something more than a roll in the sack with a stranger."

Gabby sat upright, feeling suddenly defensive. "Carmen isn't a stranger." Actually she was, but that was none of Olive's business.

"Did I hear my name?" All eyes turned to the stunning blonde. Carmen was a knockout in black jeans, a tight-fitting black shirt, and killer high heels.

Gabby stood and gave Carmen an awkward hug, hoping she hadn't overheard their conversation. "Hi. It's great to see you again. This is Olive and Nicki."

Nicki stepped from behind Olive and held out her hand. "So nice to meet you." Gabby couldn't blame Nicki for flashing a flirty grin. Carmen was gorgeous and would turn anyone's head...except maybe Olive, since she looked more disgusted than captivated.

"Friends of yours?" Carmen asked Gabby.

"Sort of. Olive is photographing my sister's wedding, and Nicki is her friend."

"Just the *pre-wedding* events," Olive said.

Gabby frowned. "Mr. Finkelmeier's doing?"

Olive nodded.

It was disgraceful how he pushed Olive around and gave her all the crappy jobs. She was a talented photographer who could be making top dollar at her choice of agency. She deserved better than Say Cheeze. Why she'd never left the island was beyond Gabby. Not that Gabby cared, but she suspected Olive had some reason other than her love of Avalon.

"We should get out of your way," Olive said. "Nice meeting you, Carmen." Olive grabbed Nicki's arm and pulled her along. Nicki nabbed a table within eyeshot, which didn't seem to suit Olive, considering she glanced at Gabby several times before settling into a chair.

Carmen slipped onto the stool next to Gabby and snapped her fingers at the bartender. "I'll take your finest Bordeaux."

The bartender stared, perplexed. "We have red or white."

"What *type* of wine is it, dear?"

He grabbed a bottle, looked at the label, and said, "Merlot."

"From what region?"

He looked like she'd just asked him to mentally divide a trillion by a gazillion. Carmen reached over the counter, grabbed the bottle out of his hand, and scrunched her nose.

"Not good?" Gabby asked.

"Napa Valley. Typical. I drink only merlot from France."

"Ah. This place is probably more about quantity than quality. If you—"

"Do you have ionized water? Or Icelandic Glacial natural spring? How about Lauquen Artes mineral water?"

"We have tap or fizzy," the bartender replied, stone-faced.

"What about coconut water? Everyone has that."

"We could go someplace else if you'd like," Gabby said.

Carmen waved a hand. "This is fine. I'll take sparkling...or rather *fizzy*, as you called it...with organic lemon."

Gabby shot the bartender an apologetic look. "I'll have a Bud Light. Thanks." Gabby glanced at Olive, who had a big smirk on her face. Had she overheard the wine/water debacle?

"I wouldn't have taken you for a beer drinker."

"I'm pretty easy to please." Gabby took a sip out of the frosted mug the bartender placed in front of her.

Carmen scooted closer, her thigh pressed against Gabby's leg. "Is that so? I usually like a challenge, but easy might be fun, too." Carmen placed a hand on Gabby's knee.

Could the woman be any more obvious? It wouldn't take much to get her into bed. Come to think of it, from the glint in Carmen's eyes she'd probably do it sprawled out on top of the bar. This was Gabby's dream girl: easy and uncomplicated, unlike Olive. With that thought, Gabby glanced at Olive, who was staring right at her, the smirk replaced with a scowl.

Gabby forced her eyes back to Carmen. "You don't mince words, do you?"

Carmen slowly ran her hand up Gabby's thigh, stopping dangerously close to the apex of her legs. "I know what I want. I'm looking for no-strings-attached, short-term entertainment. I don't need to know what you drive, what your favorite color is, or what you ate for breakfast. The only thing I'm interested in is what you like in bed."

A chuckle bubbled in Gabby's throat. Carmen might be the most straightforward woman she'd ever met.

Carmen took a slow sip of water. "Are you game?"

Gabby's eyes obviously had a mind of their own when they immediately darted toward Olive. Why she kept taking peeks at the Say Cheeze photographer was beyond her. She held Olive's gaze for several seconds until she realized Carmen was waiting for a response. Was she game? Hell, yeah! She'd be crazy not to be. She just had to make sure of something first.

"One question and please give me an honest answer. Are you married?"

"No," Carmen replied, without hesitation.

Gabby released a satisfied breath. She was a player, but she'd never mess around with a married woman. "Count me in."

Carmen's wide smile suddenly dropped when her cell phone dinged. She read the screen and groaned. "Fuck. My first night off in weeks and now this."

"Anything wrong?"

Carmen looked at Gabby, disappointment clouding her blue eyes. "Duty calls." She stood and slipped the phone into her purse. "I'm sorry, but I need to take a raincheck."

"No problem. Business before pleasure. I understand."

Carmen leaned over and claimed Gabby's mouth. What was probably meant to be a quick peck turned into something far steamier. Within seconds, Carmen had slipped her hand around Gabby's neck, pulled her close, and applied direct pressure between Gabby's legs with her knee. The woman could definitely kiss and didn't seem to mind doing so in the middle of a straight bar. After what felt like several minutes of tongue jostling, they finally broke apart.

"I'll call you." Carmen winked and sauntered out the door.

Gabby looked at Olive's table, glad to see that it was empty. For some reason, she was thankful she hadn't witnessed that brazen public display of affection.

❖

Olive had never been thrown out of a movie theater in her life. Only rambunctious teenagers and juvenile delinquents who snuck in without paying got the boot. A twenty-eight-year-old professional, well-respected citizen of the community should not be kicked to the curb, except that she was, and it was all the Italian Stallion's fault.

Olive settled into her seat, balanced a small popcorn between her thighs, and placed a large Sprite in the cup holder, ready to watch the 1979 cult-classic *Zombie Flesh Eaters*. After the sickening sight of Gabby with the blond bombshell, watching a horror movie seemed like the thing to do. They had practically mauled each other worse than the zombies would do. After their steamy lip-lock, Olive had bolted out of the bar. She didn't like watching X-rated movies on the big screen, much less seeing one up close and personal.

Olive put Gabby out of her mind, determined to enjoy the flick. She loved B horror films, mostly because they were so hilarious, with horrendous acting, crappy cinematography, and pathetic special effects. Olive stuffed a handful of buttered popcorn into her mouth, sorry she'd forgotten napkins. But what the heck. It wouldn't be a true movie experience without buttery palms. She took a big gulp of Sprite and thought she felt something hit the back of her head, probably just someone behind her trying to find their seat. Olive ducked when several pieces of popcorn rained down from above. *What the hell?* It took several more popcorn dodges for her to realize some annoying kid was using her for target practice. When Olive whisked around, a kernel hit her right between the eyes.

Except it wasn't a kid. It was Gabby.

Olive shot her a dirty look and whispered, "Are you eight? Cut it out!"

Gabby's lopsided grin looked much too cute, considering she was such a pain in the ass. "I thought you might like some popcorn."

"I have my own." Olive looked apologetically at the man sitting next to Gabby and turned around.

What's she doing here? Olive shook her head in disgust. Hadn't she had enough of the Pacellis today?

Olive drew her head back and stared, incredulous, as Gabby climbed over the backrest and into the seat next to her.

"What the hell are you doing?" She'd whispered, or at least she thought she had, until someone shushed her. "You're sitting on my bag." Olive yanked the shoulder strap under Gabby's rear end. The bag flew through the air and conked a lady in the back of the head. The woman twisted around and shot Olive the meanest "fuck you" look ever. It was Mrs. Johnson and her three boys from the zootopia photo shoot.

Olive silently mouthed, "I'm sorry," but that seemed to do little to appease the woman.

Olive gaped at Gabby's profile as she stared at the screen, chewing a mouthful of popcorn, like nothing had happened.

"Aren't you worried us sitting together is too date-like?" Olive whispered.

Gabby chuckled and responded without taking her eyes off the film. "You wish."

Olive narrowed her eyes. "What are you doing here?"

"Who would want to miss zombies? I'm surprised you're cool enough to like this movie."

"Aren't you supposed to be making out in a bar right now?"

"Carmen had to leave. Some work thing."

Olive glanced at the screen for a few seconds, then back at Gabby. "I've never seen her before. Where's she from?"

Gabby shrugged.

"Where does she work?"

"She didn't say."

"What a sec. You don't know where she lives or what she does. I'd bet a million dollars you don't even know her last name."

"Shhh," someone behind them said.

"We didn't have time to talk," Gabby whispered.

"The way she was coming on to you, I bet you would have ended up in bed without knowing anything about her."

Gabby turned to face Olive. "As a matter of fact, I would have. Haven't you ever slept with someone just for the fun of it? Without any hidden agendas or expectations?"

"A complete stranger? No. I believe in actually dating and getting to know someone before I sleep with them."

Mrs. Johnson turned and glared at Olive. "Would you shut the fu…" She glanced at her three boys. "…be quiet!" *She can't cuss in front of her sons, but she can take them to a gory flesh-eating movie?*

Olive hunkered down in her seat. Maybe she was being judgmental. Just because she didn't have one-night stands didn't mean it was wrong. Some women liked having casual relationships. So why did it annoy Olive so much that Gabby was one of them?

They watched the film in silence for a while. Olive actually forgot that Gabby was sitting beside her, until a bloody zombie unexpectedly burst through a door, scaring the crap out of her. Olive jumped and instinctively grabbed the nearest thing, which, unfortunately, was Gabby's left thigh. Fingertips squeezed hard muscle like a vise. Obviously, the Italian Stallion worked out.

"Are you okay?" Gabby whispered.

"I was *not* expecting that."

Gabby chuckled. "Luckily, I've seen this one before so I knew it was coming. Feel free to grab anything you want of mine." Gabby looked at Olive's hand, which was still on her thigh.

"Oh, sorry." Olive jerked her arm back.

Olive glanced around when she heard an annoying beeping sound. It didn't take long to figure out where it was coming from when Gabby pulled out her cell phone, the bright light from the screen shining like a beacon. Gabby typed something and laid the phone on her leg. After a few moments, it beeped again, and Gabby entered another message. This went on for several minutes…beep… type…beep…type…the screen glowing like a bonfire.

"Did you read the sign?" Olive whispered. "Cell phones off."

"This is work," Gabby said as she typed.

"You're not at work, hot shot. Stop ruining the movie for everyone."

"I'm not ruining anything."

One more beep and Olive was going to steal that freakin' phone.

Beep…that was it…Olive grabbed Gabby's cell out of her hand.

"Hey! I need that." Gabby snatched it back. "Eww. Why is it slippery? Is that butter? Don't you use napkins?"

The phone slipped out of Gabby's hands and clanged to the floor. Mrs. Johnson glared at Olive, shot out of her seat, and stormed up the aisle.

"Help me find it." Gabby dropped to her knees.

Olive sighed, leaned over, and felt under her chair, the floor disgustingly sticky.

"All right, you two. Out." An attendant stood in the walkway shining a flashlight in Olive's eyes. "Come on. We've had several complaints about noise."

"I can't find my cell," Gabby said, still dithering around on the floor.

"We'll find your phone. But I need you two to get up and leave now."

This guy wasn't fooling around. Olive grabbed her bag, squeezed past several people, and walked up the aisle, passing a sneering Mrs. Johnson along the way. Olive entered the lobby, her heart beating erratically. Hopefully, they wouldn't call the cops. She'd hate to tell Mr. Finkelmeier she couldn't come to work because she was in the slammer.

After a few minutes, Gabby burst out of the door, waving her cell at Olive. "This is all your fault, you know."

"What?! You're the one illegally texting."

"It's not a law. It's a suggestion."

"They certainly *suggested* we leave."

"What a wasted night. No Carmen and now no *Zombie Flesh Eaters*," Gabby mumbled and shook her head as she walked out of the theater.

This day off sucked. First, Gabby had invaded her privacy at home, her night out at Frank's was a bust, and now she couldn't show her face at the movie theater again. The only good thing was that Gabby's hadn't hooked up with Carmen. Olive paused, tempted to analyze why that made her so happy, but instead she bought another bag of popcorn and headed home.

CHAPTER NINE

SWEET AND SOUR

They looked like the Shirelles, the 1960s rock-'n-roll group, with bouffant hairdos, thick black mascara, and caked-on blue eye shadow. Olive couldn't have been more amused, mostly because Gabby looked so miserable. The Pacelli sisters were sitting in Patsy's Hair Salon, getting a pre-wedding makeover. Mamma Pacelli flitted from one daughter to the next, inserting her opinion and most times pushing the hair stylist out of the way to make adjustments. Olive had never known the true meaning of a *helicopter mom* until she met Mamma Pacelli. Olive snapped impromptu photos of the women as they were dolled up. When Olive approached Gabby, she was met with an icy glare that resembled her *Godfather* impression from the day before.

"Don't you dare," Gabby said sternly when Olive pointed the camera in her direction.

"Just doin' my job." Olive snapped several photos, probably a few hundred more than necessary just to irritate Gabby.

Gina twisted her head every which way, examining her hair and makeup in the mirror. "What do you think, Mamma?"

Mamma Pacilli looked down the line of women. "*Le mie belle figlie!* Olive, aren't my daughters beautiful?"

"Gorgeous. It's the perfect look for a wedding." Actually, it was bizarrely over the top, but Olive wasn't about to cross the Pacellis. Her job was to keep her mouth shut and take photos.

All of a sudden, Gina yelled, "Baby's breath! That's what we're missing."

A few of the stylists rushed off and came back with handfuls of small white blossoms. They stuck twigs in each woman's hair, which didn't help Gabby's mood any. She probably wasn't the flower type.

Mamma Pacelli grabbed Gabby's chin. "Why is my baby so sad?"

"Seriously? I'm wearing a wig, an inch of makeup, and dainty flowers."

"When it's your wedding you can do what you want." Mamma Pacelli smiled and winked at Olive. Obviously, Gabby hadn't clued her in on the fact that they were rivals.

"Are we done now?" Gabby popped out of the chair and tugged at her wig.

Mamma Pacelli slapped her hand. "Stop! We have to take a group photo."

"Can we hurry? I have to be somewhere, and I want to wipe this gunk off," Gabby said, obviously agitated.

After Olive took several photos of the gang, Gabby disappeared into the back of the salon as the remaining sisters stood in a circle and complimented each other's looks. Mamma Pacelli sat in a chair and stared wistfully at herself in the mirror, strangely quiet.

"Are you okay?" Olive stood behind Mamma Pacelli and looked at her reflection.

"I was going to have my own salon someday." Mamma Pacelli spoke in an uncharacteristically quiet monotone. "My sweet mamma taught me everything I know about hair. When I was a little girl I'd sit on the counter and watch her. All the women in our neighborhood would come to her for a cut, color, and styling. I couldn't have been more than seven years old when I declared I'd have my own salon." Mamma Pacelli's eyes flicked to Olive in the mirror. "I've never told that to anyone before. Silly dreams."

"It's not silly. Why didn't you do it?"

"I fell in love. Alberto wanted to start a family right away. There was no time. No money."

"You still could—"

"No. That was the past."

Olive was about to protest again when Mamma Pacelli stood, forced a smile, and joined her daughters. The pain in her eyes tugged at Olive's heart. She knew all too well what it was like to give up on a dream.

Olive was packing up her camera and tripod when Gabby reappeared, wiping her face clean of any remaining makeup. She leaned against a wall and stared Olive up and down, which made Olive wonder what in the world she was thinking.

"You enjoyed that, didn't you?" Gabby asked.

"What?"

"Immortalizing my discomfort on film."

"Now that you mention it…yeah, a little bit." Olive couldn't hide her grin.

Gabby sneered, opened a container, threw something into the air, and caught it in her mouth. Normally, Olive would ignore the Italian Stallion, but curiosity got the better of her.

"Just what is that?"

"Spezzatina," Gabby said, as though that explained it.

Gabby tossed up another item and again it landed in her mouth, only this time she gagged and her eyes bugged. Gabby grabbed her throat, panic in her eyes. Immediately, Olive's insides twisted and her heart pounded. Gabby wasn't breathing, and the alarm had now turned to terror. Olive knew that look, that feeling, all too well. Gabby was suffocating. Olive needed to do something…and now, but she couldn't. Her feet were cemented to the floor.

Olive heard muffled voices, someone yelling to call 911, but they didn't have time for that. Gabby looked like she was about to hit the floor like a brick. It was one of the hardest things Olive ever had to do, but she forced shaky, noodle-like legs to take a step… and then another. Everything after that was a blur. Olive ran on automatic pilot as she grabbed Gabby from behind with trembling hands and performed the Heimlich maneuver, which she'd learned at a continuing-education seminar. With every thrust, Olive held her breath, not wanting to inhale until Gabby could do so as well.

After what felt like hours, something shot out of Gabby's mouth, and she began coughing uncontrollably. Relief washed over

Olive. Thank God she'd done the procedure right and Gabby was breathing again. It wasn't until Olive's pulse returned to normal that she noticed Mamma Pacelli and all the sisters encircling them, squealing and yelping. Olive stood back from the crowd and took a deep, shaky breath.

Mamma Pacelli embraced Olive. "You saved my baby's life! How can I ever thank you? You're an angel from heaven." After a never-ending forceful hug, she finally released Olive.

Olive looked down, suddenly embarrassed. "I wouldn't go that far. I did what anyone else would do."

Mamma Pacelli shook her head vigorously. "No…no…Alberto sent you to save our daughter."

"I'm happy I could help." Olive glanced at Gabby. She seemed to have recovered, but her eyes remained fearful. Something as scary as smothering could stay with a person for days, years even.

Olive tentatively approached Gabby. "Are you okay?"

"Yeah. That was…unexpected. Thanks. Mamma's right. You saved me."

Olive put a hand on Gabby's arm. "I'm just glad you're all right."

Gabby waved off her sisters. "I'm fine now, everyone. Go back to whatever you were doing."

Everyone dispersed and resumed discussing hair and makeup. Gabby looked suddenly uneasy and a little embarrassed, even though she had no reason to be.

"What exactly did I save you from?" Olive asked.

Gabby grinned sheepishly. "Candy."

Olive smiled, glad things had lightened up a bit. "At least you risked your life for something worthwhile. What'd you call it?"

"Spezzatina. It was my papa's favorite sweet treat. He never went anywhere without a box in his pocket."

"Just like you do now?" Olive's heart melted a little at how Gabby mimicked something her father did.

Gabby nodded, sadness in her eyes. She blinked rapidly, maybe to hold back tears, and looked at the clock. "Oh, my. I'm going to be late."

Olive knew where Gabby was headed, which was the same place she was going. The Catalina Chamber of Commerce was holding a contest orientation.

"Mamma, I'll see you later."

"Where are you off to in such a hurry?"

"I have to leave, too," Olive said.

"For a date? Together?" Mamma Pacelli beamed.

"No," Gabby said, sternly.

"Then where are you going?"

Gabby stared at the floor and shuffled her feet. Considering Gabby's request to keep the contest a secret, she probably didn't want to mention the orientation. What would they do if Gabby won and quit her job? Olive could just imagine the yelling that would provoke.

Before Olive could stop herself she said, "Actually, we have plans to do some sightseeing." She wasn't sure why she felt the need to save Gabby, but there it was.

"Why didn't you say so? Go, go! Have fun." She pushed them both out the door.

They stood awkwardly outside the salon until Gabby finally spoke. "Thanks. Guess that's twice you saved me."

"It looked like you needed a little help."

"Yeah. It's not easy to lie to Mamma." Gabby ran her fingers through her hair and sighed.

"She's definitely a strong personality. Why haven't you told them about the contest?"

"Isabella knows."

"But no one else?"

Gabby shook her head. "So, do you wanna...you know...walk together, since we're going to the same place?"

Obviously, she didn't want to discuss her family. "Sure. Why not?"

The streets of Avalon were empty as they strolled through town. This was Olive's least favorite time of the year. She preferred summer months, when the town was bustling with people and activities. It made her feel less isolated and alone.

"Olive! Over here!"

She heard someone calling but wasn't sure where it was coming from. Olive scanned the area until her eyes landed on the source. "Hello, Mr. Piccolo," Olive yelled and waved.

"Ooh, snow cones." Gabby's eyes lit up. "I haven't had one of those since I was a kid. Do we have time?" Gabby was pretty cute when she got excited. Come to think of it, this was the happiest she'd ever looked. Usually, she was arguing with her family or putting on a suave act. Who knew it'd take SnoCone Zone to let her guard down?

"We'll make time," Olive said, not wanting to disappoint her.

Gabby practically skipped to the brightly colored stand, her eyes roaming up and down the one hundred flavors while she licked her lips.

"Who's your friend?" Mr. Piccolo asked.

"This is Gabby. Gabby, meet Mr. Piccolo, the king of frozen fun."

"Hi," Gabby said, never taking her eyes off the menu. "There's so many choices."

"I'd suggest the Grape Ape, Ocean Breeze, Jelly Belly..." Olive said.

"Olive named my newest creation," Mr. Piccolo said, proudly.

Gabby peer at Olive sideways. "Really? Which one?"

"Tongue Twister," Mr. Piccolo said before Olive could respond.

Gabby chuckled. "Kinda cute."

"*Kinda*? It's genius," Olive said.

"Okay. I'll have that one then."

"You might want to rethink that." Olive couldn't imagine anyone liking that sour concoction.

"Why? That's the one I want."

"Right, but it's a little on the tart side. Don't you want to try a taster first?"

"No. I know what I want."

"God, you're stubborn. Not to mention combative," Olive mumbled.

Gabby narrowed her eyes and looked like she might respond, probably with something snooty, when Mr. Piccolo handed her the shaved ice. Seemingly forgetting about Olive's comment, Gabby opened her mouth wide and took a big bite. Her face immediately contorted, the sparkle in her eyes dimmed.

Gabby cleared her throat and said, "The name is quite fitting."

Mr. Piccolo's face dropped. "You don't like it?"

"No, I do. It's...tasty." Gabby managed a lopsided grin. She held the snow cone up like she was giving a toast. "Thanks, but we better get going."

When they were far enough away from Mr. Piccolo's stand, Gabby chucked the ice into the trash. "You're dying to say I told you so, aren't you?"

"Nooo." Olive shook her head.

"Yes, you are. Go ahead. Get it out of your system."

Olive paused for three full seconds before she blurted, "God, yes, I so wanted to say it. Told ya so." Olive sighed dramatically. "I feel much better now."

They both chuckled and crossed the street to walk along the shoreline. It was a beautiful day, pleasantly warm and not a cloud in the sapphire sky. Olive breathed in the ocean's scent and gazed out at the sparkling turquoise water.

"Do you know everyone on the island?" Gabby asked.

"Pretty much all the permanent residents."

"I still can't believe you've *never* left Catalina. What gives? There must be some reason."

"I told you. I love it here."

"Still, though. It's so small."

Olive pointed at a massive, white-washed, round building—known as the Casino—which was where the orientation was being held. "We better pick up the pace."

They walked in silence to one of the most prominent landmarks on Avalon. Despite its name, it'd never been used for gambling. The Casino housed a glamorous movie theater, art deco murals, a 1929 pipe organ, and a spectacular second-story ballroom with a balcony that had amazing views and was considered the most romantic spot on Catalina. In fact, the ballroom was where Gina's reception would be held.

The meeting had already started when they entered the theater, so Gabby and Olive grabbed seats on the back row.

"Sure a lot of contestants here," Olive whispered, scanning the crowd.

"I'm not worried," Gabby said, confidently.

Olive craned her neck so she could see Mrs. Albright from the Chamber of Commerce, who was standing onstage at the podium. A man stood beside her, but she couldn't quite make him out from the back of the room.

"...largest competition we've had, and we're very excited to have *Journeys* magazine as a sponsor. The theme this year is the Isle of Love. All entries must depict the romance of Catalina. As always, this contest is for amateur photographers. If you make over two thousand dollars a year selling your photos, you're not eligible to enter."

Gabby leaned close to Olive and whispered, "Why aren't you considered a professional?"

"The pictures I take at Say Cheeze don't qualify as personal sales. You're not getting rid of me that easy."

"Like I said, I'm not worried."

Olive rolled her eyes. Could the woman be any cockier?

"The first runner-up will receive a thousand dollars and a two-year subscription to *Journeys*," Mrs. Albright said. "And the grand prize winner will be awarded a position as travel photographer for the magazine."

Gabby and Olive leered at one another like two prize fighters in the ring. Gabby's eyes filled with desire and determination. She wanted this just as much as Olive did. And who could blame her? It was a life-changing opportunity.

"And here to tell us about the grand prize is world-renowned photographer Robert Klein." Mrs. Albright stepped aside so the man could take the podium.

The theater erupted in applause and whistles, but Olive was too stunned to do either. All she could do was open her mouth wide and point.

"What?" Gabby asked. "Is something wrong?"

Olive looked at Gabby, her eyes probably the size of CD discs. "That's my favorite photographer!"

"He's all right." Gabby shrugged.

Olive elbowed her hard. "All right?! Have you seen his black-and-white landscapes?"

"Yes and ouch."

"They're perfection. You can't possibly mean just *all right*. What photos of his have you seen?"

"I dunno. The seascape ones, I guess."

"And what did you think?"

"He's good."

Good? Olive shook her head, completely speechless. Gabby was obviously insane, but no more than Olive, since she was wasting time arguing when Robert Klein was actually speaking. Thanks to Gabby she'd missed half of his speech already.

"You've taken many of *Journeys'* photographs," Mrs. Albright said. "Tell us what your favorite photo shoot was."

Mr. Klein pursed his lips. "That's a tough one. They've all been unique in so many ways. I'd say my favorite, though, was Angel Falls in South America."

Olive remembered that centerfold spread. She must have looked at it for hours, visualizing herself under the world's highest uninterrupted waterfall.

"What did he say? I wasn't listening," Gabby whispered.

"Angel Falls."

"Where's that?"

"You're the world traveler, not me. It's in Venezuela."

"I make pizza. I don't travel."

"Would you be quiet? I'm trying to listen."

The guy sitting beside Olive shushed them both.

"Oh, great. You're going to get us thrown out of here, too." Olive sneered.

"Me? You're the one that got us kicked out of the theater."

Everyone clapped as Olive watched Robert Klein exit through a side door. Olive shot Gabby a dirty look for making her miss her favorite photographer.

"You'll find information packets at the back of the room, and anyone at the Chamber of Commerce will be happy to answer any questions you may have. Good luck." Mrs. Albright smiled and departed the stage.

Everyone shot up and headed for the packets, except Gabby. She approached Mrs. Albright, who beamed the moment she saw Gabby. After a quick embrace, they chatted for a bit. Olive was too far away to hear what was being said, but she noticed lots of smiles and head nodding. Considering what had happened last year, Mrs. Albright looked awfully happy to see Gabby. A pang of uncertainty shot through Olive's gut. Maybe what Gabby had said was true. Maybe she hadn't cheated.

After Gabby exited the theater, Olive cornered Mrs. Albright.

"Do you have a minute?" Olive asked.

"Of course, dear."

"The person you were just talking to...Gabby..." Olive glanced around to make sure no one was listening. "You know that I'm the one who turned her in last year. But...wasn't what I saw accurate? She was disqualified from the competition, right?"

Mrs. Albright cocked her head, pursed her lips, and scratched what was probably a nonexistent itch on her forehead. "Actually... she wasn't."

Olive felt like a grand piano had fallen ten stories and landed on her head. She held up a hand. "Wait a minute...I saw the judge and Gabby all over each other at a bar and then go back to Gabby's hotel room. We're not supposed to talk to the judges, much less cavort with them."

"In the end there were extenuating circumstances."

"Please, Mrs. Albright, this is important. What happened?"

"We were a bit too hasty in our decision. It seems that the judge had too much to drink and was the one pursuing Gabriella. When she tried to call the woman a taxi, she wouldn't reveal where she was staying, and Gabriella didn't want to leave her at the bar in an inebriated condition. So, she took her back to her hotel room to sleep it off. The judge collapsed in the bed and Gabriella slept on the couch. This, of course, was all corroborated with the judge after the unfortunate disqualification."

Olive couldn't believe what she was hearing. Gabby hadn't done anything wrong. In fact, she was being a Good Samaritan. Olive had totally jumped to conclusions and had convinced Mrs. Albright to do the same.

"I don't know what to say. I had no idea. I just knew what I'd seen." Olive stared at the floor, regret weighing heavy on her chest. "Why didn't you reverse the decision after you found out the truth?"

"Oh, we did! And we were prepared to admit and rectify our error, but Gabriella said not to bother and then completely disappeared." Mrs. Albright snapped her fingers. "She wouldn't return calls, so we let things stand as they were."

"Why would she do that? Wouldn't anyone want to be vindicated after being falsely accused?"

Mrs. Albright shrugged. "We were going to tell you, but there was really no point, and we didn't want to mar your achievement."

What achievement? Gabby won, not me. And not only that, but I stripped her of the title.

Olive took a deep breath. "I just…I'm sorry I said anything…"

"Don't beat yourself up, dear. It wasn't your fault."

But it was Olive's fault. None of this would have happened if she'd kept her big mouth shut or had asked Gabby about it before snitching. But then again, she wouldn't have believed anything the Italian Stallion would have said. Olive had already made up her mind that Gabby was a womanizer who'd do anything to win. Olive had been judgmental and so very wrong.

CHAPTER TEN

WHITEWATER

It was like trying to talk to a tree stump. Why was Olive attempting a conversation with Nonna when she knew she wouldn't get any response? Probably because they were the only two people at Say Cheeze, waiting for the gang to arrive. The elderly woman sat stiffly across from Olive's desk, clutching a shiny, black purse in her lap.

"Sooo, the wedding is in a couple of weeks. Are you excited?"

No answer.

"I heard Gabby say that Tony, Gina's fiancé, is a dream."

Still nothing.

"Hmm...so do—"

Nonna pointed to the front door, then Olive, and crossed both arms over her chest, as she'd done at dinner a few nights before. Olive knew exactly what the woman meant.

"No, no," Olive said, shaking her head. "Your granddaughter and I are not in love. We're not even friends. Don't get me wrong. I like Gabby. Quite a lot, actually." Olive stared at the camera on her desk. "I was really wrong about her. I mean, she can certainly be obnoxious, but she's different than I thought she'd be. More...I dunno...nice and sorta fun. And anyone would be blind not to see how gorgeous she is. I mean, *really*..." Olive's cheeks flamed. She'd been absentmindedly rambling, and to Gabby's grandmother no less. Olive glanced at Nonna, who was sporting a smile and a knowing twinkle in her ebony eyes. Before Olive could do damage control, Gabby burst through the door and scanned the office.

"Seriously?" Gabby asked. "They're not even here yet? I thought I was going to be late."

Gabby exhaled and gave Nonna a kiss on her wrinkled cheek. Nonna tugged Gabby's shirt and whispered something in her ear. Olive tensed, hoping the woman wasn't revealing how hot she thought her granddaughter was.

"Do you have a restroom?" Gabby asked Olive.

"Yeah. Through that door."

Nonna's frame creaked as Gabby helped her stand and walk to the bathroom. Olive remembered what Isabella had said at Sunday dinner. What if Nonna was right? What if her life was nearing the end? She looked awfully ancient and decrepit. Olive pushed the thought aside. The Pacellis would be devastated if that happened, especially Gabby, since they seemed so close.

"Ugh. I need caffeine." Gabby headed to the coffee machine and poured a cup. She took a long sip and swallowed hard. "Ahhh. That hits the spot." Gabby leaned against the wall and closed her eyes, looking like she could doze off at any moment.

Olive took the opportunity to appreciate Gabby unnoticed, letting her eyes travel from long eyelashes, to round, firm-looking breasts, and down tan, toned legs. Olive skipped Gabby's white shorts since she abhorred anything of that color. Her pulse stampeded when she stared at Gabby's mouth. Olive had no doubt she was a passionate kisser. No one could look like she did and not have talented lips. Olive could only imagine what it would be like to actually kiss her...not that she was imagining that, of course.

Suddenly, Gabby's eyes popped open, which caused heat to creep up Olive's neck. She looked down and fiddled with the buttons on her camera.

"I need to tell you something," Olive said, never taking her eyes off the camera. "After the orientation yesterday, I asked Mrs. Albright about the contest last year...and she told me what happened." Olive met Gabby's eyes. "I'm sorry I didn't believe you."

Gabby pushed off the wall and sat in a chair across from Olive. "I want to win just as much as anyone, but I'd never cheat to do it."

"I know that now. I'm sorry you had to go through that last year."

"It's not your fault. I'm just glad you know the truth."

But it *was* her fault. Olive hoped Gabby couldn't see the guilt in her eyes. She should come clean, tell Gabby everything...but she couldn't.

"Why didn't you let them reverse the ruling? Why'd you let me win?"

"That's when Papa died. I had to rush back to LA and could have cared less about the competition or money when that happened."

"Oh, my gosh. I'm so sorry." Olive felt lower than the bottommost, slimiest, creepiest creature on the face of the earth. She couldn't have been more wrong about Gabby.

"Don't worry. You don't owe me a thousand dollars." Gabby yawned and stretched her arms high overhead.

"Did you have another date with the blond bombshell last night? You look beat." Olive wasn't sure why she'd brought up Carmen, since it was the last thing she wanted to hear about.

"No. I just stayed up too late."

Mr. Finkelmeier opened his office door. "Olive, there's been... oh, hello, Gabby."

Gabby's posture stiffened, her eyes shooting invisible darts directly into Mr. Finkelmeier's forehead. At least that was one thing they had in common: an intense dislike for Olive's boss.

"I was wondering," Gabby said to Mr. Finkelmeier. "Why isn't Olive photographing Gina's wedding? I mean, she's doing all the other shoots."

Mr. Finkelmeier looked a little shell-shocked before he said, "Oh...well...I'm the professional and we want the best—"

"Olive is a professional, too. The photos she takes here aren't even half of what she can do. Have you seen her work? She's amazing."

Olive's heart warmed. Not only was Gabby standing up to for her, but complimenting her as well. It took all Olive had not to climb over her desk and give Gabby a big smooch on the lips…or cheek. Yes, cheek. That would be more appropriate. Maybe not as much fun, but definitely more appropriate.

"Yes, but—"

"Would you let her photograph the wedding if Gina agrees?"

"Well, I…" Mr. Finkelmeier darted to Nonna when she opened the door. He helped her take a seat and then went into his office, completely ignoring Gabby's question.

Gabby chuckled and shook her head, probably at her boss's quick disappearing act.

"Thanks," Olive said. "Why'd you do that?"

Gabby shrugged. "I don't like the guy. Plus, consider it payback for saving my life. Not that it probably had any impact on him."

"Probably not." Olive sighed and looked at Mr. Finkelmeier's closed door. "But I appreciate the gesture."

Mr. Finkelmeier opened his door and popped his head out. "Olive, I remember what I was going to tell you. There's been a change of plans. The Pacelli photo shoot this morning will be a BS." Olive and Gabby exchanged curious glances. "You're supposed to meet them at the dock." Mr. Finkelmeier slammed his door shut.

"BS?" Gabby asked with a chuckle. "Like bull sh…" Her eyes darted to Nonna. "You know what I mean."

"I have no idea what it stands for, but I guess we better get going."

Olive had an uneasy feeling as she packed up her camera and tripod. Why would they meet at the dock? That's where the cruise ships and sailboats were. Someone should have told her the plan beforehand. She didn't like surprises.

Luckily, Gabby helped Olive carry the equipment across town to the beach. It wasn't a long walk, but Nonna slowed them down a bit. When they reached the ocean, Mamma Pacelli and her daughters were sitting in folding chairs under a palm tree. The dock, which extended from the shoreline out into the ocean, sprawled directly in front of them. At the end of the long wooden plank was a yacht with the words RENT ME written in big letters across the side.

Olive tentatively approached, never taking her eyes off the boat. "What's going on? Why are we meeting here?"

Isabella stood, offered Nonna her chair, and said, "Gina actually had a good idea. For once."

Gina jumped up. "I *always* have good ideas."

That's when it hit Olive. BS stood for boat shoot. Her heart rate escalated from normal to danger zone within seconds. *No, no, no... this would not happen in a million, gazillion years.*

"I rented the yacht for a couple of hours for a sunset cruise," Gina said. "We can take photos out in the ocean."

"On...the boat?" Olive hated the sound of her voice, shaky and horribly fearful.

A chill crept from Olive's head to her toes, and goose bumps appeared on her arms and legs. Her chest constricted and her lungs burned as she attempted to take deep breaths. Gabby put a hand on Olive's arm and asked if she was okay, or at least that's what Olive thought she'd said. It felt like her ears were stuffed with cotton balls. There was no worse feeling than not being able to breathe.

"Everyone stand back. She needs air." Gabby waved the Pacellis away since they'd encircled her like a gang of hungry sharks. Gabby guided Olive to a chair and directed her to put her head between her legs. She gently rubbed small circles on Olive's back. "Just take it slow, sweetie. Long, deep breaths."

Who knew Gabby had such a calm, soothing voice? And did she just call me sweetie?

Olive focused on the sound of Gabby's tone and did as instructed. Within minutes her heart rate was almost back to normal.

Gabby tucked a strand of hair behind Olive's ear and caressed her cheek. "Are you okay?"

Olive sat upright and nodded. She closed her eyes as Gabby continued to rub her back in the most comforting way ever. Olive couldn't remember the last time anyone had taken care of her. In fact, it probably wasn't since she was a kid. This was nice. Really nice. She wouldn't mind sitting there all day. Unfortunately, Mamma Pacelli's piercing voice snapped Olive back to reality.

"What happened? Did you faint?"

Olive's eyes popped open. She stared at the yacht, her pulse immediately accelerating. "I...I have to go." She tried to stand but Gabby held her down.

"Not so fast. Let's make sure you're okay first."

Olive sat back in the chair and rubbed her face. "I'm fine. I just feel...sorta sick. I can't...I'm not...I can't do this right now."

Gina cast a shadow over Olive when she stood in front of her. "You *have* to go. I already paid."

Olive dropped her spinning head between her knees. Ahh. There was that soothing hand on her back again.

"Can't you see she's sick? Don't be so selfish, Gina," Gabby said.

Olive stared at Gina's pink painted toenails, which matched the color of her sandals perfectly.

"How hard is it to press a button?" Gina asked.

Olive felt Gabby's hand form into a tight fist.

"Everyone get on the boat, and Gabby will take Olive home." If Mamma Pacelli hadn't chimed in, Gabby probably would have slugged Gina, not that Olive would've minded.

Gina's pink toenails turned and stomped to the yacht. How could two sisters be so different? Gabby was nothing like Bridezilla.

Mamma Pacelli haphazardly patted the top of Olive's head. "I hope you feel better." She certainly didn't have the soft touch of her youngest daughter.

After the Pacelllis headed to the yacht, Olive sat upright. "You don't have to drive me home."

"Don't argue. You know how stubborn we Italians can be." Gabby cupped Olive's elbow and helped her stand.

Gabby sure was being attentive, which surprisingly Olive didn't mind one bit. Maybe having Gabby drive her home wasn't such a bad idea after all. She still felt weak and shaky. And maybe, if she was lucky, Gabby would call her sweetie again.

❖

They drove in silence, Gabby behind the wheel of Olive's golf cart. Every once in a while, she'd take sideways peeks at Olive, probably to make sure she hadn't fainted. Olive wanted to thank

Gabby for helping her but didn't want to initiate a conversation where she'd have to answer questions about what had happened. Instead, she laid her head back and closed her eyes. She felt drained, physically and emotionally. And she felt embarrassed. Talk about a scaredy cat. She hadn't toughened up much over the years.

Olive recalled what she'd learned at one of Harmony Moondrop's workshops to release tension, so she visualized her "happy place." She was walking through a beautiful field of sunflowers. It was a perfect day, sunny, warm, and bright yellow as far as the eye could see. Slowly, Olive's muscles relaxed and melted into the car seat. The scene transformed from sunflowers to the ocean.

Olive stood at the shoreline gazing into the water. The waves were unusually high, but it was such a hot day she wanted nothing more than to immerse herself in the cool, refreshing turquoise sea. Besides, Olive was an expert swimmer and could handle rough water. She had waded up to her waist when an overpowering surge came out of nowhere. It grabbed her like a monstrous hand and pulled her under and farther into the ocean. Fear immediately gripped Olive as she struggled, ferociously flapping hands and feet but going nowhere from the force of the water. Salt burned her eyes as she pried them open, seeing nothing but white everywhere. How quickly the beautiful turquoise water had turned into a violent, chaotic scene. With that thought, another wave tossed Olive around like a paper doll in a tornado. It sucked her deeper into the ocean. Instinctively, she opened her mouth to scream, but no sound came out as water rushed in, panic rising even further. Her lungs ached, and her arms and legs felt like hundred-pound weights from fighting the current. As she drifted downward, the water was so cold she could no longer feel her body. Within seconds, darkness closed in, and that's when it hit her. *I'm drowning. This is how my short life will end.*

Olive felt something vigorously shake her. When her eyes opened, she was staring into anxious honey-colored eyes.

"Are you okay?" Gabby asked.

Olive's heart pounded, and she was drenched in sweat. She felt pressure on her throat and realized that her own hands were clutched around her neck. She lowered her arms and asked, "Where am I?"

"We're in front of your condo. You were having a bad dream."

No, it wasn't a dream. It was a memory.

"Come on," Gabby said. "Let's get you inside."

Thankfully, Gabby took Olive's keys and opened the front door. She didn't think she'd be able to do so with shaky hands. Hadn't she gotten over this yet? It'd been more than ten years. Olive had been kidding herself by entering the photography competition. Even if she won she'd obviously never be able to accept the *Journeys* position. She might as well withdraw now and save herself the embarrassment.

Gabby awkwardly stood in the doorway as Olive tossed her camera bag onto a chair.

"Please, come in," Olive said and motioned for Gabby to sit on the couch. Gabby entered and put her hands in her pockets. "Would you like something to drink? Coffee? Tea? Or maybe something stronger?"

"Whatever you're having is fine."

"Make yourself comfortable and I'll be right back."

Olive went into the kitchen and poured two glasses of wine. What she really wanted was a shot of whiskey, but that might be a little much, considering it wasn't even six p.m. yet. When she got back into the living room, Gabby was perched on the edge of the sofa, appearing uneasy. Olive handed her a glass and sat beside her.

After a few moments, and several gulps of wine, Olive said, "Thanks for driving me home. And…just…everything else."

Gabby placed her glass on the coffee table and turned to face Olive. "You weren't really sick, were you?" Olive didn't respond. "You didn't want to get on the boat, did you?"

Olive stared into her wine, hoping none of the other Pacellis had caught on, too. "No, I didn't."

"Why?"

"I just…I didn't want to."

Gabby laid her arm across the back of the couch and lightly touched Olive's shoulder. "There isn't anything to be ashamed of. A lot of people have a fear of boats."

Olive's eyes shot up to Gabby. "I'm not scared of boats. It's… the ocean." Was it too late to slurp those words back into her mouth?

Olive had long ago stopped confiding in anyone. If one more person told her to "get back on the horse" she'd have to slap them.

A light flashed across Gabby's eyes. "Oh…so, that's why you've never been off the island?"

Olive nodded.

"But…you're surrounded by water. You must feel so trapped."

"I wasn't lying when I said I love living here, but…yes…it's the reason I've never left."

"You don't have to tell me, but did something happen?"

Olive placed her drink of the table and crossed her arms. She'd gone this far. She might as well tell all. Well, not *all*. Not how terrified she'd been. Olive couldn't recount that moment without hyperventilating, and Gabby had seen her freak out enough already.

"It was a long time ago, when I was thirteen. A storm brewing in the Pacific had caused unusually high surf. Everyone was warned not to go into the water, but I was headstrong…" Olive was transported back to that day.

"Olive? Tell me what happened." Gabby's gentle voice urged her to continue.

"I hadn't been in the water more than a minute when a big wave pulled me under and out to sea. It was so powerful." Olive shook her head and winced. "I tried desperately to get to the surface, but I couldn't. There was nothing but white water everywhere."

"White?" Gabby asked and laid her hand on Olive's knee.

"Like the worse rapids you can imagine." Olive's pulse quickened and goose bumps appeared on her arms. She needed to pick up the pace and wrap up this little horror story before she started shaking…or worse.

"I was pulled down farther into the ocean, and then I passed out. When I woke up I was in the hospital. I found out later that Mr. Piccolo saved me."

"The snow-cone guy?"

"Yeah. He risked his life to save mine."

"God, that's horrible. I can see why you'd have an aversion to the ocean."

Really? She isn't going to tell me to get back on the horse?

"So it's not just swimming? You don't get on boats or even helicopters?"

"No. I freak out, as you saw. I tried to ride a helicopter a few times, but that was even worse. I kept imagining it crashing into the ocean." Olive grabbed a pillow and clutched it to her chest. "I had resigned to live out my life on the island until I heard about the contest grand prize. I figured it was either now or never…but after today…"

"You can't give up." Gabby sat upright, fire blazing in her eyes.

"Um. Did you forget who you're talking to? I'm your biggest rival. If I drop out you'll win for sure."

"Oh, trust me. I'll win." Gabby grinned. "I'm not scared of a little competition. But you can't stay trapped forever. This isn't Alcatraz."

She'd never thought of it that way, but Catalina was her own personal prison, just like the San Francisco Bay Island that had housed a penitentiary until the 1960s. She was no different than the men isolated and confined to Alcatraz, completely surrounded by water.

"I don't know. I've tried therapy, read books, and spent enough at self-help workshops to buy the Wrigley mansion on the hill. I'm just a big wimp."

"You are not!" Gabby spoke with such conviction, Olive almost believed her. "What happened must have been terrifying. It's an understandable reaction. But you're an amazing photographer, Olive, and there's a whole big world out there just waiting for you."

"Why are you being so nice to me?"

"When you were hyperventilating, I knew a little of what that felt like when I choked. Not being able to breathe was the scariest feeling I've ever had. I thought for a moment I might actually die. But then you were my Mr. Piccolo." Gabby looked down and tugged a thread on the back of the couch. "And…well…let's just say I know a thing or two about feeling trapped."

"Your family?"

Gabby's head jerked toward Olive. "Guess you've been around us Pacellis long enough to pick up on that. You want to talk about being a wimp?" Gabby pointed to her chest. "I'm the president of the club. I'm twenty-eight and can't even stand up to my own mother."

"Are they not supportive of your photography?"

Gabby chuckled but looked anything but pleased. "You wouldn't understand."

Olive tossed the pillow she'd been hugging into a nearby chair. "Let me guess. You're expected to get married, have kids, work at the family business, and not live more than two miles from your family. How am I doing so far?"

Gabby nodded. "Pretty darn good. It's just...they rely on me now that Papa's gone..."

Olive squirmed in her seat. She wanted to ask something but was afraid the topic was either too nosey or too painful. She had a feeling, though, it had something to do with the pressure Gabby felt. "Umm, can I ask you something?"

"Sure. I may not answer it, but give it a shot."

"Fair enough. Isabella told me about the importance of your family's last words before someone dies." Gabby's eyebrow shot up in surprise. Hopefully, Olive hadn't gotten Isabella into trouble. "And...she also said that your father spoke his last words to you. I was just wondering what they were. If you want to tell me."

"Izzy has a big mouth." Gabby shifted positions and crossed her legs. After a few moments she spoke. "He said it was up to me to take care of the business and the family."

"Wow. I don't mean to be unkind, but how could your father lay all that on your shoulders? What if you wanted to do something different with your life?"

"Mamma Pacelli's Pizza was everything to Papa. He not only loved it, but it's our livelihood. My parents took out a huge loan to put me through business college. Just me...none of my other sisters. At the time, I had no idea what I wanted to do, so I jumped at the chance. That changed, though, when I took a photography course. I fell in love and knew it was what I wanted to do with my life."

"Did you tell your parents?"

"I tried. Many times. But they saw it as a silly hobby. And then Papa had a stroke and couldn't work as much, so I took over."

Gabby shrugged. "I kept telling myself that I'd work just one more month, but then the months turned into years, and then Papa died. And now…I don't see a way out."

"The contest is your way out. If you win, surely your family wouldn't hold you back from such an amazing job offer."

Gabby took a deep breath, letting it out slowly. "We'll see."

Olive chuckled. "It's sorta funny. We have the exact same issue. We're both trapped, except mine is salt water and yours takes the form of a large, slightly scary, overbearing Italian woman. No offense, by the way."

"None taken. That's a pretty apt description of Mamma."

Olive suddenly sat upright. "Hey! Maybe we can help each other overcome our fears."

Gabby narrowed her eyes. "Why would you want to help the enemy?"

"I'm not afraid of a little competition, either. I have no doubt I can take you down."

"Is that right?" Gabby's eyes sparkled in amusement. "But… so…what would we do?"

Olive stared at the ceiling. "I'm not sure yet, but I might have an idea when it comes to you."

"Why do I get the feeling I'm not going to like it?"

"You need to think more positively. See that?" Olive pointed to a plaque on her living-room wall. "It says, 'What you're most afraid of doing is what will set you free.'" Olive purposefully left out that it was a Harmony Moondrop quote. Gabby didn't seem like the self-help type.

Gabby nodded, seemingly taking in the information. "So… what? We'd like…be *friends*?"

"You make it sound like a disease. Haven't you ever had a friend before?"

"Yeah, but not one I wanted to get into…"

Olive couldn't stop the grin that crept across her lips. "Into what? Bed?"

A deep flush rose to Gabby's cheeks. "All right. Fine. I admit it. But that was *before* I found out you're my rival."

"I see it this way. One, we agree that we aren't afraid of the competition. Two, we agree that sleeping together would be a bad idea under the circumstances. And three, we're in the same boat—no pun intended—so why not help each other out?"

"I suppose we could—" Someone opened the front door.

"Knock, knock." Nicki stuck her head into the condo "Oh. I didn't know you had company."

"Come on in, Nick." Olive stood to greet her friend.

Nicki tentatively entered, not hiding her shock at seeing the Italian Stallion sitting on the couch. "I wanted to see if you were okay. I went by Say Cheeze, but Mr. F said you had to leave early."

Gina had no doubt filled Olive's boss in on what had happened. Now she'd have a million questions to answer tomorrow at work. She could always claim seasickness, which was her routine excuse to get out of ocean shoots.

"I'm fine."

Gabby stood and said, "I should probably get going. Oh... wait...I drove you here in your golf cart."

"That's right. Nicki can drive you back down. Right?" Olive looked at Nicki, who still had a what-the-hell expression but did manage to nod her approval.

"So, friends?" Olive held out her hand.

Gabby paused a few moments before she shook. "You'll be the first friend I've ever had who I wanted to sleep with but didn't."

"Oooh, your first. I like that." Olive smiled and looked at Nicki, whose jaw was practically on the floor. Olive would have a lot of explaining to do later.

After Gabby and Nicki left, Olive sat on the couch and finished her wine. She wasn't sure why she'd pushed to be friends with Gabby, except that she felt terribly guilty about last year. Maybe she could make up for it by helping Gabby with her family. Also, if Olive was completely honest, she was more than a little curious as to what was underneath the sexy, confident, suave exterior of the Italian Stallion.

CHAPTER ELEVEN

SLY AS A FOX

Most people would think Gabby was insane. She'd been up since five a.m. backpacking through the wilderness searching for a pocket-sized, elusive creature: the Island Fox. This was no ordinary fox, though, since it didn't exist anywhere else in the world except on Catalina. Aside from that, what made the critter so special was that getting a decent photo was near impossible since they're nocturnal, don't travel in packs, and are quicker than Speedy Gonzales. But Gabby loved a challenge—especially when it came to wildlife photography—which was why she was tiptoeing through waist-high weeds hoping she didn't step on a snake in the near darkness.

Gabby stopped when she saw movement out of the corner of her eye. False alarm. It was just a squirrel. She took a swig of water and looked up at the indigo sky. Dawn was fast approaching. If she didn't spot the fox soon she'd have to give up for now. Second on her "must photo" list were the bison. In 1924, fourteen buffalo had been brought to Catalina for a film shoot. The production company ran out of funds and couldn't afford to take the ten-ton extras back to the mainland, so they were left on the island. Since then, the herd had multiplied to over one hundred and fifty. Gabby had yet to see even one buffalo, but they were probably on higher ground. Maybe she could ask Olive where to find them.

Gabby sat on a tree stump, her head swimming with thoughts of Olive. Her insides coiled as she recalled what a young Olive had experienced. Her accident had probably been much more traumatic than what she'd relayed. As terrifying as choking on the Spezzatina had been, Gabby couldn't imagine drowning. She shivered at the thought. She wasn't sure what she could do to help Olive, but oddly enough, she wanted to. No one deserved to be trapped on an island, no matter how beautiful it was.

Two spotted doves perched on a branch prompted Gabby to zoom in and snap several photos. She lowered the camera and watched them for several minutes. They lovingly rubbed necks and purred like kittens. One took his beak and scratched the top of the other's head and then down his back. Gabby wasn't the mushy type, but even she had to admit it was an endearing scene. An "aww" almost escaped her lips. She propped her chin on her fist, never taking her eyes off the doves.

For some reason Gabby's thoughts returned to Olive. She felt conflicted about her friendship offer. Gabby hadn't wanted to admit this, but she didn't have any female friends aside from her sisters. What did friends even do? Go shopping at the mall? Chat about where to get their nails done over a couple of salads? Text each other in acronyms like LOL, TTYL, and OMG? Nope, Gabby wasn't the BFF type. Hell, she didn't even get that close to the women she slept with. On the other hand, an unexpected warmth settled in the pit of her stomach at the thought of spending time with Olive. Undoubtedly, she was beautiful, talented, and intelligent, but it was more than that. Something about her drew Gabby in like a magnet in an unsettling, unexplainable way. She had felt it the moment they met, when she looked into those soulful green eyes. Yep, she'd have to play this friend thing by ear.

Gabby sat upright and shook her head. Enough about Olive. She needed to concentrate on the contest. It was less than a month away, and she had no idea what to photograph. It had to be something original, unique, something that showed the passion of the island. That was the problem right there. Romance wasn't really her thing. She loved wildlife.

Suddenly, Gabby bolted to her feet. "That's it! Why didn't I think of this before?"

Love wasn't exclusive to just people. It also abounded in the wild and was happening right before her eyes with the two doves. She could do a collage of human and animal couples and maybe even put a caption that said Love Has No Limits On Catalina or an equally mushy line that the judges would eat up. She'd have to get Mrs. Albright's approval, but Gabby didn't remember reading anything about being restricted to one image. What a relief. She'd been stressing about her entry, but now that she had a plan, the pressure was off. All she had to do was take amazing photos, which had never been a problem.

With a sudden jolt of energy, Gabby continued her hike. She hadn't walked more than twenty feet when she abruptly stopped, her heart pounding. Standing right in the middle of the trail was an Island Fox. Gabby raised her camera in slow motion so as not to scare the little fellow and took several photos. He was adorable, mostly gray but with white fur on his throat and half of his face, and a black stripe down his tail. Gabby zoomed in and looked him dead in the eye. What she saw there surprised her. Instead of fear she saw wisdom, courage, and confidence. Gabby had a feeling the little fox could teach her a lot.

"Tell me," Gabby whispered. "What does it feel like to be free?"

The fox darted away in a blur, so fast she almost doubted he was ever there. He'd answered her question. Freedom was running with the wind, going anywhere you want, whenever you want. Gabby envied him. She hoped he knew how lucky he was.

❖

Gabby purposefully delayed taking a shower and getting dressed after her hike. She'd rather hike ten miles barefoot than participate in the afternoon's events. Did she really have to do this? Gina was a pain in the ass. Out of everything for her damn wedding, this was the most dreaded. Gabby leaned across the sink, stared at the bathroom mirror, and channeled Don Vito Corleone. Satisfied that she was wearing her best game face ever, Gabby headed out to the Love and Lace Bridal Boutique for a fitting.

Opening the boutique door triggered a music-box rendition of *The Wedding March*. As the song died down, she stood in the entrance, trying to take it all in. The store certainly lived up to its name. It was like stepping into a Hallmark Valentine's Day card. Red and pink hearts abounded, and ivory lace covered the walls. Gina was standing on a podium wearing a wedding dress while Mamma Pacelli barked orders at the seamstress. A few of her sisters were in hideous puffy, hot-pink bridesmaid dresses, and the remaining were probably in the dressing room. The only pleasant sight was Olive, snapping photos of Gina. She looked awfully cute in jeans, sandals, and a blue T-shirt with JUST BREATHE written across the chest. Gabby took a deep breath and entered the shop.

"It's about time you get here." Gina shot Gabby a stern look in the mirror. "You're late. As usual."

"I went on a hike this morning." Gabby acknowledged Olive with a quick nod. In return, Olive smiled—the kind of smile that made her eyes sparkle...and Gabby's pulse accelerate.

Gabby forced her gaze away and focused on her sister. "Your dress is beautiful."

Gina opened her mouth but snapped it shut, seemingly taken aback by the compliment. Gabby had genuinely meant it, though. She looked gorgeous.

Gabby studied the display on her cell as it vibrated. "Hey, Tony, what's up?"

"They did it again. Rotten tomatoes."

"Dammit. That's it. Send 'em back and we're cutting them off."

Mamma Pacelli wagged a finger. "Watch your language, young lady. When was the last time you went to confession?"

Gabby rolled her eyes.

"Is that Tony? Ohhh, let me talk to him." Gina grabbed the phone out of Gabby's hand. "Hey, lover boy. In a week and a half you'll be tied to me for all eternity. Are you ready?"

"Problem at the restaurant?" Olive asked Gabby.

"You could say that."

"So you handle everything there?"

"Pretty much. Come on, Gina. Give me the phone back." Gabby held out her hand.

"But you have other employees, right?" Olive asked.

"Yeah, but they're pretty much useless." Gabby pulled the phone out of Gina's hand, which resulted in high-pitched yelps. "Call Frank, tell him to pick up the cartons, and let's go with the produce supplier we talked about."

"We...uhh...what?" Tony asked.

"Go to my Outlook contacts, look up Purcell Produce, and phone in a new order."

"Okay. Got it."

"Call me if you have any problems." Gabby disconnected, fully expecting another call from Tony within the hour. He probably didn't even know how to turn on the computer.

Gabby sighed and glanced around the boutique. "Where's Nonna?"

"She wasn't feeling well," Mamma Pacelli said.

"She's been tired a lot lately." Gabby never vocalized her concern, but she worried about her grandmother. Nonna had always been a bit precognitive, so it was unnerving when she said her time on earth was nearing an end. Her grandmother had certainly lived a long life, but letting her go wouldn't be easy.

"Don't worry." Mamma Pacelli kissed Gabby on the cheek.

Gabby halfheartedly grinned at the way her mamma could always read her mind. And apparently Olive could as well, since she gazed at Gabby with compassion.

"You went on a hike?" Olive asked a little too brightly, probably trying to lighten the mood.

"Yeah. Oh, and guess what I saw. An Island Fox!"

"Seriously?"

"Not only that, but I got several photos, too."

Olive's eyes widened. "Do you know how hard it is to see one, much less photograph it?"

Gabby puffed out her chest. "I know. I got some really great close-ups. It's like he was posing for me. Next up are the buffalo."

"You'll have to go into the mountains to see those."

"Maybe you could show me sometime?"

"Sure. I'd love to. How about Saturday? I'm off."

"Perfect," Gabby said.

There was that beautiful smile again, and the way it lit up Olive's face was mesmerizing. Gabby usually didn't like glasses, but on Olive they looked adorable. The red matched her hair and accentuated her emerald eyes, plus they made her look intelligent, which was always a turn-on. Gabby liked cute, but the woman also had to have brains.

"What are you looking at? Do I have a smudge somewhere?" Olive wiped her face.

Gabby wasn't sure how long she'd been staring, but Olive appeared uncomfortable. "No...just...your hair looks good tied back. You should wear it like that more often."

"Oh, thanks." Olive touched the back of her ponytail, a blush on her cheeks.

"Here." Gina thrust a bridesmaid dress at Gabby.

They'd been through this at least a dozen times. Gabby didn't do dresses. She didn't feel comfortable in them, and she wasn't going to pretend to be something she wasn't just to please Gina. She wasn't backing down now.

When Gabby didn't accept the pink-chiffon nightmare, Gina narrowed her eyes and took a step forward. "This is my wedding, and what I say goes."

Gabby straightened her posture and crossed her arms. Gina jerked toward Mamma Pacelli, who held up a hand and said, "You two are grown-ups. Deal with this yourself."

Gina's face turned bloodred as she pointed a finger at Gabby. Before she could speak, Olive stepped between the two women, which was probably the craziest thing ever. Maybe she didn't have any brains after all, 'cause this could get ugly...and dangerous.

"If I could make a suggestion," Olive said.

"You might want to stay out of this." Gabby placed a hand on Olive's shoulder, ready to yank her back if Gina took a swing.

"No, no...I think this might help. If I know Gina, and I think I do, I'd guess that she's up on the latest wedding fashions. Am I right?" Olive looked at Gina, who stared in a non-blinking, wild-woman sort of way. "Right...well...I'm sure you know that the trend is to ditch the traditional bridesmaid dresses and be more forward thinking. What's in now are pants suits."

Gina put a hand on her hip. "What the—"

"Hear me out. It's the Hollywood fashion craze. All the celebrities are replacing dresses with something more cutting edge."

Gabby smiled to herself. What a load of crap, but it was sweet of Olive to give it a try.

"You're just saying that to help my sister out."

"Hey. I don't care one way or another. I'm just letting you know what all the celebrities are doing."

"What celebrities?" Gina looked skeptical, not to mention irritated, but she had a tiny glimmer of interest in her eyes.

Olive paused and seemed to hold her breath. "The...uhh... Kardashians."

Gina's eyes widened. "Kim?" Olive nodded. "Who else?"

"Umm...the girl who played in *Friends*...what's her name..."

"Jennifer Aniston?!"

"Yep, that's it."

Gina cocked her head and studied Olive for several uncomfortable moments. "Are you putting me on?"

"Swear to God." Olive put her hand over her heart.

Gabby suppressed a giggle when she looked down to see Olive's fingers crossed behind her back.

"And you know the best part?" Olive asked. "With the bridesmaids in pants, the bride stands out even more. And really, the day should be all about you. You're the star of the show."

Gina stared at Olive and slowly nodded. After a few moments she turned and walked away.

"I can't believe you did that," Gabby said through a chuckle. "Do you think she fell for it?"

Gina grabbed the boutique owner's arm and pulled her into a corner. They couldn't hear what was being said, but from the horrified look on the woman's face, Gina was probably demanding a last-minute wardrobe change.

"Looks like it," Olive said proudly.

"I owe you big-time." Gabby narrowed her eyes and studied Olive closely. "You're a sly one. And a pretty good little liar. So, tell me…have you told me any lies?"

Olive's smile dropped, her complexion ghostly pale. "No, of course not."

"Hey. I was just kidding."

Gabby playfully nudged Olive with her shoulder, but when her smile didn't return, Gabby wondered if she really had lied about something.

CHAPTER TWELVE

HARMONY MOONDROP

Olive rang the Pacellis' doorbell, hoping it wasn't too early. Within seconds, one of the sisters…maybe Rose Marie… opened the door.

"Good morning. Is Gabby awake yet?"

"She's on the patio with Nonna."

The woman bounced up the stairs, leaving Olive alone to maneuver through the living room and kitchen. Olive halted before sliding the glass door open, touched by what she saw. Gabby kneeled at Nonna's feet, tying her shoes. After she made the final loop, she lightly patted one foot and flashed her grandmother a sweet smile. Gabby's eye caught Olive, and her smile widened. If Olive didn't know better, she'd think Gabby was happy to see her.

Olive swooshed the door open. "You girls are up early."

"We're going to take a stroll around the block. Want to join us?" Gabby stood upright, steadying her grandmother by grasping her elbow.

"I wish I could, but I need to get to work."

Nonna took a wobbly step forward, grabbed Olive's chin with a shaky hand, and kissed both of her cheeks before she disappeared into the house.

"Nonna likes you. She's pretty stingy with the kisses."

Olive resisted the urge to ask if Gabby liked her as well. *Focus. That's not why you're here.*

"Is she strong enough to take a walk?" Olive asked.

Gabby chewed the inside of her cheek, worry etched on her face. "It's good for her to get out. We won't go far."

"You really love her, don't you?"

"Of course."

"I mean, you seem closer to her than your sisters do."

Gabby shrugged, looking embarrassed. Obviously, she wasn't comfortable with sentimentality. "What brings you here so early?"

"Guess what I have?" Olive grinned and raised her arm, a tightly clutched piece of paper in her grasp.

"What's that?"

Olive closed the glass door for some privacy. "The answer to all your problems with your family."

Gabby crossed her arms and raised an eyebrow.

"Take a look at this." Olive handed Gabby the flyer.

Gabby's eyes flickered over the print before she focused on Olive, obviously perplexed. "Who the hell is Harmony Moondrop? And what's the Tribal Beliefs Workshop?"

"She's an amazing self-help guru. And she's doing a seminar in Catalina."

"Sooo, you're telling me this, why?"

"We're going." Olive smiled brightly.

"What!? No way. I don't do self-help."

"This is kismet. It's meant to be. What are the odds that Harmony is in Catalina and talking about tribal beliefs? It's perfect!"

"No…no…" Gabby backed away. "I'm not a group kinda person…and Harmony Moonbeam? Seriously?"

"Moondrop. Why can't anyone remember that?" Olive sighed. "I said I intended to help you. Besides, you owe me after yesterday at the bridal shop. You're going. It's tonight at seven."

"Tonight? Can't make it. I have a date." Gabby shook her head.

A date? For some reason that didn't sit well with Olive. "With that blond bombshell from last week?"

"Her name is Carmen."

"Carmen is an Italian name. She probably isn't even Italian, and I'd bet that isn't her real name."

"And I care why?" Gabby got a steamy, faraway look in her eyes. *Ugh.* She was probably picturing the woman naked.

"Do you want to work at Mamma Pacelli's Pizza for the rest of your life?"

A dark shadow zipped across Gabby's face. Olive knew that'd bring her down to earth and out of Carmen-land.

"Harmony can teach you the skills you need to talk to your mother. I think you should give it a try."

Gabby huffed out a breath and stared at the clouds for several seconds before looking at Olive. "And you'll go with me?"

"Of course."

"All right, but if Harmony Moonlight is as weird as her name, I'm outta there."

"Moondrop! All right, deal. What about Carmen?"

"I'll reschedule. It'll just give me something to look forward to later." Gabby wiggled her eyebrows.

Ugh. Olive was certain Gabby was picturing the woman naked now.

❖

"Where have you been?" Gabby tapped her watch and glared at Olive as she rushed toward her. She'd been standing outside the hotel where the workshop was being held for at least fifteen minutes.

"I'm sorry," Olive said, out of breath. "I had to work late."

"Mr. Finkelmeier again? You need to stand up to him."

"You're one to talk."

"That's a low blow!"

"I'm sorry. You're right." Olive did look genuinely regretful. "We better get inside."

They entered the hotel, maneuvered through the lobby, and found a closed door with a sign that read, ENTER IF YOU'RE READY TO LIVE COURAGEOUSLY. Gabby rolled her eyes. This was going to be so lame. Hopefully Harmony what's-her-name didn't demand that they walk on hot coals barefoot or hold hands and sing *Kumbaya*.

When Olive opened the door, all eyes turned to them. *Great.* The room was packed, and the only available seats were on the front row. Only nerds and teacher's pets sat at the front. Gabby was more of a back-row kinda gal. Olive slipped into a chair with Gabby beside her.

"Sorry we're late," Olive said to the woman at the front of the class, who was undoubtedly Harmony.

"No problem. We're just about to get started," Harmony said brightly. "Isn't it...Olive? You've been to several of my workshops."

Olive nodded and beamed at the recognition. "This is my friend, Gabby."

"Welcome." Harmony flashed a saccharine smile big enough to sweeten ten lattes.

Gabby sank into her chair, not particularly wanting to be pointed out.

Harmony took a deep breath and held out both hands, like Jesus on the cross, then scanned the audience. "Welcome to Tribal Beliefs. Are you living an unauthentic life? A life without passion?"

Gabby observed Harmony as she droned on and on. Her name certainly fit, considering she looked like she'd just stepped out of a hippie commune. She wore tattered, faded jeans with a peace-sign patch on the leg, a rainbow tie-dye T-shirt, sandals, and braided, butt-length hair. Gabby resisted the urge to shoot Olive a what-the-hell look. She did, though, peek at Olive out of the corner of her eye, not surprised she was sitting on the edge of her seat hanging on Harmony's every word. Still, though, Olive looked adorable all innocent and wide-eyed.

"Tribal beliefs are beliefs handed down by parents, grandparents, and ancestors. Do you have dreams that excite you but you're afraid to go against your family's beliefs?"

Maybe Gabby should listen to this chick. She certainly fit in that category. As though reading her mind, Harmony locked eyes with Gabby, which had her uncomfortably shifting in her seat.

"Gabby. What about you?"

Gabby glanced around, hoping another person with her name was nearby. Unfortunately, she was pretty sure hippie-chick was talking to her.

"What about me?"

"Do you have familial beliefs that are holding you back?"

Gabby looked at Olive, who silently urged her on. "Yeah, I suppose."

Harmony never broke eye contact, patiently waiting for Gabby to continue. Well, she'd have to wait a long time, because the last thing Gabby wanted to do was share her life story with a bunch of strangers.

"Tell us about it." It wasn't a question but a demand.

"Ummm..." Gabby shifted positions and crossed her legs. She didn't like being in the spotlight.

When Gabby didn't respond further, Harmony asked, "Who *is* Gabby?"

This chick was annoying, with the persistence of a stubborn bull.

"I'm Gabby Pacelli, and I manage my family's pizza chain. I... uhhh...have five sisters, a grandmother, and a somewhat overbearing Italian mother." *There. That should suffice.*

Harmony nodded and regarded Gabby thoughtfully before she turned her attention to everyone else. "Class, did you notice that Gabby's definition of herself included nothing but her family?"

Gabby shriveled in her chair, feeling like she'd just flunked a test. Hippie-chick was right, but it was the first thing that had popped into her head. What else was she supposed to say?

Harmony returned her attention to Gabby. "Who would you be if you weren't a Pacelli?"

What an inane question. She *was* a Pacelli, so why would she imagine that she wasn't? Gabby cocked her head and gazed up at the fluorescent light, her mind blank. The room was so quiet she could hear the gentle clang of Harmony's quartz-crystal necklace as she toyed with the beads.

Come on...think. Everyone is waiting.

But nothing came. Gabby had no idea who she'd be if she weren't a Pacelli. It was her identity. And how could it not be? From the day she was born she'd been bred to take over the family business.

"I don't mean to put you on the spot, Gabby," Harmony said.

Yeah, right.

"Tell us. Is there something you'd rather do than work for your family?"

"Yeah. I want to be a photographer."

"Great!" Harmony clasped her hands together, probably happy to get a genuine response. "And would you feel guilty if you did that?"

God, yes. It didn't take a genius to figure that out.

"Ponder this for a bit," Harmony said. "Guilt is tied to the ego. Maybe you're bringing it on yourself by thinking your family can't survive without your help. Less ego, less guilt."

Was this chick crazy? Gabby wasn't egotistical, and Harmony obviously hadn't met her brothers-in-law. Pacelli's Pizza would go up in smoke, literally, without her. Wouldn't it?

"How about we all do an exercise?" Harmony sat on the edge of the desk. "Everyone get out some paper and a pen."

Ugh. This couldn't be good. Maybe Gabby would be exempt since she didn't have anything to write on...until Olive handed her a tablet and pencil. Figured she'd be prepared.

"I'd like everyone to write your own eulogy."

What? Had Gabby heard right? That seemed a bit morbid. Gabby glanced at Olive, who looked pleasantly intrigued. She'd definitely heard wrong.

Gabby cleared her throat and raised her hand. "Did you say... eulogy? As in funeral?"

Harmony nodded enthusiastically. She was much too happy, considering she'd just asked Gabby to pretend like she was dead. Everyone's heads immediately dropped as they frantically scribbled. Gabby stared at the blankest, whitest piece of paper she'd ever seen. She looked at Olive, whose hand was flying across the page. She considered copying, but that'd be impossible with Harmony looking right at her. Just another reason the front row sucked. Gabby put the pencil in her mouth and chewed on it, leaving teeth-mark indentions in the soft, yellow wood.

How hard could this be? It's my eulogy, not someone else's.

Gabby placed the tip of her pencil on the paper. She could write about her accomplishments at work, college, and winning photography contests. But then again, someone from her family would probably be giving the eulogy, and they wouldn't mention photography. She could write about what a devoted daughter and sister she'd been. Most tributes also included partners, but Gabby had never had one of those. She couldn't very well list all the women in her little black book. An unexpected sadness washed over her, which she quickly pushed aside. Not that she wanted a wife, but it was a little disheartening that she'd never been in love. Shouldn't she experience that at least once in her life before dying? After she was gone, no one would miss her, except for her family. Gabby pressed the pencil down hard until the lead broke. Just as well. She didn't know what to write anyway.

Harmony jumped off the desk. "Is everyone done?"

Gabby folded the paper into a tiny square and stuck it in her pocket.

"This may have seemed like an odd exercise." Harmony glanced at Gabby. If she didn't know better, she'd think the woman could read minds. "But I wanted you to see that it's not too late to rewrite your life script. You can live the life you want by removing limiting beliefs. We disempower ourselves when we identify with a given role. Internal conflict comes when you do something different than what your inner being wants."

Gabby hated to admit it, but Harmony did make sense, except when it came to that ego stuff. She was sure the pizza parlor would fail if she wasn't in charge—not that she wanted to be.

CHAPTER THIRTEEN

WHERE THE BISON ROAM

I think I should tell her," Olive said as she typed an invoice on her computer at Say Cheeze.

"Tell who what?"

Olive froze and gaped at Nicki, who was sitting across from her desk flipping through a *Journeys* magazine. "What have I been talking about the last fifteen minutes?"

"Wow, look at this." Nicki held up a centerfold photo of the Sphinx. "You'll be the one taking this photo pretty soon."

"If I win. I haven't even taken any pictures I'd consider entering yet."

"You'll think of something."

"Should I tell Gabby I was the one who turned her in last year?"

Nicki closed the magazine and tossed it onto the desk. "I still can't believe you're friends with her. She's your competition."

Olive shrugged. "We have a lot in common, except for the fact that she's gorgeous."

"Don't short-change yourself. You're cute as a button."

Olive inwardly groaned. Who wanted to be cute as a button? What did that even mean? Buttons aren't necessarily cute. Most are plain and lackluster. Olive wanted to be alluring, irresistible, drop-dead gorgeous. No one would ever describe a button that way.

Olive turned off the computer and stared at her reflection in the screen. Her cheeks were too chubby, her complexion pale, and her glasses screamed dorky, not sexy. Olive removed her spectacles, ran her hand through her hair, and flashed a smile. At least she had good teeth. Who was she kidding? She'd never be anything other than "cute as a button."

"Uhh, Ollie, what are you doing?"

Olive's head jerked to Nicki. She'd forgotten she wasn't alone. "Oh, just...nothing."

Nicki laughed. "You were totally checking yourself out."

"Nooo, I was just—"

"You were fixing yourself up for the Italian Stallion."

"I was not!"

Olive grabbed an eraser and threw it at Nicki, who, of course, caught it with one hand, being the ultimate athlete that she was. Nicki tossed the item back, which struck Olive's chest and landed in her lap. She couldn't see a damn thing without her glasses. Olive put her specs back on and sneered at Nicki.

"Olive has a crush on Gabby," Nicki repeatedly said in a sing-song voice.

"Good God. Are you thirteen? I don't have a crush on her."

As the words escaped Olive's lips, she knew that was a lie. But who wouldn't have a crush on Gabby? Not that Olive would do anything about it, of course. Gabby slept around and avoided real relationships. Olive couldn't imagine having sex with someone she didn't feel a connection with. From what she'd observed, Gabby seemed like a caring person. The way she took care of her grandmother and family was admirable, and her sensitive side shone through any time she talked about her father. So why wouldn't she want to get close to a woman? Maybe she'd been hurt in the past? Either way, Olive was curious.

"Should I tell her about the contest last year or not?"

"Hell, no." Nicki stood up and stretched her long legs. "Didn't you say she was angry at the unknown person who ratted on her? Keep your trap shut. If you want to be friends, that is...or get her into bed."

Olive rolled her eyes at the bed comment. "I dunno. It seems wrong not to say anything."

Nicki put her hands on her hips and stepped forward in an impressive lunge.

"Sorry I'm going to miss your volleyball game, but I promised to take Gabby on a hike this afternoon. She wants to photograph the bison."

Mr. Finkelmeier opened his office door, looked curiously at Nicki, and shook his head. "Olive, when you finish the invoices, I need you to order a StudioFX 2400-watt photo light with a boom arm. And put a rush on it. The Pacelli wedding is in a week."

"Uhh, this is my day off, remember? I only came in today as a favor to finish the invoices." Mr. Finkelmeier stared blankly, as though Olive had spoken in Chinese. "In fact, I've worked every day off for the past two weeks."

Mr. Finkelmeier raised an eyebrow. "Are you saying you don't want to do your job and order the lights?"

What began as a bubble in the pit of Olive's stomach quickly evolved into a boiling, steaming pot of take-this-job-and-shove-it. Olive abruptly stood, so forcefully that her chair rolled back and crashed into something, probably equipment she'd have to pay for later, but right now she didn't care. Gabby had been right. It was high time Olive stood up to her overbearing boss. She'd put up with his abuse far too long. Olive clinched her fists and glared into his beady eyes with such ferocity that Nicki stopped lunging, stood upright, and looked like she might wet herself.

"What I'm saying, Mr. Finkelmeier, is that I'm tired of working on my days off, and for no extra money, I might add. What I'm saying is that I'm leaving because I have plans this afternoon, and frankly I shouldn't have had to come into the office in the first place. What I'm saying is that I won't be taken advantage of *any more!*" Olive spoke eloquently, controlled...until the last word, which was booming and unmistakably resolute.

Olive's words reverberated through the small space long after she'd stopped talking. She crossed her arms, stood her ground, and felt completely vindicated when Mr. Finkelmeier shrank to the size of a snail, turned, and wordlessly slinked into his office. Olive took a deep breath, feeling lighter than she could ever remember.

"What the hell was that?" Nicki rushed to Olive and almost knocked her over in an embrace. "I'm so proud of you! It's about time you put that wienie in his place." Nicki threw an arm around Olive's shoulders. "Let's get out of here. I have a game to play, and you've got a hot date."

Olive rolled her eyes again. "It's not a date!"

❖

The house was eerily quiet, which meant only one thing—the Pacelli sisters were gone. Gabby scarfed down the last bite of turkey sandwich and went in search of her camera bag, since Olive would be here soon. As Gabby passed her mamma's bedroom, she heard mumbling so she peeked into the room. Mamma Pacelli was on her knees beside the bed with a string of rosary beads draped through her fingers as she quietly recited prayers with her eyes closed. Growing up, Gabby had seen that image a million times. Her parents had always been religious, and even though Gabby no longer considered herself Catholic, she admired her mamma's devotion. Considering the other family members were such staunch worshippers, Gabby was lucky they didn't condemn her for being a lesbian. If anything, her mamma was more disappointed that she wouldn't become a nun. Gabby's heart ached when she saw a worn, black-and-white photo of her papa on the bed. Her parents used to pray the rosary together, so that must be her mamma's way of having her husband with her.

Gabby wished she could do something to ease her mamma's pain. Anything she said sounded trite, especially "I understand how you feel," since that was a complete lie. Gabby had never let herself get that close to anyone. No one really knew who she was—her fears, passions, desires. Even though she was incessantly surrounded by family, she often felt alone.

Mamma Pacelli made the sign of the cross, leaned over, and kissed Alberto's photo. She opened her eyes and placed a hand over her heart when she saw Gabby standing in the doorway.

"Child, you almost gave me a heart attack."

"Sorry, Mamma." Gabby walked into the room, plopped down on the bed, and studied her papa's photo.

Mamma Pacelli struggled to rise and stood over Gabby. "That was taken right after we got married."

"Papa was handsome."

"That he was." Mamma Pacelli's eyes filled with tenderness and admiration as she gazed at the picture. She sighed and tucked the photo away in a gold box on her nightstand.

Would someone ever look at Gabby that way? With emotion-filled, adoring eyes? Someone who knew every inch of her, the good and bad, and still loved her?

"Are you hungry?" Mamma Pacelli asked. "I'll fix you something to eat."

"No, thanks. I just ate a sandwich."

"That isn't lunch. How did I get such skinny girls?"

Gabby reclined in the bed and jumped almost two feet when Mamma Pacelli clapped her hands louder than a cymbal.

"Shoes off the quilt! What are those gargantuan things you're wearing, anyway?"

"They're hiking boots." Gabby swung her legs off the bed. "Olive and I are going—"

"Ohhh, you and Olive." Mamma Pacelli smirked.

They both looked at Nonna when she entered the bedroom. With a twinkle in her eye she crossed her arms over her chest.

"See," Mamma Pacelli said. "You and Olive belong together. Your grandmother agrees, and she has the seeing eye."

"Seeing eye?" Gabby asked sarcastically, even though she knew what it meant.

"Nonna knows things. She predicted me and your papa's marriage before we even met."

"Really? I never heard that before." Gabby looked at Nonna, who nodded. "Well, Olive and I are just friends."

As though on cue, the doorbell rang, prompting Gabby to jump up.

"Be sure to invite Olive to dinner tomorrow night. We're meeting at Luigi's."

Gabby groaned. She hated going to Italian restaurants with her mamma. She always critiqued the cuisine, which, of course, never lived up to her standards, and she certainly wasn't shy about letting the staff know. Gabby always felt the need to leave an enormous tip to make up for the embarrassment.

"What dinner?" Gabby asked. "You didn't mention anything before."

Mamma Pacelli smiled coyly. "It's a surprise."

"For who? Gina?"

"Now never you mind."

"Nonna will tell me." Or not…since her grandmother pretended to zip her lips, lock them, and throw away an imaginary key. Gabby had a bad feeling about this, a really bad feeling.

"Now get going. Your girlfriend is waiting." Mamma Pacelli pushed Gabby out of the bedroom.

"She's not my girlfriend!"

Those two would never give up. Gabby had to admit, though, that if…and that was a *big* if…she ever settled down, it'd be with someone like Olive. Too bad they hadn't met twenty years later, when Gabby might actually consider the idea.

❖

They must have climbed two thousand feet. Okay, maybe it wasn't that much, but that's what it felt like to Olive. She and Gabby had been hiking up a steep incline for an hour. She was getting flashbacks of the time she'd lost her mind and hired a Hitler-like trainer who incessantly yelled, "No pain, no gain! Feel the burn!" Well, she felt the burn…everywhere, in her legs, arms, hips. Even her hair hurt. Still, though, Olive hated pointing out that fact to Gabby—someone who was obviously in better shape than an American gladiator. Maybe she could use the ruse of needing water so they could take a break for five minutes.

"Can we…umm…stop for a minute?" Olive trailed behind Gabby as she barreled down the path.

Gabby halted and turned around.

Christ. She isn't even breathing hard or sweating.

"You need a break?"

"A drink would be nice."

Gabby frowned, looked at her watch, and then down the trail. She certainly had a one-track mind. No wonder she always won the photography contest. She never gave up.

"The bison aren't going anywhere," Olive said.

Gabby managed a quick grin and followed Olive to a shaded spot under an oak tree. Olive collapsed into the cool grass and looked up at Gabby, who was still standing.

"Yo, Italian Stallion." *That got her attention.* "Put it in park for a minute." Olive patted the ground next to her.

Gabby finally acquiesced and sat. Olive grabbed a water bottle from her backpack and took several swigs. She glanced at Gabby, who was staring straight ahead, seemingly deep in thought.

"Hey," Olive said, nudging Gabby with her elbow. "You okay?"

"Yeah."

That didn't sound very convincing.

"How was your morning?"

"Fine."

Getting Gabby to talk was like trying to force a corner puzzle piece in the middle of the picture.

"Aren't you going to ask about my morning?"

Gabby looked at Olive like she hadn't heard a word she'd said.

"Fine. I'll play by myself." Olive cleared her throat. "So, Olive, what did you do today?"

"Wait a second," Gabby said. "Is that supposed to be an imitation of me?"

"Yes, and a damn good one. I went to work on my day off and told my boss to stick it where the sun don't shine."

The expression on Gabby's face as it transformed into astonishment was almost as good as telling Mr. Finkelmeier off. Almost.

"You didn't. Did you?! Did you cuss? Please tell me you told him to fuck off."

Olive thought for a second. "No, I don't think I cursed, but trust me...the fuck was implied. He got the message loud and clear."

"I'm so proud of you." Gabby leaned over and gave Olive a quick hug. "What did the little worm say?" Gabby's toffee-colored eyes twinkled.

"Not a thing. He looked stunned, went into his office, and closed the door."

Gabby laughed. "I wish I'd been there to see it."

"I may not have a job tomorrow, but I honestly don't care anymore. And I have you to thank."

"Me? What did I do?"

"You're the only person who's ever told me to stand up to Mr. Finkelmeier. You made me realize I didn't have to be his slave just because I work for him."

"Glad I could help. You're too good of a photographer to work there."

"Do you really think so?"

"Of course. Don't you?"

Olive averted her gaze, feeling suddenly exposed. Gabby probably didn't have a fearful bone in her body. She always seemed so self-confident, except when it came to her family. She wouldn't understand doubts, uncertainties about her talent.

Gabby leaned back against the tree and said, "Let me tell you a little story. The first year I entered the Catalina competition, I was so sure I'd win. Talk about cocky." Gabby chuckled. "I'm not surprised you came up with a nickname for me."

Olive looked at Gabby apologetically. Now that Olive knew her a little better, she regretted having made snap judgements. Gabby had more substance than Olive had given her credit for.

"So, there I was," Gabby said, "acting like the Catalina Queen as I walked through the Casino smugly disregarding each entry hanging on the wall...crappy composition...boring subject... unoriginal style...but then my eye caught a photo that literally stopped me in my tracks. It was a picture of an elderly man playing ball with two kids. The lighting, the action, the expression on their faces, everything about that photo was perfection. And even more than that, it had something that my entry didn't have...emotion. No one could look at that photo and not feel something. I must have stood there for thirty minutes. I couldn't take my eyes off it."

Olive's heart raced. The photo Gabby was describing had been hers. Olive had no idea Gabby had been affected by her entry, much less even noticed it.

"That was the first time I doubted that I was the best," Gabby said. "The first time I thought someone else deserved to win. I don't know what the judges were thinking when they gave me the award."

Gabby sat upright, faced Olive, and gazed into her eyes. "I didn't recognize you when we met, because when we were competing I didn't want to know your name or what you looked like. That wasn't because I was conceited. It was because I was scared of you."

Olive couldn't believe what she was hearing. Gabby was afraid of *her*?

"What about now? Are you sorry that you know me?" Olive tensed, afraid of the answer. She was getting attached to Gabby and didn't really want their friendship to end. Olive eased a bit when Gabby looked at her warmly, placed a hand on her arm, and lightly squeezed.

"No. I'm not sorry we're friends."

Olive opened her mouth to speak, but no words came out. She was entranced by the sincerity in Gabby's eyes, mesmerized by the tiny mahogany flecks that shimmered in the sunlight. Olive's gaze dropped to Gabby's lips. Even her mouth was perfect. Heat flooded Olive's body at the thought of kissing those lips. Were they as soft as they looked?

"Did I embarrass you?" Gabby asked.

"No." Olive responded much too quickly and placed her hands on her cheeks, feeling heat on her palms. Great. She was probably as red as a stop light. What was she doing looking at Gabby's lips? Or, more importantly, entertaining the thought of kissing her?

Gabby leaned back against the tree. "I can't believe I told you that. Something about you makes me want to spill my guts, which is highly disconcerting. I'm not really one to open up to people."

"You seem close to Isabella."

"Yeah, but she's about the only one."

"What about women you've been with?"

Gabby outright laughed. "I share less with them than anyone."

That was the strangest, saddest thing Olive had ever heard. How could Gabby give her body to someone but not what was in her heart? Gabby was undoubtedly gorgeous on the outside, yet Olive doubted anyone had ever glimpsed the beauty inside.

"Why?" Olive asked.

Gabby silently gazed into the distance, as though she'd never considered the question before. Finally, she said, "I guess the women I've been with aren't interested in much more than having a good time…if you know what I mean." Gabby wiggled her eyebrows, probably trying to lighten the mood, but Olive wasn't letting up.

"Great sex is…great, but don't you want something more? A connection? An understanding? Love?"

Gabby visibly tensed. She shifted positions, raised her knees, and hugged them. Olive waited patiently, determined to get an honest answer.

"Well," Gabby said. "You know when we had to write our eulogy, which—by the way—was the weirdest thing ever, in the workshop yesterday? For a moment, I felt regret for not having someone special in my life." Gabby chuckled "See what I mean about you? I can't believe I just admitted that."

"This is what friends do. They share their innermost thoughts. What made you sad about it?" Olive spoke softly, hoping Gabby would continue.

"I didn't say *sadness*, but regret. Most times I feel like I'm in a tug of war. On one hand, I crave what my parents had. They were so in love. But then on the other side, I'm scared of what they had. The relationship took away their freedom."

"Do you mean your mom giving up her dream of opening a hair salon?"

Gabby's head jerked to Olive, confusion etched on her face. "What are you talking about?"

Why did Olive suddenly feel like she'd revealed a secret? "Your…uhh…your mom told me she'd always wanted to open a salon, but then she got married and had kids. I thought that's what you were referring to."

Gabby stared at Olive, incredulous. "What? I've never heard that before. Seriously?"

Olive nodded. "She told me when everyone was at the hair dresser. She seemed sad about it, but she said she loved your father too much not to marry him."

"Huh. I had no idea."

"Forgive me, but you have a really fucked-up notion of relationships."

Gabby laughed. "Do I now?"

"Totally. It's possible to be in love and not tie each other down. What if you met a woman who wanted to travel like you? Just because you have a partner doesn't mean you have to buy a house in the burbs and have six kids."

"Are you making an offer?" Gabby flashed a devilish grin.

"Huh? No...I...wait...what?" Olive wasn't sure if she was more flustered by the question, Gabby's smile, or the fact that it conjured images of her and Gabby together.

"Relax. I was joking," Gabby said. "What about you? Why don't you have a girlfriend?"

"I've dated, but no one seems to want to settle down on Catalina, so it never lasts."

"Hmm. So describe your dream woman. I'm sure you have a list and probably even a vision board, right? Pictures of your fantasy bride pasted on a poster hanging above your bed?"

Olive wanted to wipe Gabby's smug expression off her face. She was totally making fun of her. All right, yes, Olive had made a vision board after a Harmony Moondrop seminar on manifesting a soul mate, but Gabby didn't need to know that.

"Just when I start to like you, you say something that makes me want to pinch you."

"Ooh. Sounds kinky." Gabby laughed and held up her hands in defense. "I'm sorry. Really. I wanna know what you're attracted to."

Olive peered at Gabby. "Why? So you can make fun of me some more?"

Gabby waved a hand in front of her face and looked at Olive solemnly. "No more joking. I promise."

It took all Olive had not to crack a smile at Gabby's gravely serious expression and big, brown, puppy-dog eyes. She really was adorable. Exasperating, but adorable.

Olive comfortably settled into the grass and recalled her list. "Let's see…I want someone compassionate, gentle, creative, not afraid to speak her mind. Someone who likes spending time together but also gives me space to pursue photography. I want someone that I connect with mind, body, and soul. I want a relationship that's fun and passionate, with someone who's willing to put in the work it takes to be in it for the long haul."

Whoa…Olive had just described Gabby, except for that last part. Olive glanced at her, surprised to see sadness brimming in her eyes.

"That sounds nice actually," Gabby said in almost a whisper.

"Maybe it's what you want, too?" Olive asked tentatively… and maybe a little hopefully.

Gabby paused for a couple of heartbeats before she waved her hands and scoffed. "Pshaw."

"Oh, right. You don't have girlfriends or relationships."

Gabby silently nodded before bolting to her feet. "We should continue the hike if we want to see some buffalo." Gabby held out her hand and pulled Olive upright.

"They're bison. Not buffalo," Olive said as they began walking down the trail.

"Isn't that the same thing?"

"No. They belong to the same family, but they have physical differences. Bison have a large shoulder hump, massive heads, and smaller horns."

They walked in silence for a while until Olive stopped suddenly and pointed at a hill. Eight bison were either standing or lying on the ground.

"Wow." Gabby's eyes widened. "Can we get closer?"

"Trust me. You don't want to get too close." Olive surveyed their surroundings. "We could hike this way a bit and around those trees. You should be able to get some good shots with the zoom lens from there."

Gabby darted down the path before Olive finished speaking. She'd never seen her so excited before. Olive jogged to catch up and grabbed Gabby's arm.

"Slow down, hot shot. And walk a little quieter. The last thing we want is for them to feel threatened."

"Sorry. But this is so cool. I've never photographed buffa…I mean, bison before."

Olive smiled widely. Gabby's excitement was contagious. "You like taking pictures of wildlife, huh?"

"It's my favorite. In fact, I had a great idea for the contest." Gabby looked sideways at Olive as they walked side by side. "Oops. Guess I shouldn't share my flash of genius with the competition."

Great. Gabby had a brilliant concept in mind. Olive? She had nothing. Not even an inkling of what she'd enter.

When they reached a spot with a clear view of the bison but far enough away to be safe, Gabby unpacked her camera and began snapping pictures.

"I had no idea they'd be so huge," Gabby said. "Aren't you going to take any photos?"

"Trust me. I already have plenty. Several are hanging in my condo. The bison are my animal totem."

Gabby lowered her camera and looked at Olive. "Your what?"

"A totem is a natural or mythical being that you feel a close connection with. The bison have an indomitable spirit and are legendary for overcoming adversity. They're a symbol of power, freedom, and the will to face any challenge."

"I like that. Would you share your totem with me?"

"Gladly," Olive said with a smile, warmth filling her heart.

If anyone else had asked, Olive probably would have hesitated, but for some reason she really liked the idea of having the same animal spirit as Gabby.

CHAPTER FOURTEEN

THE SECRET COVE

Olive's stomach churned as she stood outside of Luigi's waiting for Gabby to arrive. When Gabby had invited her to Sunday dinner with the Pacelli clan, Olive had happily agreed. The Italian family must have been growing on her. She needed to do one thing first, though, and that was tell Gabby the truth about last year. They were becoming friends, and Olive liked her too much to keep something that big a secret.

Olive took a deep, shaky breath. This wouldn't be easy. Gabby had made it clear that she despised the person who'd ratted on her. What if she told her to go to hell and stick her friendship where the sun don't shine? Then again, maybe that would be for the best since they *were* rivals. But no. Olive didn't like that option one bit. The thought of never seeing Gabby again was disheartening. Olive could only hope that her well-prepared speech would convince Gabby to forgive her. She'd stood in front of the mirror and practiced it for an hour. She couldn't have been any more prepared.

Olive closed her eyes and leaned back against the cool brick wall of the restaurant. If anyone had told her just a few weeks ago that she'd be friends with the Italian Stallion, she'd have thought they were insane. Yet here she was, desiring the companionship of someone she cared about far more than she wanted to admit.

"Hey."

Olive's eyes popped open, her pulse racing at the sight of Gabby just inches away. *You can do this. Just recite what you practiced a gazillion times.*

"What are you doing out here?"

"I…uhh…" This was so much easier when Olive was looking at her reflection in the mirror instead of the real-life, flesh-and-blood Gabby.

"Are you okay?" Gabby placed a hand on Olive's arm, her caramel eyes dripping with concern. Apparently, she wasn't going to make this easy by being attentive and caring. Why couldn't her annoying side rear its head about now?

Olive blurted out, much too loud and forcefully, "I need to tell you something."

"Okaaay…"

Olive filled her lungs with air, let it out slowly, and gulped.

"It can't be that bad," Gabby said with a nervous chuckle.

I just hope you still think that after I spill my guts.

"This is something that—"

"Hey, you two," Gina said as she joined them. "The party is inside."

Olive sighed. Bridezilla had the worst timing ever.

"Party?" Gabby asked. "What's this dinner about anyway?"

Gina pursed her lips and appeared to be irritated and mischievous at the same time.

"Come on, Gina. What gives?"

Gina silently shook her head, with a slight grin and a flash of anger in her eyes. "Don't keep Mamma waiting," Gina said as she entered the restaurant.

"What was that about?" Olive asked.

"No idea, but I guess we should find out." Gabby placed her hand on Olive's back and guided her toward the door. "Oh, wait. You were going to tell me something."

"I'll…uhh…I'll tell you later." Olive wasn't chickening out… or at least that's what she told herself. What Gina had said was true. They shouldn't keep Mamma Pacelli waiting.

When they reached the table, everyone was seated and perusing the menu. Mamma Pacelli shook her head in disgust and made "tsk tsk" sounds. Upon seeing Gabby, though, she smiled brightly.

"You sit here." Mamma Pacelli patted the empty chair at the head of the table. "And Olive, you sit next to Gabby."

Olive slid into the seat across from Mamma Pacelli.

Gabby stood stiffly, glanced at Nonna at the other end of the table, and then at her mother. "You always sit at the head of the table."

"Not tonight. Sit...sit."

Gabby eyed her mother suspiciously as she lowered herself into the chair.

"Can you believe this menu?" Mamma Pacelli's face contorted.

"Everything looks yummy," Olive said as she scanned the selections.

"A *real* Italian restaurant would never serve Caesar salad. Salad is not an appetizer in Italy," Mamma Pacelli said. "This restaurant is a cliché! And would you look at these red-and-white-checkered tablecloths? *Che schifo!*"

"Mamma, inside voice, please," Gabby whispered sternly.

"What would you suggest I order?" Olive asked Mamma Pacelli.

"Pizza. We order pizza."

Gabby groaned. "I've had enough pizza to last a lifetime."

As though on cue, the waiter appeared with a pad and pen. The sisters yelled out their selections, which Mamma Pacelli completely ignored. Instead, she peppered the waiter with questions like it was the Inquisition.

"Do you use a wood fire? Is it thin crust? Do you have *burrata*? Every Italian restaurant should have *burrata*."

The waiter stared, dumbfounded. "Bur-what?"

A jumble of Italian words spurted out of Mamma Pacelli's mouth so fast Olive couldn't understand one syllable, except she was pretty sure they included a few profanities.

"What's bur-whatever?" Olive asked Gabby.

"It's like mozzarella but lighter, softer, and more flavorful."

"Ohhh, cheese." The waiter's face lit up. "We have the finest mozzarella."

"Huh. Nothing beats *burrata*."

"Mamma, can we just order, please?" Gabby asked, obviously irritated.

"Fine. We'll have a Margherita with sausage, Pizza Ai Quattro Formagi, and Marinara Neapolitan for Gabby, since she's lactose intolerant. And two bottles of champagne."

"Champagne?" Gabby asked. "We never drink that unless we're celebrating something. What gives?"

Mamma Pacelli smiled coyly. "Not until everyone has a glass in their hands so I can make a toast."

Gabby flagged down the waiter and asked him to put a rush on the drink order. Within minutes everyone had pink champagne.

Mamma Pacelli stood and cleared her throat. "Everyone, shush! I'd like to make a toast to the new president of Mamma Pacelli's Pizza!"

Gabby peered around the restaurant as though expecting someone to appear. When she focused back on the table, all the color drained from her face when she realized everyone was staring at her, with ginormous smiles...except Gina, who looked annoyed.

"When our dear Alberto left us, he not only put a big hole in our hearts, but also in the family business," Mamma Pacelli said. "Since then, Gabby has taken over as general manager and made us even more successful." Mamma Pacelli cupped Gabby's chin. "This is what your papa would want."

"But...you're the president. That's the way it should be." Gabby looked like she wanted to crawl under the table and stay there the rest of her life. "What about Tony? He could do it."

Gina nodded enthusiastically. That explained her irritation. She probably wanted her fiancé to get the position.

"No," Mamma Pacelli said resolutely. "It's your place to lead the family business now. Just as your papa did." Mamma Pacelli raised her glass high in the air and said, "To Gabriella!"

Everyone cheered and took a drink, except Olive. This wasn't good news. It'd be even harder now for Gabby to tell her family she was leaving. Olive wanted to ask Gabby if she was okay but didn't want to call attention to her I-want-to-die-now expression, so instead she flashed a sympathetic gaze.

When the pizza arrived everyone chowed down. Everything was delicious and even passed the strict Mamma Pacelli pizza standards, despite the absence of *buratta*. No one noticed Gabby's lack of appetite and quiet demeanor except Olive. After the last crumb was consumed, the Pacelli sisters headed to the beach to watch the sunset, while Mamma Pacelli and Nonna went back to the house, leaving Gabby and Olive alone in the restaurant.

Gabby stared at the melting ice cubes in her glass. "What am I going to do?"

"Gabby, look at me." Olive scooted her chair closer and didn't continue until she had Gabby's full attention. "You're going to do exactly what you planned. This doesn't change anything."

"This changes everything. Do you know what it means for Mamma to make me president? I can't leave now. I'm so fucked." Gabby groaned and hid her face in her hands.

"You can't give up now. What about your tattoo?"

Gabby placed her hand over her heart, which was where her tattoo was located, and looked quizzically at Olive.

"Remember? I caught a glimpse of it at Say Cheeze when you were seductively leaning over my desk."

"Seductively?" Gabby grinned and raised an eyebrow.

"You were still trying to get me into bed then, so yeah... seductive. Anyway, I remember it was a bird with the word freedom underneath. Are you really going to ignore something forever engraved over your heart?"

"I can't abandon my family. They're counting on me." Gabby's voice cracked with emotion.

"Remember what Harmony was saying about the guilt and ego connection at the workshop? Do you think that might be true in your case?" Olive flinched, afraid of Gabby's response.

"No. Of course not." Gabby's jaw muscles visibly tightened.

Olive had to tread lightly here. No one wanted to be referred to as an egomaniac. "But could it be possible that you don't trust anyone else to run the business because you like being in control?"

"You don't know my brothers-in-law. They're useless."

"Have you tried to teach them instead of doing everything yourself?"

Gabby started to say something but then paused, her eyes filled with an emotion Olive couldn't pin down.

"Just think about it, okay?" When Gabby didn't respond, Olive pushed her chair back and tugged Gabby's arm. "Come on. Let's get out of here."

"Where?"

"To the beach."

"I don't want to be anywhere near my sisters, or anyone else."

"I'm taking you someplace no one knows about. There won't be another soul there. Come on. Some fresh salt air will help clear your head."

Olive pulled Gabby out of her chair, excited to show her a place she'd never taken anyone before.

❖

"How much farther?" Gabby asked, or rather whined.

They'd driven down a bumpy dirt road for twenty minutes, hiked a narrow trail surrounded by tall weeds for God knows how long, and now they were climbing over boulders. At least Gabby hadn't thought about what'd happened at dinner since she was too preoccupied with where the hell Olive was taking her.

"I'm not exactly dressed for a ten-mile excursion," Gabby said.

"Don't be such a baby," Olive yelled over her shoulder. "We're almost there."

Within minutes they stepped into a clearing that revealed a view that made Gabby's jaw drop. It was one of the most beautiful places she'd ever seen. The sand was so white it almost hurt her eyes and the ocean an inviting, sparkling turquoise that made her want to strip and go skinny-dipping. Darkness had almost settled, with a half-moon hanging overhead and what seemed like thousands of twinkling stars in the indigo sky.

Olive removed her shoes, which prompted Gabby to do the same. The sand was so soft it was like walking on cotton balls. Gabby practically ran to the shoreline and allowed the clear water to wash over her bare feet. She could see tiny crabs burrowing into the sand and colorful fish darting about. She'd heard once that salt water heals everything, and hopefully that was true. She certainly needed something to erase all her worries. Realizing she was standing alone, Gabby turned to see Olive sitting in the sand several feet away snapping photos. Olive lowered her camera and gazed at Gabby with an intense expression. Gabby was about to suggest that Olive join the fun when she remembered Olive's fear of water. She probably hadn't even touched the ocean since the accident when she was thirteen. How sad to be surrounded by the thing you were most afraid of.

Gabby sat beside Olive as she snapped photos of the breathtaking scenery. Olive was undoubtedly one of the most beautiful women Gabby had ever met. Not only did she have enticing features, but a benevolent heart as well. Gabby had opened up to Olive more than she had anyone, even Isabella, and had been touched by her support. Because they were competitors, anyone else in her position never would have offered friendship. In a weird way, Gabby was glad Olive had turned down her advances when they first met. They would have slept together a couple of times, gone their separate ways, and Gabby wouldn't have had any idea how incredible Olive was.

"What is this place?" Gabby asked.

Olive lowered her camera. "I call it the Secret Cove. Just a few locals know about it, but they never come here because it's too difficult to reach."

"It's like our own secluded, castaway island." Gabby settled her gaze on Olive's profile.

"Yes," Olive whispered. "Just you and me."

When Olive locked eyes with Gabby, warmth spread through her, which was weird considering the chill in the air. The longer they maintained eye contact, the faster Gabby's heart raced.

Feeling suddenly uncomfortable, Gabby looked down. "Do you come here often?"

"Mostly when something's bothering me or I have to think. That's why I thought it might help to bring you here."

Right. The promotion. Gabby had almost forgotten about it.

"Has your mom, or anyone in your family, ever seen the photographs you take?"

"No."

"Maybe if she saw how good you are she'd be more supportive."

"You know Mamma. Do you really think that would happen?"

Olive pursed her lips and shook her head. "Probably not."

Despite her current predicament, Gabby couldn't resist grinning. "You have the cutest dimple when you frown."

"I do not." Olive turned a pretty shade of pink and swatted Gabby's hand away when she tried to poke her cheeks.

Gabby laughed, a real, deep-down, belly laugh. She hadn't done that in…forever. "You are so cute." Now it was Gabby's turn to blush. The compliment had unexpectedly slipped out. Definitely time to change the subject.

Gabby regained her composure. "Does it bother you to be this close to the water?"

"No. It's just when I get *in* it that I freak out."

"I've been falling down on my friendship duties," Gabby said. "I'm supposed to be helping you overcome your phobia. The contest is less than a month away. How about I take you on a boat this week?"

Olive's shoulders stiffened and she stared straight ahead. "I…I dunno…"

"Let's just try it, okay? I won't force you, and if you get scared we can stop."

"Maybe. I'll see."

"Orrrr…the ocean is just right here. We could—"

"What?" Olive's head jerked around.

"We could put our feet in the water."

"Now!?" Olive made it sound like Gabby had suggested she dive off a cliff.

Gabby placed a hand on Olive's arm and looked into her eyes. "Olive, do you trust me?"

Olive stared, her long eyelashes batting wildly. "Yeah. Actually, I do." Olive seemed just as surprised by that admission as Gabby was.

Gabby stood and held out her hand. Without hesitation, Olive took it and allowed Gabby to pull her upright. Olive's skin was warm and soft, which made Gabby wonder if the rest of her felt the same. Gabby laced their fingers together, and they walked hand in hand toward the edge of the water. The closer they got, the more Olive's grip tightened and her breathing quickened. Gabby lightly stroked Olive's skin with her thumb. It had seemed to calm her when she'd panicked before, so hopefully it'd help now. Several feet from the ocean, Olive stopped abruptly. Luckily, the waves were calm, so the chance of water rushing toward Olive until she was ready was slim.

"We'll just put one foot in, okay? Just up to the ankle." Gabby was surprised by the softness in her voice, the tender feeling in her heart. She'd never taken care of anyone, never *wanted* to take care of anyone, but more than anything, she wanted Olive to feel safe and secure.

Olive peered at Gabby sideways and nodded. When Gabby released her hand, Olive let go for a moment but then grabbed it again. Gabby smiled to herself, touched that Olive wanted her support. They both took baby steps forward until their toes barely touched the water. Olive immediately jumped back.

"Are you okay?" Gabby asked.

"Yeah, but the water is freezing. I had forgotten how cold it can be. How numbing…how powerful…"

Gabby could see in Olive's eyes that she was reliving the near-drowning. "Don't think about that. It's the past. Just be here with me now, in the moment."

Olive focused on Gabby and nodded. She inched forward until the water barely covered her feet.

Gabby noticed Olive's uneven breaths. "Slow, deep breaths. You're doing awesome. How about a little farther?"

"Easy for you to say," Olive said with a nervous chuckle.

"Don't give me that. You're braver than you think."

Olive took two steps, until the water was up to her ankles. She was as stiff as a mannequin and squeezing Gabby's hand so hard she probably cut off the blood circulation, but that didn't matter. Olive had done it, and Gabby couldn't have been prouder of her. She could only imagine how frightening it must be to face a horrifying fear.

"Look at you!" Gabby said.

A slow smile crept across Olive's lips as her face lit up. She looked younger, happier, and more breathtaking than Gabby had ever seen. Too bad she didn't have her camera to capture the image, although it was one Gabby wouldn't forget any time soon.

"I did it!" Olive's eyes jumped from her feet to Gabby. "I mean, it's not much, but I did it, and I'm not even freaking out."

"I'm so proud of you!"

Without thinking Gabby scooped Olive into her arms and lifted her out of the water. Olive held her hands high overhead and howled at the moon as they both laughed. Slowly, Olive slid down Gabby's body until she was once again standing. Gabby tightened her grip around Olive's waist and held her close, so close she could feel the pounding of Olive's heart against her chest. Olive bit the inside of her cheek as her eyes dropped to Gabby's mouth.

Kiss her, you fool. She wants you to kiss her. Doesn't she?

Uncertainty…and was that nerves…gripped Gabby. This wasn't like her. She didn't get nervous around women and never had trouble making the first move. Even if Olive turned her down, it'd be no big deal, right? Plenty of other women wanted to kiss Gabby. Like…like…what was her name? The woman from the boat. For some reason the name escaped her, but the woman obviously wanted to do more than kiss. So why did Gabby feel disappointed at the idea of Olive pulling away?

Olive's gaze jumped from Gabby's lips to her eyes. There. Right there. Desire and passion brimmed in those beautiful green eyes. Gabby was sure of it. It was time to make her move. The moment couldn't have been more perfect. The sound of the waves, a glowing moon, hundreds of stars, and a gorgeous woman in her arms. It didn't get more romantic than that. Maybe that was the problem. Gabby didn't do romance. This felt too…

relationship-like. Still though, the desire to feel Olive's lips against hers was overwhelming. It was...

And that's when it happened. Olive tilted her head, closed her eyes, and kissed Gabby. Momentarily shocked, Gabby stilled her lips, which didn't last more than a few seconds the way Olive worked over her mouth. Warm lips caressed, sucked, and nibbled. Obviously, photography wasn't Olive's only talent. The woman practically melted Gabby into a puddle. Just when it couldn't possibly get any better, Olive gently pried Gabby's lips apart with the tip of her tongue and deepened the kiss. Gabby's heart rate spiked, higher than if she were running full speed on a treadmill. She'd certainly been kissed by plenty of women in the past, but something about being devoured by Olive made her sizzle. Much more of this and Gabby would end up on her ass in the ocean when her jelly-like legs gave way. Still though, she didn't want Olive to stop...ever.

Suddenly, in a very unfortunate move, Olive jerked her head back, and a torrent of jumbled words tumbled out of her mouth. Had Gabby heard correctly? Her mind was still reeling from one of the most passionate kisses she'd ever had. Surely the sweet lips that made her swoon seconds ago hadn't just said what Gabby thought they'd said.

"W-What?" Gabby slightly shook her head, hoping the movement would clear her ear canals.

"I said I'm the one who turned you in to the judges last year." Olive spoke fast, her expression fearful.

Oh my God. Gabby *had* heard correctly, but apparently she was a glutton for punishment and needed to hear it one more time.

"What!?"

"I'm the reason you got disqualified, but—"

"Wait a second...wait a second..."

Gabby needed time to think. First, Olive should not still be in her arms after what she'd just said. Second, Gabby's lips should not still be tingling and her body vibrating with desire. And third...well, there had to be a third and probably even a fourth, but all Gabby could handle were the first two. She took a big step back to distance herself from Olive, slipped on seaweed, and landed in the water. Gabby knew she'd end up on her ass one way or another.

"Are you all right?" Olive reached for Gabby, but she pulled away, splashing cold, stinging salt water in her face. Great. Not only was her backside drenched but her front, too.

"I don't need your help."

Gabby tried to stand but fell again. Obviously, she did need assistance but wasn't about to accept anything from Olive. Finally, she managed to remain upright, drenched and with seaweed hanging from her hair. Gabby stomped out of the water and quickly slipped her shoes on, Olive following close behind.

"Let me explain," Olive said.

"I have no desire to hear anything you have to say."

"Just give me—"

"I can't believe you didn't tell me this before." Gabby faced Olive head-on and glared into her eyes. "I guess lying is your definition of friendship. First, you didn't reveal who you were when we met, and now this."

"If you just—" Olive attempted to explain, but it was too late. Gabby was halfway down the trail.

Freakin' friendship.

Gabby never should have agreed to such a thing. You bare your soul to someone, tell them your dreams and fears, only to have them slap you across the face. Nope. This wasn't for Gabby. She was better off alone. And what was with that kiss!? That tantalizing, arousing, mind-blowing kiss. How dare Olive come on to her *before* revealing her deep, dark secret.

Freakin' women.

Gabby shivered in the night air. It was Olive's fault she was soaking wet, her teeth were chattering…and her heart ached. Somehow, somewhere, Olive had wormed her way into Gabby's life and under her skin. She'd swooped in and sprinkled light and joy and fun and sexiness all over the place like confetti, and now it was gone. Just like that. This was why Gabby never got involved with anyone. Not that she and Olive were involved, but you could have fooled Gabby after that major lip-lock that turned her insides to mush.

When Gabby reached Olive's golf cart she sat in the passenger seat, crossed her arms, and rocked back and forth, hoping the action would help her warm up in the open-air vehicle. Olive arrived a few minutes later, slid into the seat, and stared at the steering wheel.

"Can we go? I'm freezing here."

Olive looked as though she was about to say something but then refrained. Guess she was smart enough to know that Gabby was far too angry to hear anything she had to say. Instead, Olive started the engine and sped away, frigid air swirling around Gabby.

CHAPTER FIFTEEN

SOMETHING'S FISHY

Olive peeked into Say Cheeze, glad to see Mr. Finkelmeier nowhere in sight. This was her first day back at work since her meltdown. In retrospect, it probably wasn't such a smart thing to blow up at her boss. He did pay her salary and provide benefits. Olive slinked into the office and hunkered down in her chair. She had a few minutes before the first appointment arrived. It was a family photo shoot with the McGregors, which shouldn't be too hard since their three boys seemed relatively well-behaved.

Olive reclined in her chair and stared at the ceiling. She'd really screwed up with Gabby. Could she have blurted out the truth at a more inopportune moment? They were in the most romantic setting ever, in a steamy, heart-stopping embrace, when Olive had suddenly decided to reveal her secret. *What an idiot.* In retrospect, Olive should have been shocked that she'd even kissed Gabby. She wasn't exactly the forward type. But Gabby had looked so beautiful in the moonlight, lips luscious and inviting, and she was being so supportive. And what a kiss it had been, passionate—which wasn't surprising—but also tender. That had been a shock.

Gabby seemed more like the wham-bam-thank-you-ma'am type, not someone who'd plant affectionate kisses on her lips and make her heart swell with emotion. Olive didn't blame Gabby one bit for the way she'd reacted after the bombshell. She should have told Gabby when they first met, or at least before she practically mauled her. She needed to find Gabby soon and try to apologize, if she'd even talk to her. At least the Pacellis had a final photo shoot on Friday before the wedding Sunday, so Gabby would be forced to see her then.

The door opened, and Mr. McGregor and his boys piled in dragging a humongous ice chest. Olive eyed the item suspiciously before standing to greet her clients.

Mr. McGregor paused to catch his breath, winded from pulling the obviously heavy chest into the office. "Sorry we're late, but this was a bugger to drag through town."

"What…uhh…what's in there?" Olive had a feeling she wouldn't like the answer.

Mr. McGregor beamed and yanked open the lid. A nauseating stench immediately wafted to Olive's nostrils. She gagged, pinched her nose, and peered inside. It was the largest, ugliest, deadest fish she'd ever seen.

"There is a bit of a smell, but isn't he a beauty?"

A bit!?

"It's…big." Olive released her nose, and her stomach churned as bile shot up her esophagus.

"Dad caught it off the pier," one of the boys said excitedly.

"Biggest halibut I've ever snagged." Mr. McGregor puffed out his chest and put his hands on his hips, doing a great impression of Mighty Mouse.

"Maybe we could put the lid back on?" Olive tried to breathe through her mouth so as not to faint from the disgusting odor.

Mr. McGregor drew his thick eyebrows together. "I brought him to be in the photo with me and the boys."

Seriously? It's not like the bug-eyed, scaly, dead creature was his fourth son. But then again, the way Mr. McGregor was acting, maybe it was.

"Boys, help me lift 'er up." They each grabbed the end of a large hook in the fish's mouth and hoisted it out of the crate. Ugh. It smelled even worse than before. The beast had to be at least four feet tall and probably weighed a ton, since their arms were shaking.

"Where should we stand?" Mr. McGregor huffed and puffed.

Before Olive could respond, Mr. Finkelmeier opened the door. He stopped abruptly, eyes bouncing from the humongous halibut to Olive. She expected him to immediately turn and dart out the door. Instead, he coughed—probably to cover a gag reflex—and walked into the office.

"Hello, Mr. McGregor. That's quite a catch you have there." Mr. Finkelmeier held out his hand but then dropped it when he realized there was no way the man could shake while holding a child-size, dead-as-a-doornail fish.

"Let's put 'er down for a second, boys." They lowered the creature back into the crate as Mr. McGregor flexed his hand. "I caught him off the pier."

"Mr. McGregor would like a photo of him, the boys, and the halibut," Olive said, giving Mr. Finkelmeier a heads-up that he should disappear into his office to escape the reeking photo shoot.

Mr. Finkelmeier paused for a few beats. "Olive, why don't you take a break, and I'll attend to this."

It took Olive a full ten seconds to realize what Mr. Finkelmeier had just said, and she still didn't believe it.

"Do…I mean…what?"

"I'll photograph Mr. McGregor and the…uhh…fish." Mr. Finkelmeier put his finger under his nose and cleared his throat, looking like he might barf.

Olive stared, her mouth agape. He'd never once offered to take over an undesirable photo shoot.

"Go on," Mr. Finkelmeier said. "Take a break."

A break? She'd just arrived. Was he firing her? But no. That couldn't be the case. He didn't appear angry. Maybe her tirade the other day had actually worked. If so, she should have blown her stack years ago.

Olive grabbed her bag and headed out the door before he could change his mind. She inhaled deeply, thankful for fresh, clean air, and walked down Crescent Avenue with a bounce in her step. Olive would give anything to tell Gabby what had just happened. Maybe she could track her down and apologize.

Olive meandered through town and ended up in front of Mr. Piccolo's snow-cone stand.

"Hey, Mr. P."

"Olive! How are you, this fine morning?" Olive shrugged, which elicited a frown from Mr. Piccolo. "What's with the long face?"

Olive slumped across the counter, resting her chin on a fist. "Remember Gabby? The woman I was with last week? I kept a secret from her, and when I told her what it was she freaked. She isn't speaking to me."

"Hmmm...was the secret something bad?"

"The worst." Before Olive could stop herself she'd told Mr. Piccolo the whole sordid story, minus the kiss.

"I see. You like this girl, don't you? Maybe even a little more than just a friend?"

Olive's face immediately heated. She was about to protest, but who was she kidding? She was not only attracted to Gabby physically, but emotionally as well.

"I suppose." Tingles cascaded throughout Olive as she recalled their kiss. She shook her head vigorously. "It doesn't matter. The last thing Gabby wants is a girlfriend. And, anyway, we'll go our separate ways after the contest."

Mr. Piccolo pursed his lips, looking deep in thought. "Did I ever tell you that I was quite the playboy in my time?"

Olive suppressed a giggle. That was a little hard to fathom. Not that Mr. Piccolo wasn't a nice-looking fellow, but he didn't strike Olive as the Hugh Hefner type.

"Really," Mr. Piccolo said, probably reading the doubt on Olive's face. "When I met Eva I was immediately smitten, but I was bound and determined not to court her. No way was I ever going to settle down and get married."

"What happened?"

"I realized that jumping from relationship to relationship didn't make me happy. Not nearly as happy as I was with Eva."

"I doubt that would happen to Gabby. She wants freedom more than anything, and she thinks a girlfriend would stifle that."

"You never know. People can change."

Could Gabby really change enough to want a serious relationship? And one with Olive? It was silly to think about. All Olive wanted right now was their friendship back. She didn't need to risk her heart with anything deeper with a self-professed playgirl. But why did the thought of that make Olive feel so sad?

❖

Gabby sat in a lawn chair in the backyard staring into space with her computer perched on her lap. She was supposed to be designing her contest entry in Photoshop, but her mind was preoccupied with Olive. Gabby had been brooding since their argument. Actually it hadn't been an argument, since she hadn't given Olive a chance to say anything. There was nothing she could have said, though, to explain what she'd done.

Mamma Pacelli's voice interrupted Gabby's thoughts. "Tony called. There's a problem at the restaurant. He wants you to call him back." She stood behind Gabby and peered over her shoulder. "What are you working on? Are those lovebirds?"

Gabby closed her computer. "It's nothing. What did Tony say?"

Mamma Pacelli sat in a rocker and fanned herself with a newspaper. "The interloper you hired who burns the pizza quit today."

"Kevin!? Damn. That leaves us shorthanded."

"Watch your language, young lady." Mamma Pacelli wagged a finger.

"I need to get back to LA. I should go tomorrow."

Mamma Pacelli stopped rocking. "The wedding is Sunday. You can't leave."

"I'll be back early Sunday morning. I need to find a replacement fast."

Gabby could have handled everything from Catalina, but escaping to La-La-Land would be a win-win. She could get away from Olive and avoid any more dreaded wedding crap.

"You'll miss rehearsal Friday night!"

"I already know what to do. Gina's drilled it into my head a million times." Gabby did her best impression of Bridezilla as she said, "Small step...pause...small step...pause until I reach the altar, then slightly turn and keep a fake smile plastered on my face until the priest says, 'I now pronounce you man and wife.'"

"But you won't be in any of the photos. No. You can't go."

Gabby sighed loudly. "Don't you think we've taken enough pictures? Besides, you *did* make me president. I'm the one who needs to take care of this. Papa would agree with me." Gabby felt slightly bad about pulling the dead-dad card, but she was getting desperate.

Mamma Pacelli paused for several dreadfully long moments before she finally said, "You be back on the earliest boat Sunday, you hear?"

"Yes, Mamma."

Chalk one up for Gabby. Winning an argument with her mamma was rare.

"You'll have dinner with the family tonight if you're leaving tomorrow."

"I don't think I can. I might have plans."

"With Olive?" Mamma Pacelli's eyes lit up.

"No. We had a fight."

"Gabriella Maria Pacelli, what did you do?"

Gabby sat upright. "I didn't do anything! It was all her!"

"Is that why you've been pouting all day? Your bottom lip is hanging so low it's dragging on the floor. Apologize and make up with your girlfriend."

"She's *not* my girlfriend. And I have nothing to apologize for."

Gabby crossed her arms and stared at her closed laptop, irritated by the *tsk-tsk* noises coming out of her mamma's mouth.

"Are you hungry?" Mamma Pacelli rose from the rocker, after a couple of attempts, and hovered over Gabby.

"No."

"You have to eat. It's lunchtime."

"Fine. I'll make myself some scrambled eggs."

"Grilled cheese isn't food. I'll fix you something." Mamma Pacelli disappeared into the house.

You win some, you lose some. She'd probably have to down a five-course meal for lunch, knowing her mamma. Gabby opened her laptop and worked on her contest photo, which was beginning to look amazing. She was glad Mrs. Albright had approved a graphic-design entry as long as every element was a photo Gabby had taken. No one else would think to combine pictures, along with a caption. Once again, she'd live up to her reputation for originality. Gabby really needed to confront her mamma sooner rather than later. Not right now, of course, but after the wedding for sure. Or maybe right before the contest...or after.

After working for a while, Gabby closed her eyes and leaned her head back. Her heart ached at the thought of Olive's betrayal. If anyone other than Olive had turned her in, it wouldn't have bothered her so much. Probably even more than the betrayal, though, Gabby was disappointed about the end of their friendship. She'd miss Olive more than she'd like to admit.

With that thought, Gabby grabbed her phone and pressed the speed dial of the only person who could take her mind off Olive.

"Hey, Carmen. I'm sorry I haven't returned your messages until now."

Carmen had left her at least six voice messages dripping with sexual innuendos over the weekend since she'd canceled their date Friday.

"If it isn't the spicy Italian. I thought you'd forgotten about me."

"Not for a minute," Gabby lied. Actually, she hadn't given Carmen much thought, but she didn't want to hurt the woman's feelings. Okay, maybe it was more like hurting her chances for a roll in the sack. "Are you free tonight?"

"I could be. What'd you have in mind?"

"How about we meet in front of the pier and then grab a bite to eat? Say seven?"

"I'll be there. I'm in the mood for a little spicy Italian for dinner."

Gabby heard a click. No good-bye, no so-glad-you-called, no see-ya-later. Carmen just abruptly disconnected. That woman had a one-track mind, which was fine with Gabby. That was exactly why she'd called her. The last thing Carmen wanted was to be her girlfriend.

❖

Gabby smelled something fishy, which wasn't unusual considering she was sitting on a bench by the pier. Still, though, that was an awfully strong smell. She sniffed several times and glanced around, surprised to see Olive standing behind her. She peered at Gabby with frightened but breathtakingly beautiful emerald eyes.

"What do you want?" Gabby winced at the harshness of her tone. She was still angry but hadn't meant to sound so mean.

Olive looked like she was about to bolt but instead took a shaky, deep breath. "Can we talk?"

Gabby turned around, her back to Olive.

"If you just let me explain." Olive walked around and faced Gabby. "Just—"

"What *is* that smell?!" Gabby pinched her nose.

Olive stepped back a few paces. "Oh, God."

"It's like…rotting whale carcass."

"It's halibut. A child-size, dead-as-a-doornail halibut."

Gabby leaned forward and took a big whiff. "Christ. Is that you?"

"We had a photo shoot this morning, and apparently, the smell stayed in the office and in my clothes."

"You took pictures of a dead fish?"

"No. Mr. Finkelmeier did. It was a family photo…of sorts."

"And your boss did the session instead of you?"

The corners of Olive's mouth quirked upward. "Yeah. I guess my little outburst the other day worked."

Gabby puckered her lips and nodded. "I'll be damned."

"Good thing your mamma isn't here. She'd tell you to go to confession for using that kind of language."

Gabby started to smirk but then quickly scowled. Olive wasn't allowed to make her smile.

"I don't have anything to say to you." Gabby stared straight ahead at hundreds of sailboats, hoping Olive would get the hint that this conversation was over. Obviously, that tactic didn't work since she took several steps forward and stood close to Gabby.

"Jesus. Can you back up?" Gabby hid her nose in the crook of her arm.

"I'm not going anywhere until you hear me out." Olive sat beside Gabby, who slid as far over as possible without tumbling to the ground. "I know I was wrong not to tell you the truth before, especially since we're friends. I apologize for that. And as for turning you in, put yourself in my place for a moment. What was I supposed to think when I saw a contestant hanging all over one of the judges?"

"She was the one hanging onto *me*! She was drunk."

"I know that now, but that's not how it looked. And...well... you kinda have a reputation for being a lady killer. We're not even supposed to talk to the judges, much less take them back to our hotel room."

"She wouldn't tell me where she was staying. I couldn't just leave her lying in the street."

"I'm just trying to get you to understand my position. If the same thing happened this year, I wouldn't question your motives. I didn't even know you last year."

Gabby looked directly at Olive. "And you know me now?"

Olive's long eyelashes blinked several times, and she never broke eye contact. "I believe so. I know you wouldn't do something dishonest to win. It's not who you are."

The air sparked with electricity as they gazed at one another. Gabby could practically hear the snap, crackle, and pop of the sizzling energy flowing between them. What the hell was that? It was the same thing that had happened the moment before they'd kissed. Gabby's heart pounded, and she felt breathless and weak. Maybe she was getting sick. She didn't even smell the dead fish anymore. Her senses were probably weakening, which happened sometimes when she got a cold. Fearing she might faint, Gabby broke eye contact and glanced down at her tightly clinched hands. Since when was she a hand-wringer?

"Am I forgiven?" Olive whispered and flashed kind, pleading eyes.

Gabby wasn't sure if she was ready to forgive the Benedict Arnold who'd cost her the title, a thousand dollars, and extreme embarrassment. But then again, apparently she had a soft spot in her heart for Olive since she melted a little at the sincerity in her voice. When Gabby didn't respond, Olive abruptly stood.

"Right. Well, see you around." Olive walked away.

Just like that? She was leaving? Olive hadn't given her a chance to let everything sink in. Gabby needed time to adjust to the idea of forgiveness. She couldn't be expected to change her mind within seconds.

"Wait!" Gabby yelled and bolted off the bench.

Olive stopped and turned around, a slow smile forming. When Olive looked past Gabby, her smile suddenly dropped. Gabby followed Olive's gaze until it landed on Carmen, who approached and kissed her cheek. When Gabby looked back, Olive had already disappeared into the crowd.

❖

"*Est-ce que vous avez une spécialité?*"

Did Carmen really have to speak French? Everyone in the restaurant obviously was fluent in English, plus the menu wasn't even written in a foreign language.

After the waiter rattled off the specials—in English—Carmen pursed her lips and studied the menu. Finally, she said, "*Je voudrais deux salade de chèvre chaud.*"

Gabby recognized the word "deux," which meant Carmen had ordered for them both. Plus, another word sounded familiar.

"Wait," Gabby said. "*Chèvre.* Isn't that cheese?"

"Goat cheese, darling. You'll love it."

"I won't love it because I'm allergic to dairy."

Carmen dropped her menu, gawked at Gabby, and burst out laughing. "An Italian who can't eat cheese?"

Yes, yes…Gabby had heard it all before. She didn't need a reminder of her inadequacies. Carmen dotted the corners of her eyes with a napkin. She'd laughed so hard she was crying.

"You're a treasure," Carmen said and placed her hand over Gabby's.

Why would being dairy-intolerant make her a treasure? Okay, Gabby was obviously in a bad mood, and anything Carmen said at this point would annoy her. She was still ticked off at Olive, and seeing her again hadn't helped any. Gabby sat upright and mentally scolded herself.

You're with a gorgeous woman who is a sure thing. Get your act together and don't blow it.

"*Je prends deux coq au vin,*" Carmen told the waiter. "*Et une carafe de vin rouge.*"

The waiter nodded, took their menus, and walked away.

"Can I ask what you ordered for me?" Gabby asked.

"Rooster cooked in sherry and vegetables. The sauce is very rich, if they prepare it right. And red wine."

"Have you been to France? You're certainly fluent in the language." Gabby took a sip of water.

"I've been all over."

That was vague.

"What do you do for a living?"

"Oh, this and that."

That was even more vague. This is going to be a long dinner.

And it was. Carmen's desire to keep things simple resulted in the most mind-numbing hour of Gabby's life. Luckily, she hadn't dozed off and was able to mask several yawns. Thank God, dinner was over and now the real fun could begin. A quick, or maybe not so quick, roll in the sack was just what Gabby needed.

As they stepped out of the restaurant, they walked hand in hand down Crescent Avenue toward Carmen's hotel.

"Gabby!" She heard someone calling her name but wasn't sure where it was coming from. "Gabby, over here!"

Gabby spotted Mr. Piccolo waving wildly from the SnoCone Zone.

"Ooh, how about a snow cone?" Gabby said and lifted a hand to Mr. Piccolo.

Carmen scrunched her face. "You can't be serious. That's for kids."

Gabby resisted the urge to pout. It wasn't just for kids. Olive loved snow cones, and so did Gabby.

"What I have in mind for you isn't G-rated." Carmen pulled Gabby into a dark alley, pressed her back against a cold brick wall, and kissed her forcefully.

It wasn't that it wasn't a nice kiss, erotic even, with dueling warm, wet tongues, but something about it just didn't sit well with Gabby. Maybe the fact that they were standing next to a trash can that reeked of coffee grounds and sour milk. Or because the lips attached to hers didn't make her legs wobble and her heart pound. Or maybe it was the detached, empty feeling in the pit of her stomach.

Since when do I have to feel *anything?*

Carmen broke the kiss and inched back. "Are you okay?"

"Yeah. Of course."

Gabby was obviously too much in her head, which was disrupting her ability to effectively smooch. That had never happened and was not acceptable. Gabby captured Carmen's mouth for round two, which unfortunately wasn't much better than round one. Scenes from the Secret Cove flashed through her mind: the sound of waves, hundreds of twinkling stars, and the sensuous feel of Olive's soft, sweet lips. Now *that* had been romantic.

Since when do I need romance?

Gabby pried herself from Carmen's embrace. She couldn't make out with thoughts of Olive on a moonlit beach tumbling around her brain.

"I hate to do this, but I'm not feeling very well." That wasn't a complete lie. Gabby did feel nauseous, which she hoped was from the trash-can stench and not Carmen.

"Oh." Shock, and more than a little anger, flashed across Carmen's eyes.

"Maybe a little too much rooster and wine. I better take a rain check."

"Right. Okay." Carmen took a step back, her expression stern. "Sorry if I ruined your night."

Carmen crossed her arms and looked more than a little perturbed. She'd probably never been rejected before. "You want to try this again sometime?"

"Sure. Absolutely," Gabby said, much too brightly to be believable.

"Okay, well...do you want me to walk you home?"

"No. That's okay. We're going in different directions. I'll call you next week." That would give Gabby time to decide if she actually wanted to see Carmen again. For some reason, she just wasn't feeling it with her.

"I guess I'll talk to you later." And with that Carmen was gone.

Gabby stepped out of the ally and headed to the SnoCone Zone.

"Hey, Mr. Piccolo. You're open late."

"It's never too late for a treat, Gabby. What can I get you?"

"Mmm..." Gabby perused the menu. "How about a bubble-gum flavor?" She needed something sweet after the day she'd had.

Gabby licked her lips as she watched Mr. Piccolo squirt pink syrup on a mound of sparkling ice. She bit off a big chunk, getting an immediate jolt from the sugar rush.

"I saw your friend earlier today," Mr. Piccolo said.

"My friend?" Gabby furrowed her brow.

"Olive." Mr. Piccolo flipped a switch on the ice-crushing machine, which made an enormous amount of noise. After a few seconds he shut it off. "She said you two were at odds."

"You could say that." Gabby huffed.

"I'm sure Olive meant no harm."

"Yeah, well, if you knew the whole story you'd be on my side."

"Olive told me what happened."

"She did? You mean about what she did last year?"

Mr. Piccolo nodded. "Do you think you could forgive her? She said she was sorry and that she missed you."

She misses me? That was nice to hear, no matter how angry Gabby was.

"I don't know. I thought we were friends. I told her things I've never told anyone before. I didn't think she'd be the type to betray me." *And break my heart.*

"Olive didn't know you a year ago. Tell me…if you were in her place, what would you have done?"

Gabby opened her mouth, about to defiantly defend her position, but then snapped it shut. What would she have done? *Dammit.* She would have done exactly what Olive did. She would have reported the seeming transgression to the contest organizers.

Gabby took a small bite and let the ice melt on the tip of her tongue. "So…she really said she missed me?" Gabby was pretty certain no one had ever missed her before. At least, not anyone who wasn't part of her family.

"You two are good for each other." Mr. Piccolo grinned in a way that made Gabby think he meant more than just friends. "Maybe you should talk to her. She's probably at home right now."

The man was many things if not pushy. Mr. Piccolo probably moonlighted as a matchmaker.

"Can't tonight. I'm going back to LA tomorrow for the rest of the week."

What a lame excuse. Gabby had plenty of time to track Olive down before she left, but for some reason she resisted doing so. Her anger had dissipated, but her attraction to Olive hadn't. Gabby needed to watch herself with that one. She didn't need anything distracting her from the competition.

CHAPTER SIXTEEN

PLAN B

It certainly hadn't taken Gabby long to move on. One disagreement and she was already making out with what's-her-name. Okay, so a peck on the cheek wasn't technically making out, but Olive was pretty sure they'd done more than that before the night was over. Not that Gabby and Olive were a couple, but they had shared a passionate kiss. Olive shouldn't care who Gabby went out with, but she did care. A lot. Which ticked her off more than anything.

Olive sat under a palm tree and absentmindedly watched Nicki's volleyball game. She was supposed to be taking photos of the action but wasn't in a working mood. In fact, she hadn't been in the mood to do much of anything since her blowup with Gabby. When Nicki shot her a dirty look, Olive lifted her camera and snapped a few photos to appease her friend.

During a break, Nicki stood over Olive and chugged down water.

"Let's see what you got." Nicki grabbed the camera and clicked through the photos. "You missed the one of me diving for that save. And what about that spike I made?"

"I got some good ones," Olive said, knowing that was probably a lie. She didn't even remember seeing a dive or a spike.

"What the hell is this?" Nicki turned the camera viewfinder toward Olive.

Olive's breath hitched. It was a photo she'd taken of Gabby at the Secret Cove.

"That's the Italian Stallion," Nicki said. Olive didn't like that nickname now that she knew Gabby better. She was so much more than a beautiful playgirl.

"You better get going. The game is starting again." Olive shooed Nicki back to the court.

With her friend out of the way, Olive studied the gorgeous shot. God, Gabby had looked so beautiful when they were at the Secret Cove, Olive couldn't resist capturing the image on film. Gabby gazed up at the moon with outstretched arms, flawless complexion glowing, and eyes filled with wonder. She looked like a goddess.

Isabella sat beside Olive. "Boy. You look as miserable as my sister does."

Did she just say Gabby was miserable?

"Wow. Is that Gabby?" Isabella snatched the camera out of Olive's hands. "Great shot.

Olive grabbed the camera back and stuffed it into her bag.

"I can't believe you're the one that turned her in last year." Isabella chuckled.

"I didn't even know Gabby last year. I was just…oh, never mind. So…is she here?" Olive scanned the beach, hoping to spot her.

"No. She's in LA."

Olive focused on Isabella. "Los Angeles? Why?"

"Some problem at the restaurant."

"But…she's coming back, right?"

Isabella squinted at Olive and studied her for several seconds. "You like my sister, don't you?"

Olive immediately felt her face flush. So much for being transparent.

Isabella laughed and threw her head back. "Guess you just answered my question. And yes. She'll be back Sunday before the wedding."

Disappointment overcame Olive. She wouldn't get to see Gabby, or try to apologize again, until the ceremony. And considering how hectic everything would be, they probably wouldn't talk until days afterward…if she even saw Gabby again. They didn't have any reason to get together now.

"How's Gabby doing?" *Or rather, is she miserable because of me?*

Isabella's face dropped, suddenly serious. "Aside from the squabble with you, she's pretty upset about the president promotion. That girl needs to come clean to Mamma about what she wants to do."

"I agree. I wish I could do something to help," Olive said. "Maybe if…"

"What?"

Olive shook her head. "It's nothing."

But it wasn't nothing. Olive had an idea that might just work.

Gabby would kill Olive if she knew what she was about to do. But considering Gabby was already angry and not even talking to her, what could it hurt?

Olive waited for Mamma Pacelli outside of the Casino. They were meeting under the ruse of reviewing the photography setup, since that was where Gina's reception would take place. Little did Mamma Pacelli know that Olive had an ulterior motive for getting together.

Olive watched as Mamma Pacelli made her way down the sidewalk. As usual, she greeted Olive with a smothering embrace and a kiss on each cheek. They made their way into the building and to the ballroom. It was a beautiful setting for a reception, with 1920s flower wallpaper, ornate wood-beam carvings, and lavish crystal chandeliers. Olive stood in the center of the room and whirled around as Mama Pacelli moved at warp speed, explaining how everything would be set up. Olive grabbed a notepad and furiously jotted down reminders. After all her hard work on the pre-wedding photos, she certainly didn't want to slack when it came to the wedding. Mr. Finkelmeier would shoot the church ceremony, which was fine with

Olive, and she'd be responsible for the reception, which would be the most fun anyway.

Mamma Pacelli took a deep breath after she'd barked orders for an hour, looking suddenly sad and near tears.

"My girl is getting married in three days. They grow up so fast. I wish Alberto could be here." Mamma Pacelli made the sign of the cross at the mention of her husband.

Olive put an arm around Mamma Pacelli's shoulders and gave her a squeeze. "He'll be here in spirit. I'm sure of it."

"You're a sweet girl, Olive." Mamma Pacelli flashed a weak smile, tears sparkling in her dark eyes. "Now if I can just get Gabby married. She's a restless one."

Mamma Pacelli shook her head and hoisted her purse over one shoulder, looking like she was ready to leave. Olive had to act fast if she intended to go through with her plan.

Olive cleared her throat and took a deep breath. "Maybe Gabby has other interests aside from settling down." Mamma Pacelli's head jerked toward Olive. "What would you like for her?"

"I want her to have a wife, kids, a family. She needs someone to take care of her."

Olive paused and pursed her lips. She was treading on thin ice and needed to choose her words carefully. Considering this was Mamma Pacelli, though, straightforward was probably the way to go.

"Excuse me for saying this, but…that sounds like what *you* want. Not what Gabby wants."

Mamma Pacelli's olive complexion turned bloodred, and the intensity in her eyes caused Olive to take a step back. The woman looked like a fire-breathing dragon ready to strike. Maybe Olive had overstepped her boundaries, but she couldn't believe Mamma Pacelli would be that selfish.

Olive held up her hands in defense as the words quickly tumbled out of her mouth. "You're a wonderful mother, and I know you speak out of great love, but it's Gabby's life."

Why am I risking my neck, literally, for my biggest rival, who isn't even talking to me? Olive would think about that later. Right now, she just needed to get out of this alive.

"I want her to be happy!"

"That's great, but do you actually know what would make Gabby happy?"

Mamma Pacelli put her hands on her hips and glared at Olive like she belonged in a straightjacket. This was not going well. Reasoning wasn't the way to reach this woman. Olive hated to do this, but she really needed to go to Plan B.

"Would you take a little stroll with me?" Olive asked, tentatively.

"Where?" Mamma Pacelli raised a thick eyebrow.

"Just...come with me..." Olive lightly held Mamma Pacelli's elbow and tugged her along.

They walked through the Casino and into a huge conference room. It was completely empty except for oversized, framed photos lining the walls.

"What are we doing in here? This isn't where Gina's reception will be."

"I wanted to show you these." Olive walked to the first photograph. "Come take a look."

Mamma Pacelli paused for several seconds before she joined Olive. "Why would I want to look at pictures?"

Olive ignored the question and motioned for Mama Pacelli to follow as she inched down the row of vibrant, glossy images.

"Did you take these?" Mamma Pacelli asked.

"I took some."

"This is nice." Mamma Pacelli paused and pointed to a print of a humpback whale jumping out of the ocean.

Olive smiled to herself as they continued walking. Suddenly, Mamma Pacelli stopped and examined a black-and-white photo of an eagle soaring over a snow-capped mountain.

"Beautiful," Mamma Pacelli whispered, as though she were in a sacred place and needed to be quiet. "Now that's talent. You took this?"

Olive shook her head. "No. But someone you know did."

Mamma Pacelli squished her eyebrows together and looked at Olive like she was insane.

"Look at the name tag." Olive pointed to a small, laminated sign next to the print.

Mamma Pacelli squinted and leaned forward, shock registering on her face, as she read the nameplate. "Gabriella Pacelli. 'Freedom.'"

Olive hadn't made the connection before, but she wondered if the photo had inspired Gabby's "freedom" bird tattoo.

"I don't understand," Mamma Pacelli said.

"Your very talented daughter won the Catalina photography contest two years ago with this photo. And the humpback whale... and that one...and those over there." Olive pointed to various prints around the room. "These are all photographs that have either won or were runners-up in the yearly contest."

"I knew she liked to snap pictures and entered these silly contests, but I never thought...she's good, yes?"

"She's fantastic. I think you should talk to Gabby. Ask her about her photography. This is what makes her happy. This is what she wants to do with her life."

Mamma Pacelli's eyes bore into the photograph, an unreadable expression on her face. Olive would have given anything to know what she was thinking. Without a word, Mamma Pacelli abruptly turned and walked out of the room. Hopefully, Olive hadn't just made things worse.

CHAPTER SEVENTEEN

GHOST CHAT

Gabby sat in her office at Mamma Pacelli's Pizza and absentmindedly stared at the clock. It was noon, which meant Olive would probably be on her way to lunch. Maybe she'd meet Nicki at Tito's Taco Stand or eat at her desk before a photo shoot. No. Olive liked to get outside in the sun and fresh air whenever possible. Gabby grabbed her cell and looked up the temperature in Avalon. With a high of seventy-three, Olive was probably in jeans, maybe the low-riding ones that hugged her body perfectly, and the red shirt that accentuated her assets and made Gabby's pulse race. Screw anyone who said strawberry blondes shouldn't wear red, because Olive looked amazing.

Gabby shook her head and mentally scolded herself. Why was she thinking about Olive and her assets? Probably because she felt guilty about storming away after their kiss—that titillating, heart-stopping, surprising kiss—and not even giving Olive a chance to explain. Gabby tapped Olive's name in her cell-phone contacts, fingers poised to type a text. Everything she thought of, though, sounded lame.

*Sorry about how I reacted...*not sincere enough.

*Thinking of you...*too honest and scary to admit.

What are you wearing? Gabby tossed her phone onto the desk. She'd just wait and apologize in person at the wedding.

Tony walked into the office and threw a three-inch stack of papers on Gabby's desk. "Take a look at these. They're resumes."

Gabby thumbed through the items. "Wow. How many did we get?"

"This isn't even half of them." Tony sat in a chair across from her desk. "You didn't have to come back just for this. I put an ad in the paper, and we won't hire anyone until at least a few weeks."

"I know, but I wanted to get away for a few days." Gabby rubbed her forehead.

Tony chuckled. "Gina getting to you?"

"You could say that." *Among other people...or rather person.* "Hey. Can I ask you something?"

"Sure. What's up?"

"Do you think I'm...controlling?"

Tony burst out in such a fit of laughter he almost tumbled out of the chair. Gabby stared, stone-faced, for a full minute before he regained his composure. Tony wiped his eyes and grew suddenly serious when he saw Gabby's expression.

"Oh. That was a real question. I thought you were joking."

Gabby raised an eyebrow. "I guess that's a yes?"

"Now you know you're my favorite soon-to-be sister-in-law, but let's face it, Gab. You're a control freak when it comes to the business."

"How? In what way?"

"You want to do everything yourself. You don't show me or Dante anything. We don't even know the password to get into the system to order supplies. It's like you don't trust us."

Geez. Maybe that Harmony chick had been right. Maybe Gabby was on an ego trip. But that couldn't be true. She didn't even want to be in charge or have anything to do with Mamma Pacelli's Pizza.

"I'd gladly let you two take over," Gabby said, even though she wasn't completely sure she believed that herself.

"Really? Then give me the keys to the safe. Or let me be in charge of replacing Kevin. Or a host of other tasks you insist on doing yourself."

Gabby inhaled deeply and let the breath out slowly.

"Look," Tony said. "I'm sorry, but I figured you'd want an honest answer."

"Thanks for your candor. It's not easy to hear, but I appreciate it."

Tony rose and walked toward the door.

"Hey," Gabby said, which prompted him to turn around. "271945."

"What?"

"That's the system password. Easy to remember since it's Papa's birthdate."

"Thanks, Gab." Tony smiled brightly and walked out.

Giving Tony the code left a sour taste in Gabby's mouth and her insides jittery. Maybe she *was* a control freak and Mamma Pacelli's Pizza was her safety net. Leaving her family and going out on her own was frightening. If she never left, then she couldn't fail as a photographer. And nothing would be worse than falling flat on her face.

❖

Gabby strained to climb a steep hill covered with the greenest grass she'd ever seen. If she didn't know better she'd think it was artificial. She stopped to marvel at dozens of little yellow flowers. It was a beautiful day, manicured surroundings, warm with blue skies overhead. She considered sitting on a nearby bench but instead continued the ascent. She wasn't here for the view. When Gabby reached the top of the hill, she took several deep breaths and gazed into the valley below. After resting for a moment, she walked to an oak tree and stood in front of her papa's headstone. Mamma Pacelli had insisted his resting place be in most beautiful spot in the cemetery. At first, Gabby had balked at the hilltop location, considering it was hell trying to get Nonna up here, but maybe her mamma had been right. Gabby was certain her papa would have loved this spot.

Gabby dusted a few leaves off the gravesite and sat in the cushiony grass, her back against the tree. She stared at the ground, pulled up blades, and contemplated how to start the conversation. Gabby wasn't crazy. She knew her frequent cemetery talks were completely one-sided, but she felt closer to her papa here than anywhere else. And sometimes she'd swear she could actually see him and hear his voice.

"Oh, hey. I brought you something." Gabby reached into her pocket, pulled out a tin of Spezzatina, and placed it beside the headstone. "Don't choke on it." Gabby released a nervous chuckle.

"So, Papa…I wanted to talk to you about something. You know I love the family very much, and you asked me to take care of them and the business. See…there's something else I want to do." Gabby sat upright and inched closer.

"I want to take photographs, Papa. I want to travel the world. I want my freedom. I want to live my own life." Gabby sighed and closed her eyes. "Papa, I don't want to be president, or manager, or have anything to do with the pizza parlor. God. I don't even freakin' like pizza."

Gabby's heart lurched when she opened her eyes and saw her papa sitting on top of his headstone, tossing a Spezzatina into the air and catching it in his mouth. The vision looked so real she resisted the urge to bolt toward him for a hug.

"Papa? Did you hear me?"

He smiled and looked at her with sparkling brown eyes. Gabby had missed those eyes.

"I heard you." He spoke without moving his mouth…or maybe Gabby was hearing things. "Are you happy?"

Gabby paused and considered the question. Taking photographs brought her joy. And lately she'd been happy spending time with Olive.

"Then that's what you should do," he said, as though reading her mind.

"Do what?" Gabby asked.

"Take photographs. Your sister's husbands can take care of the business. Life is too short to spend it doing something you don't love. Do you want your eulogy to be a blank page?"

Gabby gasped. "How did you—"

"And that girl? She's good for you. Ask her out on a date." He winked, tossed another Spezzatina into the air, and disappeared.

Gabby blinked rapidly. She'd just had a conversation with her dead father, which she'd done many times before, but this one had felt especially real. Gabby rose and placed her fingertips on the stone where her papa had been sitting, warmth radiating up her arm and into her heart.

"Thank you, Papa," Gabby whispered, feeling lighter than she had in years.

CHAPTER EIGHTEEN

SHATTERED GLASS

Endless, chaotic pre-wedding preparations...check.
Hour-and-a-half ceremony...check.
Hour-and-twenty-minute bridal-party photo shoot...check.

The Pacelli wedding extravaganza was almost over. Now all Gabby had to do was get through the reception. She walked into the Casino ballroom, struck by how beautiful everything looked. Flowers galore, an excellent band, and the most expensive, excessive buffet she'd ever seen. Actually, the entire wedding so far had been perfect. Gina wasn't exactly her best bud, but Gabby was glad her special day was a success. Once Gabby had even felt a pang of jealousy, something she never thought she'd feel at a wedding. It was when she'd glanced at Tony, whose eyes were filled with love and affection as he gazed at his bride-to-be. It was the same look her papa used to give her mamma. Not that Gabby wanted to get hitched—far from it—but she did long to have someone look at her that way. Maybe she was getting soft, or more likely weddings probably made a sentimental sap out of everyone.

Gabby scanned the crowd, looking for Olive. She hadn't seen her at the ceremony, but then again she didn't see much of anything standing at the altar with her sisters. Mr. Finkelmeier took pictures at the church, but Olive was supposed to photograph the reception. Hopefully she'd get a chance to talk to her in private. Gabby approached the buffet table and snatched a twist of fried dough covered in powdered sugar. Suddenly, someone slapped her hand, which caused the item to slip from her fingers.

"What the…" Gabby whisked around. "Oh. Hey, Mamma."

"No food until the couple makes their entrance."

"I'm starving. I haven't eaten all day."

Mamma Pacelli flashed her infamous head-tilt/raised-eyebrow/crazy face. It was the same heart-stopping look she used to give Gabby and her sisters when they giggled uncontrollably in church as kids.

"But I already touched it. Wouldn't it be unsanitary not to eat it?"

Mamma Pacelli paused, as though considering the notion, but then shook her head. "Five-second rule. Leave it."

Gabby sighed and locked eyes with Olive from across the room. *Wow…* Gabby's heart actually skipped a beat. She thought that happened only in romance novels. Olive looked incredible in a vibrant emerald, tight-fitting dress that showcased sensual curves, and sexy black pumps. Gabby didn't like to wear dresses or heels, but she could certainly appreciate a beautiful woman in them. Olive's hair was pulled back and…something was different about her…Oh yes. She wasn't wearing glasses. Her green eyes, the exact color of her dress, looked larger and brighter than ever. It took Gabby almost a minute to realize that Olive was eyeing her up and down as well, with a rather lustful expression, if she wasn't mistaken.

"Gabriella!"

Gabby jerked her head toward her mamma. "What?"

"You haven't heard one word I've said."

"I'm listening. Five-second rule." Gabby looked back at Olive but saw only an empty space where she'd once stood. She scanned the crowd, frantically searching for a glimpse of emerald.

"I said did you bring the vase?" Mamma Pacelli grabbed Gabby's chin and turned her head.

Gabby shook free from her grasp. "Yes. It's under the table."

"Remember. That's your job."

"I know."

They turned their attention to the entrance when everyone yelled, "*Evviva gli sposi!*" which meant *hurray for the newlyweds.* Gina and Tony couldn't have looked happier and more in love as they greeted their guests. Good. Now maybe Gabby could eat. That didn't happen, though, when everyone encircled the couple for their first dance. When that was done, Tony pulled Gabby and about twenty others onto the floor for the *La Tarantella*, a frenzied dance where everyone holds hand and races clockwise until the music speeds up, and then they reverse directions.

After about fifteen minutes, Gabby slipped off the dance floor—hot, sweaty, and winded. She plopped into a chair and spotted Olive snapping impromptu photos of the guests. Gabby followed her every move. She was radiant, smiling and laughing. As though she sensed being watched, Olive looked directly at Gabby. It didn't matter that hundreds of guests surrounded them; it felt like they were the only two people in the room. Just one glance from this gorgeous woman and Gabby's insides warmed and her pulse raced. Gabby broke eye contact and shook her head. She needed fresh air. The lack of food and the high-intensity dancing must be getting to her.

Gabby stepped onto the balcony, a cool breeze caressing her skin. She leaned against the railing and admired the deep-indigo ocean and the sparkling lights of Avalon. Olive had said that this spot was considered the most romantic location on Catalina, and Gabby could see why. It provided a 360-degree view of the breathtaking island.

"It's a beautiful night."

Gabby spun around and was inches away from Olive. She looked even more stunning up close.

"It looks like they're serving the food now, if you're hungry."

Gabby was starving, but for some reason that wasn't a priority at the moment. "Actually, I was hoping to get a chance to speak to you."

Olive's gaze dropped to the ground. "I'm really sorry. I—"

"Wait. I'm the one who should apologize." Beautiful green eyes slowly rose to meet Gabby. "I shouldn't have stormed off that night. I should have let you explain. And after thinking about it, I realize you weren't to blame for last year."

Olive's face lit up. "Really? You're not angry at me?"

"I wish you'd told me earlier, but no. I'm not angry with you."

"That's a relief." Olive's shoulders relaxed and she let out a breath. "So we're friends again?"

Gabby couldn't stop the grin on her face. "Yeah. Definitely."

"Good." Olive smiled and propped herself against the railing next to Gabby. "What do you think of the wedding so far?"

"It's really beautiful and everything is going perfectly. Did you get some good shots?"

"I got some of your fancy dance moves." The corners of Olive's mouth quirked upward.

Gabby groaned. "Those may have to mysteriously disappear."

"Why? You were fantastic."

"You must be tipsy if you thought that was good."

Olive playfully bumped Gabby's shoulder. "I'm working. I'm not allowed to drink."

"How about you? Let's see what kind of moves you have." Gabby whisked Olive into her arms and twirled her around, which caused Olive to throw her head back in laughter.

"Not bad," Gabby said as she slipped one hand around Olive's waist and threaded their fingers together with the other. They inched closer as they moved in unison to the muffled sounds of the band playing *That's Amore*. Gabby stared at Olive's lips, those very talented lips, and recalled their kiss. Her gaze jumped to Olive's glimmering emerald eyes.

Gabby cleared her throat. "Where are your glasses?"

"I wear contacts sometime."

"You look really beautiful. I mean, I like your glasses, but... tonight...you're gorgeous."

Olive smirked, wrapped her arms around Gabby, and rested her chin on her shoulder. When Olive whispered, "Not as gorgeous as you" in Gabby's ear, shivers cascaded down her spine. Thankfully, Olive's ruse had worked, and Gina had let the bridesmaids wear baby-blue satin pantsuits. Gabby wouldn't have described the outfit as sexy, but she was glad it appealed to Olive.

Gabby closed her eyes and breathed in the scent of roses, which must have been from Olive since there weren't flowers on the balcony. Gabby inwardly sighed, reveling in how amazing Olive felt in her arms, so soft and warm. As they swayed to the music, heat rose to Gabby's cheeks, making her light-headed. She had slow-danced with sexy women before but had never had this reaction. What about Olive affected her so much? Yes, she was beautiful, but it was more than that. Olive was also caring and supportive. Gabby had never known anyone who understood her so well. It was a nice feeling. Really nice.

Gabby couldn't resist the desire to tuck Olive's hair behind her ear and plant kisses on her delicate neck. When the tip of her tongue touched Olive's skin, Gabby heard a low moan. Olive caressed Gabby's back, her breathing ragged.

"You're driving me crazy," Olive whispered and squirmed in Gabby's arms.

"You smell incredible. You taste even better."

Olive growled and pressed their lips together. It was a passionate, open-mouthed kiss, which immediately caused Gabby's insides to clinch. She'd never felt so aroused by a kiss before, her body pulsating with desire. If it were up to her she'd lay Olive down right there and make love to her. The L-word was unexpected and more than a little disturbing, but not enough for her to stop feasting on Olive's delicious mouth.

Suddenly, Olive pried their lips apart. "Wait," she said breathlessly. "I need to tell you something."

Had Gabby heard correctly? This was what Olive had done the last time they'd kissed. No way were they going down that road again.

"I can't do this unless I confess," Olive said.

"No...no...no..." Gabby tried to kiss Olive, but she put a hand in front of her mouth.

"I don't want to hide anything from you. Not after last time."

Gabby dropped her head and sighed. "Seriously? You're going to do this right now? Fine. What is it?"

Olive stepped back, Gabby reluctantly releasing her hold. Olive wrung her hands and paced back and forth. This didn't look good. Half of Gabby wanted to know out of curiosity, but the other half didn't, if it meant she and Olive wouldn't resume kissing.

"I...I may have overstepped my boundaries. But I was doing it to help you." Olive stopped and stood in front of Gabby. "Honestly, I just wanted to help."

Okay. Now Gabby was beyond curious. "What is it?"

"Promise me you won't blow up." Olive looked frightened, which made Gabby want to wrap her arms around her.

"I promise."

Olive took a deep breath and spoke quickly. "I showed your mamma your winning photos and suggested she talk to you about what you really want to do with your life." Olive flinched, like she expected Gabby to deck her.

It took a second to comprehend what Olive had just said. Her first instinct was to get angry, but she'd promised not to blow up. And really, was she even angry? Gabby had always wanted to do this but hadn't had the nerve. Gabby walked to the balcony railing, her back to Olive. She had to let this news sink in.

After a few moments, Gabby turned around. "What did Mamma say about my photos?"

Olive seemed surprised. "She loved them. At first she didn't know who'd taken them, but when she looked at the nameplate, she was shocked. She had no idea you were that good."

"She really liked them?"

Olive stepped forward and put her hands on Gabby's shoulders. "She was very impressed. You need to talk to her."

"I know and I will. I did talk to Papa when I was in LA." Olive looked baffled, so she added, "Trust me. I know he's dead. It was at the cemetery."

"What did you say?"

"I told him I didn't want to work at the family business. I know this sounds crazy, but I felt like he answered me. He was supportive and said life was too short not to do something I love."

"It's not crazy." Olive lightly stroked Gabby's cheek. "I think we have a different perspective after we cross over. I'm sure your papa would be supportive. So, you're not mad at me?"

"You were a bit meddlesome, but you did me a favor. It'll be easier to talk to Mamma now."

Gabby slipped an arm around Olive's waist and inched closer until their lips were centimeters apart. As much as Gabby wanted to kiss Olive, she had a stronger urge to do something she never thought she'd do.

"Olive, would you go out with me? On a date?"

Olive drew her head back. "I...thought you didn't date."

"I'll make an exception for you."

Olive tensed in Gabby's arms, her expression unreadable but undeniably displeased. Not exactly the response she was hoping for. Gabby wished she could snatch the words back, but it was too late. She'd put herself out there, which made her feel like she was standing naked in the middle of Central Park.

"It's not that I don't want to," Olive said, tentatively. "But...is that really a good idea? I mean, the contest is in a few weeks, and either way we'll go our separate ways. Won't we?"

Gabby dropped her arms and put a safe distance between them. "Right. I don't know what I was thinking. Maybe I had a little too much to drink." Gabby chuckled nervously and hoped Olive was clueless to the fact that she hadn't had even one sip of alcohol.

This was awkward. Olive could kiss the hell out of her but didn't want to date. That was a switch. What did one do after being rejected? Cut and run? Get angry? Cry? They stood staring at each other for several uncomfortable moments until someone burst through the French doors onto the balcony.

"Gabriella!" Mamma Pacelli yelled. "It's time for the vase. Everyone's waiting."

"I'll be there in a minute."

"What's the vase?" Olive asked.

"It's a tradition. A member of the wedding party breaks a glass container, and the number of fragments represents the number of years the couple will be happily married."

"Remember to smash it hard," Mamma Pacelli warned her. "We want lots of pieces."

They returned to the ballroom and gathered everyone around. Gabby stood in the middle of a wide circle of people, clutching a glass vase. She glanced at Olive, who was peering through a camera ready to capture the action. Gabby's face heated at what had just transpired between them. Rejection was never fun, but that didn't compare to the unexpected disappointment and sadness that washed over her.

Gabby lifted the vase high overhead, looking forward to releasing her emotions in such a destructive manner. In one swift move, she threw the container down with such force the crash was deafening. The crowd gasped and backed away. Gabby viewed the shards of glass scattered around her feet, which resembled her shattered heart.

CHAPTER NINETEEN

SNOCONE ZONE SHOWDOWN

Olive flew out of Say Cheeze and down the street, late meeting Nicki for lunch. She rushed past the pier and saw her impatiently waiting in front of Who Let The Dogs Out, Mr. Sanchez's hot-dog stand.

"Why'd you want to meet here?" Nicki adjusted her Dodgers baseball cap. "I thought you couldn't look Mr. Sanchez in the eye after the little love shoot."

"I'm dropping off his photos."

"Oh yeah? Can I see?"

Olive pulled the envelope back. "Of course not! I shouldn't have even told you about it, so shush."

"So he was really in a speedo and red silk robe?" Nicki laughed.

"Hey. I give the guy a lot of credit for doing that for his wife. It was beyond brave of him. I just hope she actually likes the shots." Olive had done all she could, but trying to make Mr. Sanchez look sexy had been a challenge.

They stood in line a few minutes before reaching the counter.

"Hey, Maria. Is your dad working today?" Olive asked.

"He should be back soon. Is that for him?" Maria pointed at the envelope.

"Yeah, but it's sort of personal. I should hand-deliver it." God forbid the girl opened it and saw risqué photos of her dad. She'd be scarred for life.

After ordering two Hot Diggity Dogs and Diet Cokes, they nabbed an outside table. Nicki shoved half the hot dog into her mouth while Olive examined hers, contemplating how to eat it without getting chili all over her face and hands. Obviously, Nicki hadn't been successful. Olive grabbed a handful of napkins and gave them to her.

"You want to meet at Frank's after work?" Nicki said through a mouthful.

"I can't. Mr. Piccolo asked me to go by the snow-cone stand, which is kinda weird. He's never requested an appearance before. I hope everything's okay."

Nicki swallowed and sipped her drink. "How was the wedding?"

Technically, Nicki had asked about the ceremony, not the reception, so maybe Olive didn't have to tell her about the kiss. Hell, she hadn't even told her about the first one. In fact, Olive had purposefully avoided Nicki for three days, knowing she'd ask about the wedding. Oddly enough, though, Olive had told Mr. Piccolo all about it, maybe because she knew he'd listen without judgment, unlike Nicki, who could be pushy sometimes.

"The wedding was fine." Olive averted her eyes and played with the straw in her Diet Coke.

Nicki stopped chewing and eyed Olive suspiciously. "What aren't you telling me?"

Olive should know better than to try to fool her best friend. She picked up the hot dog and thrust it into her mouth, hoping to buy some time.

"Well?" Nicki asked.

Olive pointed to her munching mouth. Nicki patiently waited until Olive swallowed and then snatched her hot dog.

"Heyyy."

"You get this back when I get a straight answer."

Olive figured she might as well come clean. Otherwise she'd never get to finish her lunch.

She responded in one long, run-on sentence. "The ceremony was perfect, everything was beautiful, Bridezilla was happy, the reception was amazing, scrumptious food, I got lots of good shots,

Gabby kissed me on the balcony, she asked me out on a date, I said no, she broke a vase, I caught the bouquet, the end."

Olive purposefully left the part out about immediately looking at Gabby after she caught the bouquet. It had been embarrassing enough when it'd happened, like maybe Olive was expecting to marry her.

Olive grabbed her hot dog back and took a big bite. Nicki, on the other hand, had stopped eating and was staring with her mouth wide open. Luckily, she'd swallowed first.

"Gabby kissed you? And asked you out? And you said no?!"

Olive chewed and nodded.

"Wait a second. I thought you said she didn't date."

Olive took a swig of Diet Coke. "She said she'd make an exception for me." That had actually been the sweetest thing ever. Gabby had looked so sincere and shy, Olive had almost believed she'd changed her playgirl ways.

"Why'd you say no?"

Olive blinked rapidly and shook her head. She didn't know where to begin.

After several seconds of silence, Nicki said, "Ohhh. You're scared."

Scared? That wasn't one of her reasons.

"Look, Ollie. I don't blame you. You've had shit luck in relationships, but not everyone leaves. Maybe things could really work out with Gabby. You said you liked her."

Olive more than liked her, but Nicki didn't need to know that.

"I can't believe you're saying that. This is the Italian Stallion. She doesn't have long-term relationships. Besides, she'll probably win the contest and be on the first plane to Aruba in a few weeks."

"So, go with her."

Olive rolled her eyes. "Yeah, right."

Nicki pushed her half-eaten hot dog aside and leaned across the table. "She asked you out on a date. That says a lot, don't you think? And it's just a date, not a marriage proposal. Have you talked to her since the wedding?"

Olive tore little pieces off the edge of her napkin. "No. I gave the disc with all the photos to Mamma Pacelli yesterday, but Gabby wasn't around."

Olive's eye caught Mr. Sanchez walking toward them. Would she ever see that man again and not picture him half-naked?

"Hi, Mr. Sanchez. I have your photographs." Olive stood to greet him.

"Wonderful. Thank you for bringing them." He slid the envelope under his arm. "I better lock these in the safe. Don't want to ruin the surprise before Valentine's Day."

"Absolutely. See you later." Olive waved as he trotted to the hot-dog stand.

"You need to take a cue from Mr. Sanchez."

Olive slid back in her seat. "You want me to do a boudoir shoot?"

"I want you to be brave. Take a chance for once."

Olive flinched. That *for once* had stung, but it wasn't like Olive could argue the point.

Nicki stared directly at Olive. "Sometimes what you're most afraid of doing is what will set you free."

Olive hated when Nicki quoted Harmony's words back at her, especially when she was right. Maybe she was scared, but who could blame her? Gabby didn't exactly have a stable relationship history. Still, though, Olive had wanted to say "yes" with every cell of her being. She'd wanted to wrap her arms around Gabby and repeatedly kiss her until the sun came up. Her heart had been crying out for one thing, while her brain and mouth did something completely different. She certainly hadn't followed Harmony's advice, that's for sure. All right. Olive had blown it big-time. Gabby probably wouldn't even talk to her again.

❖

Gabby heaved her sister's millionth suitcase aboard the *Catalina Express*. Why she was expected to play bellhop was beyond her. Still, though, she didn't mind if it meant getting her sisters out of her hair so she could concentrate on the contest. She'd still have to contend with her mamma and Nonna, but considering she needed to have a serious talk with them about her future, she didn't mind that they were staying behind on the island.

Gabby and her mamma stood on the dock and waved as the boat pulled out of the harbor.

"Are you sure you shouldn't go back with them?" Mamma Pacelli asked. "You're the president now. You have responsibilities."

"About that…there's something I need to talk to you about."

"A problem at the restaurant?"

"Not exactly."

Mamma Pacelli flashed a worried expression. "What is it?"

"I have to be someplace in a few minutes." That wasn't a lie. Mr. Piccolo had asked Gabby to stop by, which was odd, but she wasn't one to pass up an opportunity for a snow cone. "And it's something I'd like Nonna to hear, too."

"Hmm…well, as long as there isn't a problem."

Gabby could practically feel her stomach ulcer exploding. Problem was a nice way of putting it. It'd be more like a catastrophe.

Mamma Pacelli headed back to the house while Gabby walked to SnoCone Zone. When she passed the marina, she couldn't help but think about Olive, since this was where they'd met when she first arrived. No matter how much rejection stung, it didn't change the fact that Gabby was drawn to the woman, which made her angrier than anything.

Gabby glanced at her cell phone when it rang. She considered not answering it, but she'd have to deal with Carmen sooner or later.

"Hey," Gabby said.

"Hello, stranger. I haven't heard from you in over a week."

"Sorry about that. It's been pretty busy."

"When can we get together again?"

Gabby wracked her brain to think of something to say to let her down easy. Normally, Carmen would be her dream girl, but something had changed since she'd been on Catalina. Actually, Gabby had changed, and she was pretty sure the strawberry-blond Say Cheeze photographer had something to do with that.

"Hello? You still there?"

"Yeah. Umm...you're a really great gal, but—"

"Great gal?" Carmen's voice oozed with sarcasm.

"It's not going to work with us. I'm looking for something... different." Okay. Maybe not the best choice of words.

Silence.

"Carmen?"

"What do you mean different?"

"Honestly, I'm attracted to someone else." Gabby had learned a long time ago to be honest when breaking things off.

"Really?!"

On second thought, maybe honesty wasn't the way to go, based on Carmen's angry tone.

"It's not that I don't like you."

"Right. I get it. No problem."

Except it sounded like it *was* a problem.

"I'm sorry."

"That's fine. See you around."

Carmen disconnected. Gabby hoped she hadn't hurt her feelings, but Carmen wasn't the woman she wanted.

When Gabby reached Mr. Piccolo's stand, it was empty. She leaned over the counter, thinking maybe he'd squatted down, but didn't see anything. She walked around to the back, turned the corner, and bumped into Olive.

"What are you doing here?" Gabby winced at the harshness of her tone.

"Mr. Piccolo asked me to come by."

"Me, too."

They both raised an eyebrow, probably thinking the same thing: this smelled like a setup.

Mr. Piccolo appeared out of nowhere. "Oh, good. You're both here."

"What gives, Mr. P?" Olive asked. "Why'd you ask both Gabby and me to come over?"

Mr. Piccolo went into the kiosk while they both stiffly stood by the counter.

"I need some help coming up with the name of a new flavor concoction and immediately thought of you two."

Seriously? He couldn't come up with a better excuse than that to get them together?

"I'm sure Olive can take care of it." Gabby started to walk away.

"Afraid of a little competition?" Olive asked.

Gabby abruptly halted and turned around. "Is that a challenge?"

"Sure. Why not?"

"What does the winner get?"

Olive looked awfully cute as she pursed her lips and stared at the sky, seemingly deep in thought. After a few seconds she said, "How about if I win you have to make me a famous Mamma Pacelli's pizza, and if you win you get to take me out on a date."

Gabby put her hands on her hips. "I thought you didn't want to date. And what makes you think the offer still stands?" She liked half of that deal, and it wasn't the pizza, but after being rejected she had to at least put up a fight.

"Why don't we just see what happens."

"So who decides the winner?"

"Mr. Piccolo, of course."

After a few moments, Gabby rolled up imaginary sleeves and rested her elbows on the counter. "Count me in. Show us what you've got, Mr. P."

Olive nudged Gabby out of the way with her elbow and matched her stance. They watched as Mr. Piccolo squirted bright-green syrup on top of perfectly rounded crushed ice. He handed them each a snow cone.

"We'll each come up with three names," Olive said.

"How come you get to make up all the rules?"

Olive sighed. "Fine. How do you want to do it?"

Gabby shrugged. It's not that she didn't agree, but she didn't particularly like being told what to do. "Let's just do this."

They both took a bite and stared off into space. Gabby detected a definite sweetness but couldn't isolate one particular flavor. She took another bite, allowing the ice to melt on her tongue. Nothing was jumping out at her, so maybe she could do something with the color green.

"Well?" Mr. Piccolo asked.

Gabby was about to make a suggestion but didn't want to give Olive any ideas. "I think we should write our three guesses down."

"I agree," Olive said.

Mr. Piccolo handed them each a pad and pen. Gabby turned her back to Olive and considered her choices. She could go so many ways. She needed something catchy, something that was a sure winner. Yes. Gabby wanted to win more than anything, and not just because she was competitive.

Think green.

When Gabby glanced over her shoulder, Olive was writing at warp speed. Ugh. Olive probably had awesome suggestions, considering she was the one who'd come up with Tongue Twister, which was way cuter than Gabby had admitted. Feeling suddenly pressured, Gabby jotted down three, hopefully, good entries and handed them to Mr. Piccolo.

"Let's see what we've got." Mr. Piccolo looked at Olive's paper and smiled. "Key Lime Pie, Cactus Juice, and Green with Envy. These are great."

Damn. Cute names, especially Cactus Juice. Gabby didn't stand a chance. Was it too late to withdraw?

"Now let's see what Gabby came up with." Mr. Piccolo cocked his head and didn't smile. She was screwed. "Pickle Juice, Frog Eye, and...what's this?"

Gabby's face heated. "That's...umm...Show Me the Money."

Olive laughed. "Show Me the Money?"

"It's a famous line from *Jerry Maguire*," Gabby said defensively.

"That movie is like twenty years old. Kids aren't going to know that." Olive was still laughing.

Mr. Piccolo nodded and stared at the paper. "No...no. I like these a lot. You know what? I think I'll go with Pickle Juice. It's a winner."

Was he serious? It tasted nothing like pickles. Cactus Juice was so much better. Olive looked just as shocked as Gabby felt.

"So, I guess since Gabby is the winner, you two will be going out on a date." Mr. Piccolo winked and smiled at Olive.

"I guess so," Olive said. "If the offer still stands?"

Of course the offer still stood, but Gabby didn't want to appear too eager. "I suppose I could take you out."

Mr. Piccolo clapped his hands. "Great! How about tomorrow tonight?"

Was this guy pushy or what?

"I could be free," Gabby said.

"I can make that work."

"How about I pick you up at seven?"

"Okay." Olive didn't sound very excited, but the twinkle in her eyes gave her away. She was obviously looking forward to the date just as much as Gabby was.

CHAPTER TWENTY

FLOWER POWER

I have to take flowers?" Gabby popped a couple of antacids into her mouth.

Isabella sighed on the other end of the phone. "It's a nice touch."

"What did I get myself in to?" Gabby paced in circles on the patio, clutching her cell.

"Gab, relax. It's just a date. Where are you taking Olive to dinner?"

"Umm...I dunno. Where should we go?"

"Okay, listen. Take her to Luigi's, the Italian place where Mamma announced your promotion. By the way, have you talked to her yet?"

"No. I can only handle one crisis at a time, and today it's the date. What else do I need to know?"

"Be yourself, relax, and she'll love you."

The thought of Olive loving her should have freaked Gabby out, but for some reason it didn't.

"Thanks. I'll talk to you later." Gabby slid the glass door open and entered the kitchen.

"Who was that?" Mamma Pacelli stuck an oversized pan of lasagna into the oven and set the timer.

"Isabella. She said Dante's handling everything at the restaurant really well. It's almost like they don't even need me there."

Mamma Pacelli vigorously stirred something in a large bowl.

After a few seconds, Gabby asked, "Did you hear me? I said they seem to be handling things fine without me."

Mamma Pacelli stopped stirring and looked up. "Gabriella Maria, out! You're tracking mud all over the floor."

Gabby looked down at her shoes. "Sorry."

"Dinner will be ready in an hour. You better get cleaned up."

"I'm going out tonight."

"Where? With who?"

"Olive and I are going to the Italian restaurant."

Mamma Pacelli approached Gabby, a wide smile on her face. "You and Olive? On a date?"

"Yeah...technically speaking."

"I like the Say Cheeze photographer. She's good for you. You bring her flowers, no?"

Again with the flowers? Gabby had never done that with a woman before, but then she'd never gone on a date.

"Yes. Fine. I'll get some on my way." Gabby kissed her mamma's cheek.

After showering and dressing in black jeans and a yellow shirt, Gabby hopped into the golf cart she'd rented for the night. She could have had Olive pick her up, but she was hoping for a good-night kiss, which wouldn't happen with her mamma and Nonna standing two feet away. Gabby pulled into The Floral Master, glad they hadn't closed yet. She opened the door, assaulted by scents, colors, and hundreds of varieties of flowers.

"Hello?" Gabby scanned the shop.

An elderly woman popped her head up over the counter. She didn't look like a floral master, but what did Gabby know?

"Welcome. How can I help you?" The woman beamed.

Gabby scanned the shop, the jungle closing in around her. "I need some flowers."

The woman stepped from behind the register and looked up at Gabby. "What's the occasion, dear?"

"They're...umm...for someone special." Gabby wasn't sure how gay friendly the floral master was, so best to keep it simple.

"For Olive?" The woman grinned mischievously.

Gabby's eyes widened. "How did…"

"I've seen you two together. It's a small island."

"Oh, right. Yes. They're for her."

"How about red roses?" The woman motioned to a giant bouquet.

Gabby didn't know a flower from a bean stalk, but didn't red roses represent love and all that mushy stuff? That seemed a bit much for a first date.

"Do you have anything that says something like 'let's go out and have fun and get to know each other better but with no pressure attached'?"

The master scrunched her face. "You mean like friends?"

"No. Something between friends and…well…lovers."

The master rested her chin on her hand and puckered her lips. "Hmm…"

"Hey. How about a cactus?" Gabby picked up a perfectly cute arrangement.

"Oh, my." The woman looked horrified.

"Not good?"

The master grimaced. Gabby put the prickly plant back down. Guess it wouldn't be very romantic if Olive pierced her finger on the thing.

The master grabbed Gabby's arm and guided her to a corner of the shop. "Camellias!"

"Those are pretty. Do the colors represent anything?"

"Pink is for longing, red is for the heart, and white says you're adorable."

Not that Gabby would publicly admit this, but all those fit Olive. "Can I get a dozen of mixed colors?"

The master nodded enthusiastically, gathered the camellias, and wrapped them in pink paper. With flowers in hand, Gabby was on her way. Her stomach churned as she crept up the hill to Olive's condo. What was she thinking, asking Olive out on a date? This wasn't such a great idea, considering they'd go their separate ways in a few weeks. Why get even more attached? Gabby had no answers. She just knew that for the first time in her life she wanted to date someone and wasn't going to pass up the opportunity to do so.

Gabby parked in the driveway, disappointed to feel a couple of raindrops hit her cheek. The golf cart didn't provide much protection. How would she get her date down the mountain without getting drenched? Gabby trotted to Olive's condo to avoid getting wet and rang the bell. When Olive opened the door, Gabby's gaze swept the length of Olive's body, taking in luscious curves. She looked adorable in tan pants, black fitted shirt, and sandals. Gabby jerked her head upward to find amused eyes staring back at her.

"These are for you." Gabby whisked the flowers from behind her back.

"For me?"

Gabby nodded, too mesmerized to speak by the beautiful face that lit up before her.

"I love camellias." Olive stuck her nose in the bouquet and took a big whiff. "They smell amazing. Come on in and I'll put these in a vase."

Olive disappeared into the kitchen and returned a few moments later. She put the flowers on the coffee table and sat on the couch.

Gabby walked to a photograph hanging above the fireplace. It showed a black-and-white moonlit beach with the silhouette of a couple holding hands. It was dark, moody, and romantic.

"Is that a Robert Klein?"

"Yes."

"I can see why he's your favorite. Sorry I ruined his speech for you at the orientation." Gabby glanced at Olive before returning her attention to the photograph. "His work is on display at the West Coast Photography Museum in LA. Have you been?" Gabby rolled her eyes and mentally kicked herself. What a stupid thing to ask.

As though reading her mind, Olive said, "It's okay. I'll get there one day. You can have a seat if you'd like." Olive patted the place next to her.

Gabby settled into the soft leather and admired Olive. She looked relaxed with an arm draped across the back of the sofa and one leg tucked underneath the other. Very different from the last time Gabby had been in her condo after she'd freaked about the boat ride.

"Is it raining?" Olive asked.

"Yeah. It just started."

"We could stay in if you'd like. I don't have anything fancy to offer, but I'm sure I could come up with something."

Gabby felt slightly disappointed. She'd wanted to wine and dine Olive, but then again, spending time alone instead of in a noisy, crowded restaurant sounded appealing.

"I don't want to put you out," Gabby said.

"It's no trouble as long as you like spaghetti TV dinners."

Gabby grinned. "Those are my favorite."

"Great." Olive stood up and held out her hand.

Gabby grabbed it, enjoying the warmth of Olive's skin against her palm. Reluctantly, she released Olive when they reached the kitchen.

"Can I help with anything?"

Olive opened the freezer and peered inside. "No, thanks. Stand back, and I'll impress you with my microwaving abilities."

Gabby leaned against the counter and smiled. "Your talents never cease to amaze me."

"You don't believe me, do you?" Olive opened two frozen dinners. "The key is not to follow the directions on the box."

"You? A rule breaker?"

"Hey, I've broken plenty of rules." Olive playfully bumped Gabby's shoulder.

"Oh yeah? Like what?"

Olive paused, cocked her head, and stared into space. "Plenty, and this is a good example. The directions say to puncture the plastic and microwave for four minutes. I don't puncture, and I cook for three-and-a-half minutes."

Gabby chuckled. "I didn't realize what a badass I was dealing with here."

Olive suppressed a smile. "My way makes the noodles soft, not hard. Trust me. You'll see."

"I trust you implicitly. With my spaghetti, anyway."

"Nothing else?" Olive placed the dinners in the microwave and set the timer.

Gabby whirled Olive around in a move that surprised even her. "I trust you with everything. You might be the sweetest woman I've ever met."

Olive scrunched her face and placed her hands on Gabby's hips. "Sweet? I think I like badass better. No one wants to be referred to as sweet."

"Fine." Gabby sighed. "You can be a sweet badass, although that does sound like an oxymoron."

"Mmm...I'll take it."

Everything around them seemed to still as they peered into each other's eyes. If Gabby didn't know better, she'd think they were about to kiss, but didn't that happen at the end of dates? She certainly wanted to kiss Olive, but more than anything, Gabby wanted to do this date thing right. They both flinched when the microwave dinged. *Saved by the bell.*

Olive pulled out the cartons and scooped the contents onto a couple of plates.

"Do you drink wine?" Olive asked.

"Remember who you're talking to. I'm Italian. It's a must at every meal."

"Oh yeah. Red or white?"

"Red should go nicely with spaghetti."

Olive handed Gabby the plates. "Can you take these out to the balcony, and I'll meet you there with the drinks."

Gabby walked into the living room, surprised she'd never noticed the balcony before. She opened the French doors, set the dishes on a table, and leaned against the railing. The view was breathtaking, even in the gentle rain. Dusk was setting over the ocean, and Avalon sparkled in the lights below.

"Beautiful, isn't it?" Olive placed two glasses and a bottle of wine on the table and stood close to Gabby.

"I'd sit out here all the time if I were you."

"I do. Every night. What's your place like?"

"I have an apartment. Down the street from Mamma. Too close for comfort."

"I know your family is a challenge, but I'm jealous of how tight you all are. Makes me wish I had sisters and that my parents lived closer."

Gabby's heart clinched at the sadness in Olive's eyes. She put an arm around her shoulders and gently squeezed.

Olive shook her head. "We better eat before it gets cold."

Olive lit a candle and poured the wine. Even though they weren't dining on the finest cuisine, Gabby loved being alone with Olive in the romantic setting.

"How is it?" Olive asked.

Gabby swallowed a mouthful. "I think you were right about ignoring the directions. It's great."

Olive smiled in a way that showed off adorable dimples. "I can give you a tour of my condo after we eat."

"I'd like that. I didn't get to see much of it last time I was here."

Olive shifted positions and averted her eyes. "Oh, right. I forgot you brought me home after I freaked out about the boat."

"I'm sorry I brought it up, but if you ever need someone to talk to, I'm a good listener." Gabby had a feeling Olive had told her only the bare minimum regarding her almost drowning.

Olive put her fork down and took a sip of wine. "I don't talk about it much to anyone. Aside from the fear of dying, the most frightening thing was the total loss of control, the feeling of being overpowered by something so much larger and more forceful than me. Every time I get near the water I feel those same emotions, and it paralyzes me."

"But you conquered your fear at the Secret Cove. And the next step is our boat ride."

"You'd still go with me?"

"Of course. I promised to help you."

When Olive gazed into Gabby's eyes, the air between them sizzled with electricity. After several seconds, Olive pried her gaze away. "I hope I can do it. The contest is just a little over a week from now."

"Tell me why you want to win." Gabby shoved a forkful into her mouth.

Olive chuckled. "Are you kidding? It's my ticket to freedom, adventure. I want to experience life up close and personal instead of looking at magazines or watching TV."

Gabby wanted that for Olive as well. She wanted her to have everything she desired. She'd been a prisoner on the island far too long.

"You can still have that without winning," Gabby said.

"You don't think I can beat you, do you?" Hurt flashed in Olive's eyes.

Gabby could handle anger, but not pain. She scooted her chair closer and looked directly at Olive. "I just don't want you to give up on your dream. You don't need *Journeys* to leave Catalina."

"I know. You're right. Have you thought about what you'll do if you don't win?"

For Gabby, not winning wasn't an option. She was sure she'd be the one on a plane to who knew where in a few weeks.

"Actually, I haven't. But no matter what happens, I'm going to pursue photography. I'm talking to Mamma and Nonna about it tomorrow."

"I'm proud of you. I know it won't be easy, but it's your life, and you deserve to be happy." Olive placed a hand on Gabby's arm.

"Thanks." Gabby inwardly sighed as Olive's fingertips lightly stroked her skin. It felt so good she never wanted her to stop.

"It was sweet of you to bring flowers. It's an interesting array of colors."

Gabby cleared her throat and blurted, "Pink is for longing, red is for the heart, and white says you're adorable."

Did I seriously just say that? She obviously hadn't been thinking clearly with Olive caressing her arm. Gabby took a swig of wine.

Olive grinned. "Good to know. Did you choose the colors yourself?"

"Yes," Gabby said, surprised by the hoarseness of her voice. Tingles cascaded from head to toe as Olive ran a hand up and down her arm.

"You know, when you asked me for a date, I really wanted to say yes."

"Why didn't you?"

"I guess I was scared."

"Of me?"

"No. Of course not." Olive's face softened and she lowered her gaze. "I didn't know if it would be a good idea to get closer to you with our futures so up in the air."

"I know what you mean." Gabby reached over and tucked a strand of strawberry-blond hair behind Olive's ear. "How is it that you're still single? You're beautiful, talented, sweet, caring, thoughtful...I could go on and on."

Olive's cheeks tinted pink. "I've dated but...everyone eventually leaves."

"They were obviously insane."

"Thanks." Olive smiled and regarded Gabby closely. "Do you look like your dad? I've always wondered because you don't favor your mom very much."

"Yeah. I have his features, especially the eyes."

"I bet he was gorgeous."

Did Olive just insinuate that I'm gorgeous?

"When you stepped in front of my camera on the pier, I stayed up all night thinking about your eyes, trying to describe the color." Olive lightly stroked Gabby's cheek and looked directly at her. "I finally decided that they're caramel with swirls of chocolate. They're deep, soulful eyes."

Gabby looked down, heat creeping up her neck.

"Did I embarrass you?"

"Nooo."

"And here I thought you were a Casanova." Olive stood and pulled Gabby to her feet. "Do I make you nervous?"

"A little." *Well, actually a lot.*

Olive rose on her toes, kissed Gabby's cheek, and whispered in her ear. "You took my breath away when we kissed before. Can I kiss you again?"

Gabby nodded, her stomach fluttering at the thought of their lips touching. A cascade of emotions swirled inside Gabby when

Olive kissed her softly…over and over again. She kissed her lips and her cheeks, and nibbled on her neck. Much more of this and Gabby would be hyperventilating. When Gabby stepped back, Olive's eyes fluttered open.

"What's wrong?" Olive asked.

"It's our first date."

Olive smiled and reached for Gabby's hand. "You're so cute. We've known each other for a while."

"You mean…this is okay?" Gabby motioned between them.

"More than okay."

Olive kissed Gabby slowly, sensually, sliding their lips together. Gabby opened wider, rewarded with the touch of Olive's tongue. Chills ran up and down her spine as she wrapped her arms around Olive and pulled her close. She loved the way this beautiful woman felt in her arms, so warm and soft. They fit together perfectly, like two puzzle pieces. Olive ran her hands through Gabby's hair and deepened the kiss, which heightened Gabby's desire. How could one kiss make her weak, light-headed? Gabby groaned when Olive withdrew her mouth and rested their foreheads together.

"You're an amazing kisser," Olive whispered.

"It's all you. You take my breath away."

"Do you…want to go to my bedroom?" Olive's voice trembled. She drew her head back and looked at Gabby tentatively.

Gabby wanted to tell Olive there was nothing she wanted more, that Olive was the most amazing woman she'd ever met, and that being with her would be the closest thing she'd ever come to making love. Instead, all she could do was nod.

Olive took Gabby's hand and guided her across the living room and into her bedroom. Gabby sat on the edge of the bed and watched Olive light several candles, the scent of vanilla and lavender filling the air. Gabby looked up at Olive as she stood in front of her, candlelight flickering across her face.

"You're so beautiful," Gabby said.

"So are you." Olive kissed her tenderly.

Olive laid Gabby on the bed and covered her body. As they gazed into each other's eyes, Gabby felt a strange sensation in the pit of her stomach, a mixture of nervousness and excitement along with an emotion she couldn't name. She'd never actually looked into the eyes of a lover before or felt such a connection.

Gabby reveled in the sensation of Olive's lips caressing her mouth. She'd never tire of her kisses, her lips, her tongue. Gabby slid her hands under Olive's shirt and stroked her back. Needing to feel more of her, Gabby lifted the fabric over Olive's head. Olive straddled Gabby's hips, unhooked her bra, and tossed it aside. Gabby was speechless as she feasted upon a breathtaking sight. Olive couldn't have been more perfect, with her milky, ample breasts and rosy, aroused nipples. Gabby planted soft kisses in Olive's cleavage and around luscious peaks. Olive grabbed the back of Gabby's head and pulled her closer when she traced her tongue around an engorged nipple.

"Mmm...please..." Olive said in a husky voice.

Gabby enclosed her lips over the tip of Olive's breast and lightly sucked. Olive's hips jutted forward, and she released a moan that made Gabby's pulse race. She kissed and licked her way to Olive's other breast, around the swell of creamy flesh, and nibbled until her nipple was hard and erect.

"That feels so good." Olive cupped Gabby's face and kissed her deeply. It was a hot, wet kiss that made Gabby glad she was flat on her back; otherwise her legs would give way.

"You have entirely too many clothes on," Olive mumbled against her lips.

Olive quickly undressed Gabby and showered her with urgent kisses across her stomach and upward to her breasts. A jolt shot directly to Gabby's groin when Olive lightly rolled a nipple between two fingers.

"Do you like that?" Olive asked.

"Yes," Gabby said breathlessly. "I want your mouth on me."

Olive immediately obliged, licking the hardened tip and pulling it gently between her lips. An incessant pounding between Gabby's legs caused her to squeeze her thighs together.

"I want to touch you," Gabby said as she unbuttoned Olive's jeans, slid them off, and rolled Olive onto her back.

Olive's breath hitched when Gabby slipped her hand inside her underwear.

"You're so wet...so warm..." Gabby whispered. She caressed moist folds as she kissed down Olive's neck to her heaving chest.

"Go inside. Please." Olive inched her legs farther apart and grabbed Gabby's hand, pressing it hard against her.

Gabby tickled the slick entrance before inserting two fingers, slowly moving in and out. Olive's hips undulated with the rhythm and bucked when Gabby circled her clit over and over.

"There. Right there," Olive said through jagged breaths. "Don't stop."

As Gabby increased the pressure and tempo, Olive tightened around her fingers. Gabby wrapped her arms around Olive as she shuddered and cried out in pleasure, the look of ecstasy on her face intoxicating. She kissed Olive's forehead and ran her fingers through her hair as Olive's breathing slowed. When Olive's emerald eyes fluttered open, they were filled with such tenderness and desire, the sight took Gabby's breath away. No one had ever looked at her that way before. She'd be completely happy to stare at that face, those eyes, all night...all day...forever. Gabby inhaled deeply, the scent of lavender filling her senses, thankful for the moment.

"What are you thinking?" Olive asked. "You look so serious."

Gabby couldn't tell Olive what she was feeling. It was too soon, too much. "I was thinking about how beautiful you are."

"Do you want to know what was going through my mind?"

Gabby closed her eyes, melting into a puddle, when Olive reached between her legs and lightly stroked.

"Do you?" Olive asked.

Did she seriously expect Gabby to answer that? No way could she form intelligible words into an actual sentence. So, instead, Gabby gulped and nodded.

"I was thinking how much I want to taste you."

Gabby melted even more.

"How much I want to make you come with my mouth."

Every muscle in Gabby's body went limp as Olive rolled on top of her and spread her legs. She ran both hands up and down Gabby's thighs, inching closer to the core of her being with each caress. Gabby opened wider, hoping to urge Olive to touch her and relieve the insistent ache deep within. Finally, Olive's fingertips repeatedly grazed her soaking lips. Gabby moaned low, her excitement heighted at the thought of what was to come. She didn't have to wait long before Olive's warm tongue licked the length of her and darted inside. Gabby ran her fingers through Olive's hair, clutching fistfuls every time she neared her pulsating clit. Gabby's hips rose when two fingers stroked deep within. She was torn between never wanting the sensations to end or giving way for her need to come hard and fast. The decision was made for her when Olive lightly sucked where she needed it most, sending tingles cascading from head to toe. When Olive reached up to caress Gabby's breast and tugged a nipple, endless waves of spasms washed through her over and over again. Gabby sprawled out on the bed, panting, helpless as Olive kissed her way upward to her lips.

"You're so sexy," Olive said before planting a soft kiss on her mouth.

Gabby wanted to tell Olive that she was the sensual one, that no one had ever made her feel so aroused, so cared for. Instead, Gabby wrapped her arms around Olive and held her close, hoping the moment would never end.

CHAPTER TWENTY-ONE

THE MORNING AFTER

Olive jerked awake and looked at the clock. She rolled over and admired the bare back of the woman she'd made love to over and over again. Sleeping with Gabby probably hadn't been the smartest thing under the circumstances. They'd part ways in a week, and even though Gabby had asked her out on a date, she only had one-night stands, and Olive had no reason to believe this would be any different. In fact, it was probably the only time they'd ever be together. Even with all that, though, Olive didn't regret the decision. It'd been an amazing night of heated passion and surprising moments of gentleness. Olive's body sizzled as she recalled intimate kisses and caresses they'd shared. She inched forward, wrapped her arms around Gabby, and pressed her breasts into the muscular form.

"Mmm...that feels good." Gabby lightly kissed Olive's hand. "What time is it?"

"It's five. Go back to sleep."

Gabby rolled over and laid her head on Olive's pillow. "How can you look so beautiful early in the morning?"

That had been the millionth time in the past few hours that Gabby had told her how beautiful she was. Olive thought she was cute, but a beauty? Not even close, although she was slowly starting to believe it.

"You're sweet." Olive kissed the tip of Gabby's nose. "Now get some rest."

"Sleep? Now? When I'm with a sexy, completely naked woman?" Gabby grinned.

"Oh yeah? And just what do you intend to do with this woman?"

Gabby slowly traced a finger around Olive's breast, down her stomach, and to the moistness between her legs. Olive closed her eyes and moaned. Gabby could turn her on with one simple touch. Olive lay on her back and gave Gabby full access. Within minutes, she was on fire, and every nerve ending burst as she climaxed. Astonished, Olive laid an arm over her forehead, chest rising and falling quickly as she slowly recovered from the eruption of pleasure.

"You must think I'm so easy," Olive said through gasps. "I'm usually a one-orgasm woman, and it doesn't happen this quickly."

Gabby smiled against Olive's neck and kissed her. "I love touching you."

Olive enveloped Gabby, savoring the sensation of their intertwined bodies as an unexpected sadness washed over her. She attempted to push the feeling aside but couldn't ignore the hard lump in her throat. She loved being close to Gabby—kissing, touching, talking. Olive had never felt this strongly about anyone. Letting go of lovers was never easy, but doing so this time would crush her. Relationships end, people leave, and Gabby would be no different. Olive attempted to take a deep breath, her heart constricted.

"Are you okay?" Gabby raised her head and looked at Olive with concern.

"Yeah. Still coming down from that orgasm, I think."

Gabby peered at Olive suspiciously. Before she could ask any more questions, Olive closed her eyes and pulled the covers under her chin.

"We better get some sleep. I have to be up in a few hours for work."

"Sure. Of course." Gabby scooted to her side of the bed.

Olive felt suddenly cold and alone. Resisting the urge to dive back into Gabby's arms, she reached over and intertwined their fingers. That satisfied her desire for contact without getting too close. However, she was fairly certain it was too late for that.

❖

Coffee…Olive…kisses…caresses…those were the thoughts that entered Gabby's mind as she awakened, and not particularly in that order. First, she'd shower Olive with affection, then inject caffeine into her system. Gabby reached over, disappointed when she hugged blankets instead of the warm, soft body she expected. She squinted her eyes open and glanced around the room. Maybe Olive was in the shower, although the place was awfully quiet. Gabby grabbed a piece of paper, which had her name on it, from the nightstand.

Gabby, I didn't want to wake you but had to get to work. Help yourself to anything in the kitchen. Please lock up when you leave.
Thanks, Olive

Huh. That was certainly short and not so sweet. Not that Gabby was the mushy type, but she would have expected something a little more romantic after the night they'd shared. And what was with the "thanks"? Like Gabby had done her a favor by sleeping with her. She lay on her back, hands behind her head, and tried not to read too much into the note. Olive was probably running late and had quickly scrawled it out.

Gabby turned her head and stared at Olive's pillow. God, she'd loved every second of their time together. She could still feel Olive's kiss on her lips, the taste of her. Olive's energy, her being, surrounded Gabby like an aura, even though she was nowhere near. Gabby hugged herself and curled into a ball, wishing she was wrapped in Olive's arms. These unfamiliar feelings should have frightened her, but they didn't. It was a high she never wanted to come down from. Overcome by a sudden desire to see Olive, Gabby jumped out of bed, took a quick shower, and ran out the door.

She stood outside Say Cheeze with two large coffees in each hand, jittery. Was she more excited or nervous to see Olive? Maybe a little bit of both. This was all so new for her.

Gabby balanced one cup on the other, opened the door, and caught Olive yawning with her arms stretched high overhead.

"Looks like I got here just in time." Gabby kicked the door shut with her foot.

Olive's eyes lit up for a second but then quickly dimmed. "Hey. What are you doing here?"

"I thought you might need this." Gabby handed Olive a cup.

Olive wrapped her hands around the warm beverage and sighed. "You're a goddess. Thank you. I didn't have time to get any this morning."

Gabby walked around the desk and sat on the corner close to Olive...maybe a little too close, considering she rolled her chair back.

"I did keep you busy last night so I figured I owed you. Why didn't you wake me when you left?"

"Did you get my note?"

"Yeah, but it would have been nice to see you."

"I figured you needed your sleep. Aren't you talking to your mamma and Nonna today?"

Gabby peered at Olive. "Are you changing the subject?"

"Umm. What's the subject?" Olive took a sip and flipped through a desk calendar.

"Hey, are you okay?"

"Sure. Why wouldn't I be?" Olive responded without looking at Gabby.

This was certainly a different Olive than last night. She had to be tired, but this wasn't the reaction Gabby had hoped for, considering how close they'd been.

"You seem a little distant."

Olive stopped turning pages. "Okay, look. We might as well lay it all on the table. Last night was great, but don't worry. I know it wasn't anything more than a fun night for you."

Gabby stood, scrunching her eyebrows together. "Wait... what?"

"I know we only went out on a date because of that silly snow-cone bet. I don't expect a repeat of last night." Olive turned her back to Gabby and stared at her computer screen.

"Wait a second. Are you saying you don't want to go out with me again?"

"I know you don't do relationships." Olive's voice was flat, monotone.

Gabby swiveled Olive's chair around, leaned on the arm rests, and looked directly at her. "Are you one-night-standing me!?"

Olive sat upright. "You're the one who does one-night stands!"

"Really? Then why did I come over here to ask you out for tonight? Huh?"

Olive opened her mouth in a huff but then snapped it shut. After a few moments she asked, "You're asking me on another date?"

"I was going to...but now..." Gabby backed away and crossed her arms over her chest.

"But now what?" Olive's expression softened, her eyes filling with tenderness.

Gabby threw her arms into the air and yelled, "You're exasperating!"

Olive stood and took a step toward her. "Maybe you should go ahead and ask me anyway."

Gabby cocked her head and studied Olive. Was this a trick? Gabby wasn't sure if she could take the rejection. Olive's hopeful expression, though, urged her on.

"Olive, would you go out with me tonight?"

"I'd love to." Olive's beautiful face lit up like a hundred-watt bulb.

Gabby grinned widely. "Excellent. But...what was all that before?"

"I was giving you an out. I thought it's what you'd want."

"You were wrong." Gabby placed her hands on Olive's hips.

"Good...but the contest is a little over a week away." Sadness filled Olive's eyes.

"Maybe we could play it by ear and see what happens."

Olive's head dropped. "I'm not sure I can take playing this by ear. I need more stability than that."

"Poor choice of words. I meant, let's live in the moment." Gabby lifted Olive's chin to meet her eyes. "I'm not sure what's going on between us or what any of this means, but all I know is that I want to be with you."

"I want that as well, but it's hard for me not to think about the future."

"I know." Gabby wrapped her arms around Olive and held her close. "Do you still want to go out?" Every muscle tensed as Gabby awaited a response.

"I do. Call me crazy, but I do."

❖

"Why are we eating out?" Mamma Pacelli asked. "We have leftover lasagna."

Gabby guided her mamma and Nonna into Luigi's. She'd rather break the news that she was quitting the family business in a public place, since her mamma would be less likely to cause a scene. Gabby hoped that, anyway.

Gabby pulled out a chair for Nonna and helped her into the seat. "You two need to get out of the house more."

Gabby sat across from her mamma and grabbed a menu. She rested her elbows on the table, hoping that would help steady her shaking hands.

"Pizza?" Mamma Pacelli asked.

Ugh. Pizza again? But Gabby didn't argue. It was best not to incite her mamma before she dropped the bomb.

After ordering a pie sans cheese, Gabby took several gulps of water, her stomach in knots. She wasn't sure how to start the conversation or what to say. She really should have practiced a speech.

"You're like a camel." Mamma Pacelli pointed to Gabby's empty water glass.

Had she drunk the entire thing already? At least she had a good excuse to go to the bathroom and gather her thoughts. Gabby excused herself, glad to see there wasn't a line. She leaned against the counter and focused on her reflection in the mirror.

You can do this. You have to do this.

She was almost thirty and still letting her family control her. She stood upright, puffed out her chest, and put her Don Vito Corleone game face on. This was her life, dammit, and she was ready to live it. Gabby burst out the door and plopped down into her seat.

"What's wrong with your face?" Mamma Pacelli asked. "You look like you sucked a lemon."

"Mamma, Nonna...I need to tell you something." Gabby paused and stared at the pepperoni pizza that had been served while she was in the bathroom.

"What is it?"

Gabby looked at the space above her mamma's head. It was best not to get sucked into her intense ebony eyes. "Have you ever had a dream?"

"Of course. Everyone dreams at night." Mamma Pacelli grabbed a slice and put it on her plate.

Gabby served Nonna and cut the pizza into bite-sized pieces. "No. I mean something you wanted to do or accomplish in your life." Gabby hoped her mamma would recall her aspiration of owning her own hair salon before she was married.

Mamma Pacelli pointed at Gabby's empty plate. "Aren't you going to eat?"

"In a minute. So, did you ever have one?"

Mamma Pacelli peered at Gabby as she shoved a slice into her mouth. "What's all this about?"

"Well, see...I have a dream." Gabby glanced between Nonna and her Mamma. "Olive said she showed you the photographs I took."

Mamma Pacelli dropped her pizza, took a drink of water, and folded her hands in her lap.

"Photography is my dream, Mamma." Once Gabby started, the words poured out of her like a waterfall. "You know I love the family, but pizza isn't my dream. I want to travel the world taking photographs. I entered the Catalina contest, and I'm going to win. I just know it. The grand prize is a position at a famous travel magazine."

Mamma Pacelli was as stiff and pale as a corpse. "That wasn't your papa's wishes."

"I know, but I have to live my own life."

Gabby jerked toward Nonna, who looked momentarily shocked before she smiled and patted Gabby's hand.

"Is this okay with you?" Gabby asked her grandmother.

Nonna leaned over and kissed Gabby on the cheek. She was so happy she could have cried. If Nonna was on board, surely Mamma would be, too...or not.

"Mamma? What about you?" Gabby had never seen her so quiet. It was eerily frightening. Gabby could handle arguing since that's what she was used to, but this...

"We should finish eating." Mamma Pacelli fingered the pizza on her plate.

"We need to talk," Gabby said.

Mamma Pacelli took a bite and stared straight ahead. Maybe her mamma didn't want to make a scene in public. Gabby would surely get an earful when they got home.

Except that didn't happen. Mamma Pacelli went straight to her room and closed the door. Gabby made some coffee and sat beside Nonna at the kitchen table.

"I should go talk to her."

Nonna shook her head.

"No? Maybe give her some time? I've never seen her so quiet before." Gabby stared at her mamma's door.

They sat in silence, sipped coffee, and waited for Mamma Pacelli to emerge. After an hour, Gabby gave up and went into her room to work on her contest entry on the laptop. Mostly, though, she lay in bed and stared at the ceiling. She must have dozed off because she awoke with a start. She looked at the clock, surprised it was already time to get ready for her date with Olive. At least that was one thing she had to look forward to. She rolled out of bed and heard a soft knock on the door, shocked that it was her mamma.

"Can I come in?" Mamma Pacelli looked surprisingly calm.

"Of course." Gabby stepped aside.

Mamma Pacelli walked to the window and gazed out. After a few moments she said, "I had a dream once. Before I married your papa."

Gabby sat on the edge of the bed. "Tell me about it."

"It was so long ago. I was very young. I wanted to own a hair salon." Mamma Pacelli chuckled. "I wasn't as talented as you are with the pictures." Mamma Pacelli quickly glanced at Gabby, then outside again. "I don't regret marrying your papa for a moment, but I understand more than you might think."

"You're not disappointed in me? You don't hate me?" Gabby's voice quivered.

Mamma Pacelli sat beside Gabby on the bed and took her hand. "*Mia bambina*, is that what you think?"

"I'm never going to get married, give you grandchildren, and now this."

Mamma Pacelli closed her eyes, took a deep breath, and shook her head. When she opened her eyes they were filled with tears. "I could never be disappointed in you. You have made me and your papa so proud…and now it's time for you to make us even prouder. Win the contest. See the world. You have my blessing."

Gabby threw her arms around her mamma, not even trying to stop the tears from flowing. "Thank you. You have no idea what this means to me." Gabby felt so light she could have levitated off the bed.

"You can thank your girlfriend. I had no idea you were so talented until she showed me your photographs."

Her girlfriend. Oddly, Gabby didn't feel the need to correct her mamma this time.

❖

Olive sat on a blanket at the edge of the ocean at the Secret Cove and stared into a campfire she'd made. Gabby had texted to meet her there, but she was nowhere in sight. Maybe things hadn't gone well with her mamma and grandmother. Or maybe she'd changed her mind about dating. Olive's heart sank. That was a possibility she didn't want to consider. Olive stood when she heard someone walking down the path.

"There you are." Olive practically threw herself into Gabby's arms. Amazing how one hug could make her feel so protected and cared for.

"Are you okay?"

Olive released her hold and gazed into beautiful brown eyes. "You're almost an hour late. I was worried about you."

"I'm sorry. I got tied up talking to Mamma."

"How'd it go?"

Gabby guided Olive down on the blanket. "She gave me her blessing." Gabby's mouth curved upward in a wide smile.

"That's wonderful! I'm so happy for you."

"I have you to thank. I don't think she would have been so agreeable if she hadn't seen my photographs."

"I'm glad I could help."

Gabby brushed her lips against Olive's for a sweet, all-too-quick kiss.

"That's it?" Olive asked. "That's all the thanks I get?"

Gabby's eyes twinkled as she scooted closer, wrapped her arms around Olive's shoulders, and claimed her mouth. It was a lingering, passionate kiss that left Olive hungry for more. She slipped a hand around Gabby's neck, opened her mouth, and deepened the exchange. Olive practically growled when Gabby's tongue touched hers. She laid Gabby back on the blanket and inched her fingers inside her shirt to caress soft skin.

"Are my hands cold?" Olive mumbled, never stopping the kiss.

"They feel good."

Olive snaked upward, easily finding Gabby's erect nipple through her bra. With an insatiable desire to touch her, Olive tugged the material down and ran her thumb over and around the hard peak. Gabby wrapped her legs around Olive, hips rolling with each stroke.

"Wait." Gabby pulled back, panting.

Wait? Was she kidding? There was no waiting when Olive's body was thrumming with desire.

"Here?" Gabby asked.

"We have the moonlight, a warm fire, and each other. Yes, here." Olive pulled Gabby's shirt over her head, quickly followed by her own, and melted into her embrace.

Olive didn't think being together could be any more arousing or loving than their first time, but it was. Gabby had just the right amount of passion and tenderness. She knew exactly where to touch Olive to ignite the fire within her and when to hold her close and shower her with gentle kisses and caresses. More than anything, though, Olive treasured the moments when they looked into each other's eyes and connected on a soul level.

"You're an amazing lover," Olive said as they lay wrapped in each other's arms.

Gabby kissed the top of Olive's head. "I was thinking the same thing about you. You're not like anyone I've ever been with."

Olive raised on one elbow so she could see Gabby's face. "In what way?"

"In every way." Gabby stroked Olive's arm. "Sometimes when you look at me, I think of the way Mamma used to look at Papa. With affection...with emotion."

Olive had a feeling Gabby wanted to say love. And would that have been so far off? There were certainly things she loved about Gabby, but was she *in* love?

CHAPTER TWENTY-TWO

WATER DANCE

Olive coasted down the mountain, knuckles white from gripping the steering wheel. Her stomach rolled as she neared Avalon. She was meeting Gabby at the beach so they could go in the ocean.

In the deep, dark, powerful ocean.

Olive chewed her lower lip. She'd touched the water at the Secret Cove, but today she was going to swim, if she didn't freak out and embarrass herself. Olive wasn't convinced this was necessary since they were getting on a boat in a few days, but Gabby thought it'd help her overcome her fear. She was probably right, but that didn't mean Olive couldn't be scared out of her mind.

Olive spotted Gabby the moment she parked her golf cart. She looked stunning in a red-and-black one-piece bathing suit that showed off her olive complexion, toned legs, and perfect figure. She must have taken a dip in the ocean, since her hair was wet and water beads shimmered on her skin. Olive had the ultimate pleasure of viewing and touching every part of Gabby's beautiful body, but something about her in a skin-tight, wet bathing suit did things to Olive's libido. She stood a few feet from Gabby, letting her eyes roam up and down her figure.

"Wow. You look amazing." Olive wrapped her arms around the Italian beauty and kissed her cheek, tasting salt on her lips. She held

Gabby at arm's length and peered at the ocean out of the corner of her eye. "We're really going to do this?"

"I have all the confidence in the world in you." Gabby lightly pressed their lips together.

Olive closed her eyes and sighed. If they weren't in public she'd kiss Gabby properly, or rather improperly.

"To help you along, though, I invited someone to join us."

Olive's eyes popped open. "You did what?" She didn't want anyone else here. What if she froze or freaked out? Olive trusted Gabby, but not a stranger.

"Don't worry. In fact, here she comes now." Gabby pointed down the beach.

Olive squinted and shielded her eyes from the sun. Her heart skipped a beat. Could it be...was that really...tie-dye T-shirt, braided hair. Yes, it was Harmony Moondrop!

Olive wrapped her arms around Gabby's neck in an embrace that almost knocked them both over.

"I thought you might like this surprise," Gabby said as she chuckled. "It's amazing what people will do for a free night in Avalon."

"I don't know what to say." Actually, Olive was resisting the urge to say "I love you." There was that L word again.

"You can thank me later, but right now we have a guest to greet."

Gabby held out her hand. Harmony completely ignored it and embraced Gabby in a hug that would've made Olive jealous if she hadn't been her favorite, straight, self-help guru. Plus, she had to grin at Gabby's deer-in-the-headlights expression. After what seemed like a two-minute embrace, Harmony wrapped her arms around Olive and held her so tight she wondered if she might crack a rib. *This must be one of those* heartfelt hugs *Harmony writes about in her books.* When Olive was finally released, Harmony put a hand on each of their shoulders, making Olive wonder if she wasn't going for a group hug.

"I'm so honored to be here," Harmony said and bowed her head. "Let us intend that this be a healing, joyful afternoon for all.

Let light and strength stream forth into our hearts. Allow Olive to discover that she is strong and courageous to overcome any fear she may have. And so it is."

Harmony removed a necklace from her bag and placed it over Olive's head. Olive looked down at the crystal.

"That's tiger's eye," Harmony said. "It's for willpower and strength."

"Thank you. It means so much that you're here."

"Now let's get to work." Harmony sat cross-legged in the sand, with Olive and Gabby beside her. "Why do you think you've held on to the fear of water for so many years?"

Olive furrowed her brow. "Because I almost drowned." *Wasn't that an obvious answer?*

Harmony grabbed Olive's hand. "Fear keeps us safe, but it also holds us back from moving forward. Sometimes we use it as an excuse not to do something."

Olive resisted the urge to draw her hand back. *What was that supposed to mean?* "I experienced a paralyzing terror. I don't think it's odd that I'd still be afraid of the ocean."

"There's no judgment here, Olive." Harmony paused. "If you could do anything in the world, what would it be?"

"I'd be a travel photographer."

"Excellent. When you visualize yourself doing that, what feelings arise?"

Olive gazed up at the clouds. "I'd feel free, joyful, accomplished...scared."

"Why scared?"

"I've never been off the island. I feel safe here. What if I got out into the world and failed? What if I couldn't make it as a professional?"

Harmony grinned and nodded. "Maybe you've held on to the water phobia for more reasons than almost drowning. It's easy to stay complacent."

"I've never really thought of it that way before."

"Makes sense," Gabby said. "That's part of the reason I haven't gone after my dreams."

"I want you to see that water isn't the real issue. Don't give it power over you. You need to let go, trust, and have the courage to become the person you want to be." Harmony leaned over and wrapped her arms around them both. Olive had known there'd be a group hug sooner or later.

Harmony was on to something here. Olive had always blamed the ocean for keeping her prisoner on the island, but maybe it was actually her fear of failure, anxiety of the unknown. They all stood and walked hand in hand to the edge of the shoreline. Olive's heart raced, her legs wobbly.

Olive suddenly stopped before the water reached her feet. "I don't know about this."

"We won't let anything happen to you," Harmony said. "We'll go slow and at your pace. Just remember to take deep breaths."

Gabby placed her hand on Olive's lower back, a simple gesture that gave her strength. Olive straightened her posture and mentally reminded herself that it wasn't the water she feared.

"It helps to come up with a mantra," Harmony said. "A phrase you repeat to yourself."

"Like...I am strong?" Olive asked.

"Perfect."

Olive grabbed Gabby's hand and inched closer to the ocean. She jumped when the waves washed over her feet.

"You're doing great." Gabby's voice was calm, reassuring.

*I am strong...I am strong...*Olive silently repeated the words as they waded into the ocean. After a few minutes she looked down, surprised that she was already knee-deep.

"Excellent!" Harmony said. "Now let's dance."

Was this chick high on hemp? Olive couldn't move, much less dance.

Harmony flailed her arms around and moved her feet to the beat of the muffled sound of the Beach Boys *Surfin' U.S.A.* coming from the shore. She looked so silly Olive couldn't help but giggle. Surprisingly, Gabby joined in, jiggling her hips and doing the twist. After a few minutes, Olive snapped her fingers and moved to the rhythm, shocked she could even lift her legs. Harmony twirled around them as Gabby swooped Olive into her arms and dipped her so low that her hair touched the water. Harmony kicked her leg up and splashed water in their faces. They laughed uncontrollably, which provoked several stares from nearby swimmers, but Olive didn't care. She was actually dancing in the ocean.

After they calmed down, Harmony said, "Look where you are."

Olive was shocked that she was waist-deep. She should have been petrified, but she wasn't. It'd take a while for her to do this alone, but with Gabby and Harmony beside her she wasn't even frightened.

Olive looked at Gabby and grinned. "I did it."

"Nothing can stop you now." Pride shined through Gabby's eyes.

Olive turned her attention to Harmony. "I can't thank you enough. When you said dance in the ocean, I thought you were insane."

"Any time you feel fear, dance. It helps relieve the tension." Harmony gave Olive a long, heartfelt hug and whispered in her ear, "What you're most afraid of doing is what will set you free."

After giving Gabby a hug, Harmony waded on to shore, leaving them alone in the ocean. Olive stood close to Gabby, hands around her waist.

"I'm so proud of you," Gabby said.

"I couldn't have done it without you."

"I'm not so sure about that."

Olive shook her head. "Nope. Having you with me gave me strength. And look at this." Olive surveyed the ocean. "I'm in the water and not freaking out."

Gabby kissed Olive in a way that left her aching for more.

"Mmmm…you can't do that to me when I have to go to work in a few minutes."

"On Saturday?" Gabby groaned and nibbled on Olive's ear, which made her pulse skyrocket. "You're so kissable. I could eat you up."

Shivers ran up and down Olive's spine. "Do you have plans tonight?" Olive asked through quick breaths.

"I do now. How about I come over at seven?"

"Perfect." Olive melted into Gabby's embrace.

Now this is a heartfelt hug.

Olive reluctantly pulled away. "I hate to say this, but I need to dry off and get to work."

"I know." Gabby released a sigh, grabbed Olive's hand, and waded through the ocean to the beach.

When they reached the shore, Gabby said, "Remember we have a boat ride Monday."

Olive towel-dried her hair. "Did you rent a sailboat or speed boat to go around the island?"

"That's a surprise."

Olive stilled. "I don't like surprises."

"You loved the Harmony one."

That was true, but Olive had a bad feeling about this. "Come on. Tell me. I'll already be nervous, and this will make it worse."

"Do you trust me?" Gabby batted big, brown, innocent-looking eyes.

"You know I do but—"

"Then that should be enough. You'll love it." Gabby watched Olive dry her arms and legs. "I could help with that, you know."

Olive grinned. "The mischievous look in your eye tells me I wouldn't make it to work if you did." Olive playfully snapped the towel at Gabby.

"All right. I'll let you get going. See you tonight."

Olive's body turned to rubber when Gabby placed a kiss on her lips. She'd never swooned before until she'd been kissed by Gabby. That woman certainly had an effect on her.

❖

"You're all wet!" Mamma Pacelli yelled from the couch when Gabby walked in. "Where have you been?"

"Swimming at the beach." Gabby peered over the recliner at Nonna. "Is she sleeping?"

"*Sì*. Were you with Olive?"

"Yeah. I'm going to get changed."

"Not so fast. Come sit."

"My clothes are soaking." Gabby towel-dried her hair.

Mamma Pacelli patted the place beside her. Gabby gave in, figuring her mamma didn't care about stained leather when they were just renting the place.

"You like this girl, no?"

The big, goofy grin that appeared on Gabby's face must have answered the question.

"You going to marry her?"

Gabby snorted and rolled her eyes. "We just started dating."

Mamma Pacelli raised her chin, squinted, and glared at Gabby like she was a specimen under a microscope. Finally, she asked, "What happens between you two when you win the contest?"

"There's no guarantee I'll win," Gabby said, even though she was sure she would.

"You should ask Olive to go with you."

Gabby looked at her mamma like she had spaghetti for hair. "I can't do that."

"You love her."

"What?!" Gabby bolted to her feet. She'd yelled so loud Nonna jolted awake.

"Don't make the same mistakes I did. You can have your dream and the love of your life. You don't have to choose."

"You're just talking crazy, Mamma." Gabby pulled the afghan under Nonna's chin and kissed the top of her head. "I'm going to change."

Gabby sprinted upstairs before her mamma could spout any more nonsense. It was nonsense, right? Could Gabby really ask Olive to go with her? They both wanted to be travel photographers, and the thought of leaving Olive behind made Gabby want to cry. Olive was the first person Gabby thought about when she awakened and fell asleep at night. In fact, Olive was all Gabby thought about, even more than the contest. Not to mention the warmth that radiated from her chest when Olive held her hand or kissed her.

Gabby wouldn't admit this to her mamma, but she had wondered if she was falling in love. The last thing Gabby wanted to do was leave her heart in Avalon. Maybe her mamma wasn't so crazy after all.

CHAPTER TWENTY-THREE

THE LOVE BOAT

"Did you take my green shirt and favorite jeans?" Olive frantically tapped a pen on her desk at Say Cheeze, phone tightly clutched in her hand. She'd kill Nicki if she'd borrowed her clothes again without asking. They wore the same size, and she was forever acting like Olive's closet was a free-for-all.

"Uhhh...no, I don't think so. I might still have your red shirt, though."

"How many times have I asked you not to take stuff out of my apartment?" Olive felt only slightly bad about reaming her best friend. She'd really wanted to wear her green shirt today since it was Gabby's favorite. She said it brought out Olive's eyes.

"Sorry. Won't happen again."

"Yeah, right."

"So today's the big day. Are you scared?"

Olive considered the question. She should be, since she was about to get on a boat, but knowing Gabby would be with her relieved her fears.

"Not really. Maybe once we get there I'll feel differently. Listen. I gotta do some work before Gabby gets here."

"Okay. Good luck."

Olive hung up the phone and smiled at Mr. Finkelmeier when he entered the office.

"I thought you were off today," he said.

"This afternoon and tomorrow."

"Right. Did you get the invoices done?"

Olive handed him a stack of papers for his signature. He grunted and disappeared into his office. Olive turned her attention to the computer and scanned photo files until she found her photography-contest entry. Until two weeks ago she'd had no idea what to submit. Olive opened the image in Photoshop and adjusted the contrast and saturation. It was a breathtaking photo, which, to Olive, screamed Isle of Love.

As much as she adored the picture, though, Gabby would probably win. She had no reason to think this year would be any different. Olive swallowed a hard lump in her throat. After Gabby won she'd be on the next plane to somewhere very far from Avalon.

Gabby walked in, and Olive quickly closed the file. They'd agreed not to share their photographs until they were revealed during the competition.

"Hey, sexy." Gabby dropped her backpack into a chair and bent down to give Olive a kiss. "Are you ready?" Gabby smiled mischievously and rubbed her hands together.

"You're being awfully mysterious. Just where are you taking me?" Olive turned off the computer, grabbed her bag, and slung it over her shoulder.

"On a boat."

"I know that, silly, but is it a sailboat or a speedboat? And are we going around the island?"

Gabby suppressed a grin. "You'll see."

They walked hand in hand out of the office. It was a beautiful day, warm, with an abundance of sunshine. Olive was glad she'd remembered to pack sunscreen and Dramamine in case she got seasick.

As they approached the dock, a man standing on a humongous boat waved to Gabby. "Welcome back. We all set?"

"You bet. Skip, this is Olive."

Olive raised her hand in greeting. "You rented a yacht!?" This must have cost Gabby a small fortune.

"This is a special occasion, and I know what you're thinking. It's my treat. You're not paying for it."

Olive gazed at the white, double-decker boat, feeling like the size of a green pea next to the monstrous vehicle. She smiled when her eye caught the name written in black letters on the side of the boat. "*Impossible Dream*, huh?"

Gabby grinned. "Seemed applicable."

"It's perfect. "Olive kissed Gabby's cheek and held on to her elbow. "I'm ready if you are."

As they walked the plank onto the boat, Olive's stomach clinched and her knees wobbled.

"Are you okay?" Gabby asked.

"Yeah. Just a little dizzy. I can make it inside. It'll be better if I can't see the water."

They walked down three steps before Gabby opened a door, Olive's jaw dropping. *Wow.* It was nicer than her condo. Hardwood floors, a big-screen TV, couch and chairs, a kitchen, and full bar. Olive looked at Gabby with a raised eyebrow when she saw a queen-size bed.

"I don't intend to seduce you. I swear." Gabby held up her hands in defense.

"Aww, really?" Olive pretended to pout. "This place is amazing." Olive walked to the center of the room. So much for being away from the water, though, since windows surrounded them.

As though reading her mind, Gabby said, "We can close the shades."

"No. It's okay. I just need to sit for a minute." Olive perched on the edge of the sofa.

Gabby sat beside her, slowly rubbing her back in circles. "Maybe you should lie down."

"I knew you were trying to get me into bed." Olive chuckled. "I'm okay. It's not as bad as I thought it'd be. I mean, look at me...I'm on a freaking boat!"

"I'm really proud of you."

Skip popped his head in. "We ready to take off?"

Gabby looked at Olive, who nodded. "Let's get this show on the road."

Skip tipped his sailor hat and closed the door after saying, "We'll be in Long Beach in an hour and a half."

Olive bolted to her feet. "California?!"

"Awww…I wanted to tell you." Gabby grabbed Olive's hand and pulled her back onto the couch. "Why just sail around Catalina? You've seen the island, sweetie. I'm taking you somewhere you've never been. Hollywood!"

Olive wasn't sure whether she should be scared or excited. It didn't take her long to decide when she wrapped her arms around Gabby's neck. "Where are we going? What are we going to see? What are we going to do?"

"When we arrive, we're taking a cab to my apartment to get my car, and I'm escorting you on a tour you'll never forget."

"I get to see where you live?"

"Yep. In fact, we're spending the night there."

"But…I don't have any clothes or anything with me."

Gabby jumped up and grabbed a suitcase from behind the bar. She brought it to Olive and opened it.

"That's my green shirt and jeans. Where…how…"

"I enlisted Nicki's help. I'm surprised she kept her mouth shut."

"That sneak. She did take my things, but not for the reason I thought." Olive chuckled, excitement bubbling in the pit of her stomach. "What's the plan for the day?"

Gabby sat back and folded her arms across her chest. "It's a surprise."

Olive scooted closer, nuzzled Gabby's neck, and kissed up to her ear. She traced the crevices with the tip of her tongue, lightly blew, and nibbled on her earlobe. "Are you *sure* you can't tell me where you're taking me?"

Goose bumps appeared on Gabby's arms, and her breathing increased. "I can't be coerced."

"Let's see about that." Olive pushed Gabby back onto the couch and lay on top of her, knee firmly tucked between her legs. Olive pressed their lips together while she stroked Gabby's breast with her thumb, awakening a nipple. After being thoroughly kissed, Olive lightly nipped at the erect point through her shirt, causing Gabby's hips to rise sharply.

"Now will you tell me?" Olive asked as she gazed into eyes flaming with desire.

Gabby slid a hand behind Olive's neck and pulled her down for another searing kiss. Olive felt the dampness on her panties and the throb between her legs. Much more of this and she'd forget all about her question. A knock on the cabin door interrupted them, and it took all Olive's resolve to pry herself away from the tantalizing woman lying beneath her.

Gabby sat upright and straightened her clothes. "Come in," she said, her voice ragged.

Skip opened the door. "Do you two need anything?"

"No, thanks."

"Mighty fine. We should be docking in an hour."

Had thirty minutes passed already? It was amazing how fast time escaped when they were together.

After Skip closed the door, Gabby reclined on the couch with one hand behind her head. She flashed a sexy grin and asked, "Where were we?"

Olive looked at the door. "He could come back at any moment."

"That makes it sort of thrilling, don't you think?"

"Hmm…is that a fantasy of yours?" Olive lay on top of Gabby.

"It adds an element of excitement."

"You like living on the edge, don't you?" Olive's eyes dropped to Gabby's lips.

"Sometimes." Gabby's hands crept under Olive's shirt. She closed her eyes and enjoyed the sensation of fingertips caressing and lightly scratching her back. "You're so sexy when you get turned on."

Olive's face warmed, whether from embarrassment or excitement she wasn't sure. She moaned when Gabby's hand snaked around the front and cupped her breasts. Gabby brushed her lips against Olive's cheek, which sent shivers through her body.

"Do you want me to stop?" Gabby whispered.

"Please don't." Olive ached for more. She'd possibly shrivel up and blow away like ashes if Gabby pulled away now.

Gabby's demanding tongue slipped inside her mouth. No one had ever kissed Olive with such desire and raw emotion. The kiss melted every inch of her.

"Touch me," Olive whispered, then unzipped her jeans. She almost came undone when Gabby slipped a hand inside and rubbed slick folds.

"You're so wet."

Olive groaned when Gabby sank two fingers into her tight passage. "Yes…that feels so good."

"Maybe we should stop. Skip might come back," Gabby said, a smile in her voice.

She was probably teasing, but Olive didn't want to take any chances. She kissed Gabby hungrily, which hopefully conveyed that she'd die if she stopped touching her. Olive sucked in a breath when Gabby massaged the hard bundle of nerves that throbbed, yearned to be touched.

"Don't stop," Olive said, panting.

With just a few strokes, she climaxed, bursting with pleasure. Olive collapsed against Gabby, basking in the feel of arms wrapped around her and soft kisses on her cheeks. After a few minutes, Olive sat upright and ran her fingers through Gabby's hair, looking deep into her eyes.

"What are you thinking?" Gabby asked.

"How incredibly lucky I am to have found you."

"That's funny, 'cause I was thinking the same thing about you."

Gabby brushed her lips against Olive's in a kiss that filled her heart with joy, making her oblivious to the fact that she was on a boat in the middle of the Pacific Ocean. The incredible woman in her arms seemed to easily trump her greatest life-long fear.

Olive stuck her head out of the window of Gabby's car, wind whipping her hair. She couldn't take everything in fast enough—the traffic, skyscrapers, freeways. It all looked so much bigger and more exciting in person, and very different from Avalon. They'd barely stayed five minutes at Gabby's apartment, both eager for a tour of the city.

"What's over there? Is this where the sidewalk stars are?" Olive sat upright and gazed up at a towering marque. At the risk of sounding like an annoying kid, she'd already asked a million questions.

"Yes. And that's Grauman's Chinese Theatre, where the celebrity handprints are located."

"This is so cool. Can we walk around?"

"We'll do that later. There's someplace I want to take you first."

When Gabby turned a corner, Olive immediately spotted the West Coast Photography Museum.

"Isn't this where Robert Klein's exhibit is?"

Gabby smiled. "Not only that, but he's giving a lecture in thirty minutes."

Olive's jaw dropped. "This is by far the best surprise ever." Her eyes filled with tears.

"Are you okay?" Gabby grabbed her hand.

"Everything just hit me at once. I can't believe I'm actually off the island. I couldn't have done it without your help."

"I just gave you a nudge."

"No. You provided the support I needed. I'll be forever grateful."

Gabby stopped at a red light and looked at Olive. "You did the same for me with my family."

"We're pretty good together, aren't we?"

"Yes, we are." Gabby gave Olive a quick kiss.

The museum was amazing, and Robert Klein's lecture was informative and inspiring, but that didn't compare to seeing his work in person, something Olive thought she'd never do. She must have stood in front of his black-and-white seascapes for an hour, each one more mesmerizing than the last. Olive reached for Gabby's hand and gave it a squeeze, hoping to relay how much she appreciated her thoughtfulness. Olive wouldn't have wanted her first trip off the island to be with anyone else.

They both turned when they heard a voice behind them. "Enjoying the show?"

Blood immediately rushed to Olive's head, and her throat constricted, rendering her suddenly speechless. Her favorite photographer was not only standing two feet away, but he was actually speaking to her. Thank goodness Gabby wasn't struck dumb.

"We are. Your work is amazing, Mr. Klein."

"Please. Call me Robert."

Could this moment get any better? They were on a first-name basis with a world-famous photographer.

"I'm Gabby and this is Olive, who happens to be your biggest fan." Gabby placed a hand on Olive's lower back, probably in case she fainted.

"Is that so?" Robert looked at Olive with a smirk.

"Yes." Not the most eloquent response, but at least it was something.

"We heard you speak in Catalina a few weeks ago for the photography contest," Gabby said.

Robert wagged a finger. "Wait a second. You're Gabby Pacelli. Mrs. Albright showed me your work. Very impressive."

"Thanks. I do hold high hopes of winning this year." Gabby flashed a satisfied smile.

"You'll love working for *Journeys*. Some of my best assignments have been with them."

"I can't wait. It'll be a dream come true."

What was Olive? Chopped liver? She had every chance of winning, too. Olive glared at Gabby and cleared her throat.

Gabby glanced at Olive, her smile suddenly dropping. "Oh, but I do have competition from this one." Gabby squeezed Olive's shoulders.

Yeah, right. Too little, too late.

"Well, good luck to you both," Robert said before excusing himself.

Olive put her hands on her hips and glared at Gabby.

"What?" Gabby asked, innocently.

"What makes you so sure you're going to win when you haven't even seen the entries yet?"

Gabby shrugged. "Confident, I guess."

"More like arrogant," Olive whispered under her breath.

"What was that?" Gabby furrowed her brow.

"Nothing. Let's go." Olive didn't want to mar their special outing with an argument. Besides, Gabby had plenty of other positive traits, even if her ego *was* the size of Texas.

❖

Olive sat close beside Gabby in a booth, their legs touching and hands clasped. She'd much rather still be in bed in Gabby's apartment, but they'd promised to have breakfast with Gina and Tony before boarding the boat to Catalina.

Gabby looked at her watch and sighed. "She's late on purpose."

"It's fine." Olive stroked Gabby's hand. "Let's make this an enjoyable meal. Don't get in a huff before they even get here."

"We could have spent more time in bed. Together," Gabby grumbled.

"Oh. You're right. Where they hell is she?"

It hadn't been easy prying herself away from Gabby's beautiful naked body that morning. They'd even showered together to save time, but that had turned into a steamy, wet lovemaking session, which they had to cut short so they wouldn't be late.

"I'm starving." Olive grabbed a menu. "I want everything—pancakes, omelets, sausage, French toast."

Gabby flashed a flirty grin. "You must have worked up an appetite."

"You did keep me busy." Olive glanced around the restaurant, her eye catching the lovebirds as they strolled in. "There they are."

Gina and Tony approached the table and slipped into the booth.

"Where have you been?" Gabby asked sternly.

"I couldn't get this one out of bed." Gina cocked her head toward Tony, who turned bright red.

"Eww. I don't wanna hear about your newlywed sex life." Gabby scrunched her face.

"How was the Maui honeymoon?" Olive asked and took a sip of coffee.

"Fabulous! We've vowed to go back every year on our anniversary," Gina said.

"But now it's back to the real world." Tony frowned. "And I can't believe this one is quitting! What are we going to do without her?" Tony wagged his finger at Gabby.

"I have no idea how you talked Mamma into letting you leave." Gina rolled her eyes and shook her head, seeming disgusted.

"Gabby is a grown woman," Olive said, feeling suddenly defensive. "It's her life, and she can't let her talent go to waste."

Gabby placed an arm around Olive's shoulders and gently squeezed.

"Since when are you my sister's cheerleader?" Gina eyed them suspiciously. "Wait a second. Are you two…together?!"

"Why do you sound so surprised?" Gabby asked.

Gina burst out in uncontrollable laughter, while Olive and Gabby exchanged curious glances. When Gina finally calmed down, she said, "I can't believe our Casanova is actually dating someone. You better watch this one, Olive. She's a heartbreaker."

Olive's cheeks flushed with anger. She wasn't sure if it was because she wanted to defend Gabby, or maybe because what Gina said struck a nerve.

"Ignore her," Gabby said and studied the menu.

"I'm serious," Gina said to Olive. "My little sister has never gone out with anyone longer than a week."

Olive quickly did the math in her head. They were coming up on a week. Was she about to get dumped?

"Have you decided what you want to order?" Gabby asked Olive.

"Just coffee for me." Olive put her menu down, her stomach suddenly sour. She'd lost her appetite.

CHAPTER TWENTY-FOUR

THREE TIMES THE CHARM

You did it?! You really got on a boat and went to Los Angeles?" Mr. Piccolo clapped his hands together.

Olive couldn't stop smiling. If anyone knew how much she feared the water, it was him. They'd been back a couple of days, but Olive just now had a chance to tell Mr. Piccolo about her venture off the island.

"This calls for a celebration." Mr. Piccolo scooped ice into a cup, squirted yellow syrup on top, and handed it to Olive. "This is the Gold Medal."

Olive raised an eyebrow. "I haven't seen this on the menu before."

"I needed a new flavor for when you win the photography contest. They reveal the results tomorrow, right?"

"Just the finalists. The grand-prize winner will be the next day, on Valentine's Day. I may not win, you know."

"I wouldn't be so sure about that. Maybe this is your year."

Olive turned when she heard a voice, her smile suddenly dropping. It was Carmen, the drop-dead gorgeous blonde she'd completely forgotten about until that moment. She'd never asked Gabby what had happened between them. Maybe she'd mentally blocked it out because she didn't want to know the answer.

"Oh, hi, Carmen. I better get going." That wasn't a lie. Olive needed to get home to straighten up before Gabby came over for dinner. Olive strutted down the sidewalk, with Carmen unfortunately following.

"I saw you and Gabby in the ocean together the other day. You seem cozy."

Olive peered at Carmen sideways and picked up the pace.

"Don't get me wrong. I don't mind her seeing other people. A fantastic kisser like that shouldn't be limited to one woman only."

Olive stopped abruptly and faced Carmen.

"Did I say something wrong?" Carmen cocked her head. "Surely you know Gabby isn't the monogamous type. She and I are alike that way. She even said I was her dream girl."

Olive's stomach knotted so tight she thought she might barf on Carmen's shoes at any moment. "You're dating Gabby?"

Carmen threw her head back in an evil wicked-witch-of-the-west laugh. "People like Gabby and I don't date, dear. We have... fun." Carmen smirked and nonchalantly strolled away like she hadn't just stabbed Olive in the heart.

Olive's head spun like a tornado. Fearing she'd fall face-first, she stumbled to a bench and put her head between her legs. How stupid could she have been to date Gabby? What made her think Gabby had changed just for her? She should have listened to Gina's warning at breakfast. Gabby didn't date anyone longer than a week. Once a playgirl always a playgirl.

❖

Was Gabby whistling? She'd never whistled before in her life. She didn't even know she could. Gabby bounced down the sidewalk to Olive's condo and pressed the doorbell. She felt a burst of joy when she heard the deadbolt turn. Her excitement plummeted, though, when she saw the drawn expression on Olive's face, sadness brimming in her eyes.

"What are you doing here?" Olive asked, her voice hard, emotionless.

"Didn't we have a date?" Gabby tried to enter, but Olive blocked her way.

"I sent you a text. I'm not feeling well."

"Are you sick?"

Olive flinched when Gabby put a hand on her arm. "Just... uhh...tired. I'm sorry you drove all the way here."

"That's okay. I should have looked at my phone. Do you need a doctor? I could take you." Olive looked awfully pale and seemed lethargic. Plus, her eyes were bloodshot and watery. Maybe something was really wrong with her.

"No. I just need to get some rest. Besides, Nicki is here. I'll talk to you later."

Olive attempted to close the door, but Gabby stopped it with a hand. This was not the Olive she knew. Maybe she was having a delayed reaction to being on a boat, a post-phobia something-or-another.

"Are you okay about our trip to LA? You can talk to me, you know."

Olive averted her eyes and shook her head. "It's not that. I just need to get to bed early tonight. Really, I'm fine."

"If you say so, but call me if you need anything." Gabby had an urge to kiss Olive's cheek but refrained.

Olive nodded and closed the door. Gabby stared at it for several minutes, tempted to ring the bell again and strong-arm her way in. She had a bad feeling about this. Something was definitely wrong.

❖

"Why didn't you ream her?" Nicki sat on the couch with her feet propped on the coffee table.

"I didn't expect to see her. I'm not prepared." Olive sat beside her friend.

"Man, I can't believe the Italian Stallion is sleeping around. Well, I guess I can."

Olive hugged a pillow, chest constricted and a hard lump in her throat. "I thought she was different. I thought she cared about me."

"Come here." Nicki slipped an arm around Olive's shoulder and pulled her close.

Olive flinched when the doorbell rang. "Who could that be?" Olive got up and opened the door, shocked to see Gabby.

"I know you want space right now, but I'm really worried about you. Are you okay?"

Nicki suddenly appeared beside Olive and adjusted her Dodgers baseball cap. "I should let you two talk."

"No. You stay." Olive grabbed Nicki's arm, but she pulled away.

"I'm just down the street if you need me."

And with that, Olive's safety net was gone. It was just her and Gabby. She might as well get this over with. Olive stepped aside and let Gabby enter.

"What's going on?" Gabby stuck her hands in her pockets, looking nervous.

Olive stood by the opened door. "This isn't going to work."

"What isn't?"

"You and me."

Gabby furrowed her brow. "You're breaking up with me?"

Olive could have sworn she saw hurt flash across Gabby's eyes. "I don't go out with women who sleep around."

"What are you talking about?"

Seriously? She's going to act clueless?

"I'm talking about you seeing and sleeping with Carmen while dating me!"

"What?!" Gabby scrunched her face and drew her head back.

"You heard me." Olive crossed her arms, hoping to keep her heart from jumping out of her chest. This breaking-up thing should be easier. They'd only gone out a few times. Why did it feel like Olive was calling it off with someone she'd been seeing for decades?

"I'm not sleeping with Carmen. Or anyone else for that matter."

"Really? Carmen told me herself. She even said you told her that she was your dream girl."

"Wait a minute..." Gabby waved her hands. "Carmen and I kissed once, and I broke it off with her before you and I started dating. And as for that dream-girl comment, I don't know…maybe I thought it when we first met, but that's certainly not how I feel now."

Gabby sounded sincere, and Olive had never known her to lie. Still, though, it was best to end things now.

"I can't do this any more. Let's go our separate ways now while it's easy." *What a lie. There's nothing easy about this.* "It was bound to happen sooner or later." Olive adjusted her stance, hoping to stop her legs from collapsing beneath her.

"Oh my God. You don't believe me. Fine! I don't want to be with someone who thinks I'm a liar." Gabby stormed to the door and stopped in front of Olive. "First, you accused me of sleeping with the judge last year, and now this. You don't know me at all."

Tears sprang to Olive's eyes as Gabby whisked past her. They were really over. No more friendship, no more kisses, no more hand-holding, no more anything. Olive closed the door and sat on the couch, finding it difficult to breathe. She couldn't fall apart. She had to stay strong. It was best to break it off now, when her heart could still be salvaged, or so she hoped. They would have to part ways in a few days anyway.

Olive wasn't sure how long she sat motionless until the doorbell rang again. Thinking it must be Nicki, she forced herself to stand and opened the door. Except it wasn't Nicki.

Gabby barged in. "You want me to leave, don't you?"

"Yes! I want you to leave." *Or hold me in your arms and never let go.*

Gabby stood in the center of the living room, posture rigid, hands fisted by her side. "What did you mean when you said we were bound to break up sooner or later? Are you throwing me out because of Carmen, or are you just using her as an excuse?"

"I don't know what you're talking about." Olive walked to the couch, her back to Gabby, and fluffed—or rather punched—a throw pillow. Several seconds of silence passed. Gabby was so quiet, Olive turned around to see if she'd left.

Gabby's face had softened, and she released a sigh. "You're rejecting me before I can reject you. I'm not like your ex-girlfriends. I'm not leaving you."

Olive's entire body quivered. Gabby approached and put her hands on Olive's shoulders.

"You've been pushing me away since we met. I see it now. I know you're scared, but you can't get rid of me."

Olive felt both elated and ashamed that Gabby had seen right through her. Instinctively, she'd known Carmen had been fabricating the truth.

"I can't do long-distance relationships," Olive said. "What happens if one of us wins the competition?" Olive despised the sound of her small, weak voice.

"I don't want to give up on us. You're the best thing in my life." Gabby paused and looked directly into her eyes. "I want you to come with me if I win."

Olive couldn't have possibly heard correctly. "You want me to what?"

"It's the perfect solution. We can both work on our photography and be together."

Fearing her legs might crumble beneath her, Olive sat on the couch with Gabby beside her. "Are you serious?"

Gabby grabbed Olive's hand. "I've never been more certain about anything. What do you think?"

"I think I might cry. Yes. I'll go with you." Olive threw herself into Gabby's arms, joy and excitement filling her.

CHAPTER TWENTY-FIVE

THE FINALISTS

Gabby paid for a large latte and stuck five dollars into a jar on the counter. She'd never tipped that much for coffee before. Maybe she did it because they actually spelled her name correctly on the cup, or more likely it was the result of feeling elated that she wouldn't be separated from Olive. Asking Olive to go with her after the contest had been a bit spur-of-the-moment, but Gabby had meant everything she'd said. Olive had wiggled her way into Gabby's heart from the first moment she'd seen her taking photographs by the pier. She'd even enjoyed their competitive sparring, but that didn't compare to the closeness they shared. Maybe her mamma had been right. Gabby could have it all: the profession she loved and the woman of her dreams.

With a bounce in her step, Gabby walked to the Casino. The two finalists would be announced today and the winner tomorrow on Valentine's Day. Gabby stopped. That was the day of candy hearts, mushy cards, and giant helium balloons. This was the first time in her life she'd had a girlfriend on Valentine's Day. Surely she had to do something, maybe roses and chocolate, although that seemed clichéd. Olive would appreciate something more original. Well, she didn't have time to think about it now. She had to get to the event.

Gabby walked into the ballroom, shocked by how packed it was, not only with contestants but also the press and news cameras.

Her heart lurched when she spotted Olive across the room. Gabby snuck up from behind and wrapped her arms around Olive's waist, resting her chin on her shoulder.

"You better be careful," Olive said. "My girlfriend might catch us."

Girlfriend. Gabby liked the sound of that.

Gabby placed her lips close to Olive's ear and whispered, "She'll have to fight me off because I'm not giving you up that easily."

Olive turned, a big grin on her face. "Hi."

"Hey. Did I just see you last night, because it feels like forever ago." Come to think of it, they'd spent every night together since their first date.

"It's been at least two hours. I missed you." Olive kissed Gabby lightly on the lips. "Are you nervous about today?"

"No. You?"

Olive puffed out a breath. "God. I wish I had your confidence."

"Don't you mean arrogance?" Gabby raised an eyebrow.

"Oops. Guess you heard me say that the other day after all." Olive scrunched her face.

"It's fine. You're probably right." Gabby put her arm around Olive and glanced around the room. "When are they going to get this show on the road? It's past time."

"Did you see all those cameras?"

"Yeah. Guess the prize this year makes this high-profile."

"I don't know if I'm more nervous about being a finalist or not. I hate this part of it, where we have to go onstage and talk about our entry."

"You'll do great," Gabby said, although she wasn't fond of speaking in public either.

"Where are your mom and Nonna? I thought they were coming."

"Nonna wasn't feeling well so they stayed home. Mamma is taking her back to LA tomorrow after the results are announced."

"Is Nonna okay?"

Gabby's stomach suddenly soured, her limbs heavy as cement bags. "No. Not really."

"Aww, honey. I'm so sorry." Olive wrapped her arms around Gabby's waist for a hug that made everything seem perfect, even if for a moment.

"I wanted to be with her when...you know..." Gabby couldn't bring herself to say the D word, much less think about it. "...I'm the person she has to say her last words to."

"If you win, I'm sure *Journeys* would understand about postponing your start date because of a family emergency."

"Maybe. Mamma asked if we'd both stop by the house later."

Olive nodded, her eyes misty. "Yes. I'd like to see Nonna."

Gabby instinctively knew what Olive was thinking. This would probably be the last time she ever saw Gabby's grandmother.

"We should find our place," Gabby said. "Looks like they're starting."

They walked to the section where the contestants were seated in front of the stage. Two massive framed photos sat on easels, covered with sheets. Gabby squinted, attempting to see through the cloth, but she couldn't. If the results were anything like the past three years, she and Olive would be the finalists. Gabby wasn't sure if that was good or bad. She hated beating Olive out of her dream.

Mrs. Albright stood behind a podium and tapped on the microphone a few times. She droned on for at least fifteen minutes about stuff Gabby could have cared less about. Finally, Gabby perked up when Mrs. Albright mentioned the results. She sat upright and clutched Olive's hand.

"Good luck," Olive whispered.

"You, too."

Mrs. Albright walked to one of the covered photographs. "The first finalist in the Catalina Isle of Love contest is..." She yanked the sheet off in one quick motion. "...Gabriella Pacelli!" The ballroom erupted in applause and whistles.

Yes! Gabby pumped her fist in the air. She was one step closer to winning the entire competition. In that moment, Gabby realized how important this really was. She was competitive by nature, but that was the least of it. She'd prove to her family she had the talent to succeed and it would justify her quitting Mamma Pacelli's Pizza.

Gabby gave Olive a quick peck on the cheek and bounded onstage.

After the crowd quieted, Mrs. Albright put a hand on Gabby's shoulder. "Congratulations. How does it feel to be in the running for the fourth year in a row?" Mrs. Albright jabbed the microphone under Gabby's nose.

"Pretty darn nice," Gabby said with a chuckle.

"For those of you who don't know, this young lady is quite a risk taker. We can always expect something unique from Gabby. Tell us about your entry and how you think it relates to the Isle of Love."

"As you can see, I constructed a collage of photographs I took on the island depicting human and animal couples, along with the caption LOVE HAS NO LIMITS. I wanted to show the diversity of the island."

Mrs. Albright smiled and nodded. "It's certainly creative and original. Good luck, Gabby."

Mrs. Albright approached the second covered photograph. Gabby locked eyes with Olive. She looked nervous, biting the nail of her little finger with a pained expression. Gabby winked and smiled, hoping to help her relax.

"Our second finalist is none other than…" Mrs. Albright whisked the sheet off. "…Olive Hayes!"

Relief visibly washed over Olive's face, and her chest heaved in a sigh. She'd probably been holding her breath. Tingles cascaded up and down Gabby's spine. Not only was she excited for Olive but proud of her as well. She watched as Olive walked up the steps to the stage. Gabby gave her a quick hug and kiss on the cheek before Mrs. Albright grabbed her hand.

It wasn't until then that Gabby saw Olive's photograph. She jerked back, her eyes practically bulged out of her head. Not only was it breathtaking, but it was a silhouette of Gabby! She was standing at the ocean's edge at the Secret Cove gazing out into the water on a moonlit night. The ocean was a gorgeous indigo, and hundreds of stars sparkled in the darkened sky. Olive must have secretly taken the photo before their first kiss. Everyone in the audience ooh'd and ahh'd, as they should have. The picture was stunning. A little *too* stunning, considering this was Gabby's competition.

"Wow," Mrs. Albright said. "This is an amazing shot. Tell us, Olive. Why does this signify the Isle of Love to you?"

"The Secret Cove is one of the most romantic places on the island. This was a perfect night, and...just...everything in this shot screamed love to me." Olive glanced at Gabby.

Mrs. Albright turned her attention to the audience. "As you can see, our judges have their work cut out for them. Remember to be back here tomorrow for the final results. One of these talented women will be *Journeys'* next top travel photographer."

After everyone dispersed, Gabby stood in front of Olive's photograph.

"Are you mad?" Olive asked.

"Why would I be mad?" Gabby said, never taking her eyes off the picture. It had everything—heart, soul, emotion. Gabby didn't stand a chance. What had she been thinking taking a hodge-podge of photos?

"Because it's a photo of you."

"I don't think anyone would recognize me as a silhouette." Gabby finally peeled her eyes away from the picture. "It's a perfect shot, Olive. Really amazing."

"Thank you. And yours...wow. What a unique idea. I'm sure you'll win now."

"Really?" A glimmer of hope sparked within Gabby.

"Are you kidding? It's a sure thing."

Olive sounded sincere. Maybe Gabby was being too hard on herself. Still, though, in her heart of hearts, if Gabby were a judge she'd choose Olive's photo for the win.

❖

Olive and Gabby walked hand in hand toward the Pacellis' rented house. Olive grabbed Gabby's arm before she opened the front door. Once they were inside, they wouldn't have any privacy.

"I think we need a congratulations kiss." Olive snaked her arms around Gabby's waist.

"I like the way you think." Gabby cupped Olive's face and pressed their lips together.

When they broke apart, Gabby kept her eyes closed. "Mmm... Your kisses make me weak in the knees."

Olive smiled to herself, glad she wasn't the only one affected by their closeness. They'd been dating only a short time, but Olive physically craved to be near Gabby when they were apart. More than anything, she wanted Gabby to go home with her, but she didn't want to be greedy.

"I guess you'd like to stay here tonight. To be close to Nonna," Olive said.

Gabby's eyes popped open. "I thought maybe...I mean...if you'd rather be alone, I can do that."

"No! I want you with me."

"It's what I want, too."

Olive was about to go in for another kiss when the door opened. Mamma Pacelli stood with one hand on her hip and a murderous scowl.

"How long are you two going to stay out here?"

"Were you peeking through the blinds?" Gabby asked.

"Curtains." Mamma Pacelli pulled them both into the foyer. "Well? What happened?"

"You're looking at the two finalists." Gabby smiled widely.

"*Fantastica!*" Mamma Pacelli embraced them both.

"How's Nonna?" Gabby asked.

Mamma Pacelli's expression turned somber. "She's very weak. It will be better when she's home in her own bed."

"Do you think I could see her?" Olive asked.

"She's in the room down the hall to the right," Mamma Pacelli said. "You go ahead, and I'll grill Gabby about the event."

Olive walked to Nonna's room, glad she had a chance to see the elderly woman alone. She wanted to tell her something. She slowly opened the door and tiptoed to the bed. Nonna looked so fragile lying on her back with her eyes closed that it broke Olive's heart. When Olive lightly touched Nonna's bony, wrinkled hand, she blinked her eyes open.

"I'm sorry if I woke you. Do you want a drink?" Olive asked when Nonna lifted a finger to a pitcher on the nightstand.

Olive poured water into a glass and helped her take a sip. She dabbed Nonna's chin with a napkin and looked into murky brown eyes.

"I wanted to say what a pleasure it was to have met you," Olive said. "And I wanted you to know you were right about something."

Olive pointed to Gabby in a family portrait next to the water pitcher and crossed her arms over her chest, as Nonna had done several times before. Within seconds, Nonna's thin lips curled upward and her eyes sparkled. Olive smiled as well, content to know that Nonna was aware that her granddaughter was loved. Yes. Olive had no doubt she was in love with Gabby.

CHAPTER TWENTY-SIX

WINNER TAKES ALL

G abby bolted upright in bed, alarmed by the scent of something burning. She didn't see smoke, but her heart lurched when Olive was nowhere in sight. She jumped out of bed, hurriedly put her tank top and shorts on, and was about to run out of the bedroom when Olive walked in carrying a tray stacked with an array of items.

"What are you doing up?" Olive's lower lip jutted out in a pout. "I wanted to surprise you."

"I smelled smoke."

Olive grimaced. "I sorta burned the pancakes. Hope you don't mind them crispy."

Gabby peered at heart-shaped blackened pancakes, sausage, orange juice, and a single red rose. "You did that for me? No one has ever cooked me breakfast before."

"I wanted to do something special for our big contest day. Plus, it's Valentine's. Now get back into bed."

Gabby mentally conked herself on the head. She was the worse girlfriend ever. She hadn't gotten Olive anything. "I'm so sorry. I completely forgot."

"It's okay." Olive sat in bed and balanced the tray next to her. "I usually ignore this particular holiday, even when I'm dating someone. I think couples should be romantic every day, not just today."

"Still though. I feel horrible." Gabby sat on top of the covers.

"It's fine. Really. If it makes you feel better, consider it payback for taking me to LA and helping me meet my favorite photographer." Olive cupped Gabby's face and lightly kissed her.

Gabby wanted to tell Olive how important she was, that she'd never felt so strongly about anyone before, but the words lodged in her throat. Everything was moving so fast, and being in a relationship was such a new experience. Maybe someday she'd be able to express her true feelings.

"Thank you for this. It's so sweet." Gabby gazed at the heart-shaped food on her plate.

"Don't thank me until you've tasted it."

Gabby took a big bite. Never had burnt pancakes tasted so delicious.

❖

You'd think they were Hollywood celebrities the way flashbulbs went off and reporters swarmed when they entered the Casino for the awards show. This was the moment Gabby had been waiting for. Winning this competition meant everything. It was her ticket to being self-sufficient and would provide the income she needed to support Olive. Gabby could hardly believe that in the next thirty minutes all her dreams would come true.

After answering a few questions and accepting well wishes, Gabby and Olive made a beeline for Mamma Pacelli.

"How's Nonna?" Gabby asked.

"Not well. But don't worry about that. This is you and Olive's big day." Mamma Pacelli kissed them both on the cheek.

"Your support means everything to me," Gabby said.

"Your papa would be so proud. Now you two better skedaddle. It looks like they're starting."

"We reserved a seat for you in front," Olive said.

"I'll find it. Now go…go…" Mamma Pacelli waved them away.

Gabby held Olive's hand and walked to the front of the ballroom. Mrs. Albright greeted them and pointed to two chairs onstage, where they were to sit.

Gabby faced Olive. "Are you ready?"

"As much as I'll ever be." Olive inhaled a shaky breath. "Let's do this."

They climbed the stairs to the stage and sat side by side. When Gabby's eyes adjusted to the bright lights, the first thing she saw was her mamma sitting upright with a huge smile on her face. A hard lump formed in Gabby's throat. She never thought her mamma would be proud of her for anything other than the family business. Sitting beside her mamma were Nicki and Mr. Piccolo, who gave them both a thumbs-up.

A shot of adrenaline coursed through Gabby when Mrs. Albright started the program. First, she introduced the two finalists and the judges, who each stood and took a bow. Gabby winced, recalling what had happened last year. She'd been so humiliated being falsely accused of sleeping with a judge. That was another reason this year's contest was so important. She had a chance to be vindicated and take what should've rightfully been hers.

"Now I'd like to introduce you to the *Journeys'* senior editor," Mrs. Albright said. "She's here to tell us about the grand prize."

Everything after that was a blur. Gabby heard the name, but it didn't register until she saw the woman walk onstage. And even then, she had to blink several times to make sure she wasn't seeing things. The magazine's senior editor was none other than Carmen!

Olive whipped her head around and stared at Gabby in disbelief. For a split second, anger flashed across her eyes, quickly replaced with compassion. Obviously, it hadn't taken Olive long to realize that Gabby had no idea who Carmen was. Gabby could only hope Mrs. Albright would feel the same.

Carmen strutted onstage, did a double take when she saw Gabby, and stopped right in front of her. She looked just as shocked as Gabby felt. The surprise, though, slowly morphed into something different as her lips curled into an evil grin that sent shivers down Gabby's spine. This was bad. Really bad. Carmen walked to the podium, and instead of speaking, she pulled Mrs. Albright aside. Gabby peered at them out of the corner of her eyes, sweat rolling down her back. She wanted to bolt out of the chair and explain her side of the story. There was no telling what lies Carmen was spouting. This couldn't be happening. She couldn't be wrongly disqualified two years in a row.

After the two women finished chatting, Carmen spoke like nothing had happened. Maybe everything would be all right after all. Or maybe they just didn't want to cause a scene in front of everyone. Gabby sat stiffly in the chair, the next few moments going by like a fog-filled dream. Before she knew it, Mrs. Albright asked them both to stand next to their framed prints for the results.

Mrs. Albright held an envelope in her hands and ripped it open. Gabby's heart pounded, her entire body shaking. She locked eyes with her mamma, who looked like she was about to bounce out of her chair in excitement.

"...and the winner of the Catalina Isle of Love contest is... Olive Hayes!"

The ballroom erupted in applause as Gabby's stomach turned inside out. She closed her eyes and shook her head. *Damn Carmen.* She'd obviously cost Gabby the position of a lifetime. Gabby was sure her name was written on the envelope instead of Olive's. Maybe she could talk to Mrs. Albright and explain. But then again, Gabby couldn't do that to Olive. She was beaming, and despite everything, Gabby was happy for her.

"Congratulations," Gabby said and gave Olive a quick hug and kiss on the cheek.

Olive's eyes sparkled, pure bliss and shock written across her face. Before Olive could say anything, Mrs. Albright pulled her into a circle of well-wishers. Gabby stood to the side, her eyes landing on her mamma, whose joyful expression had turned sour. Gabby's heart dropped, knowing she had caused her mamma's disappointment.

Still in a daze at the turn of events, Gabby stumbled into the ballroom for the after-awards reception. Luckily, no one cared about the runner-up, so no annoying reporters accosted her. She wanted to be left alone to sulk, but she had to at least make an appearance.

Gabby spotted Olive across the room posing for photographs. Olive motioned her to join, but Gabby pointed to the bar, indicating she needed a stiff drink. With a whiskey in hand, she stepped onto the balcony and leaned against the railing, gazing at the sparkling lights of Avalon. Within minutes, she felt Olive's arms wrap around her waist from behind.

"Hey, you. We haven't been able to talk since the results were announced." Olive rested her chin on Gabby's shoulder.

"Yeah. Pretty crazy, huh?"

Olive whisked Gabby around. "How are you holding up?"

Gabby raised her glass. "Ask me again after about ten more of these."

"I'm sorry. I know how much you wanted this."

Gabby shook her head. "Damn Carmen. I can't believe she's the senior editor."

"I know. Luckily, though, I won't report to her, and with traveling so much I probably won't ever see her."

"I'm sure she said something to get me disqualified and that's why I lost."

"Is that what Mrs. Albright said?"

"I haven't talked to her yet, but you saw Carmen whispering to her."

Olive scrunched her eyebrows together. "You don't think I could've won fair and square?"

"It's not that. I mean...well..."

"I know you're disappointed, so I'll try to overlook how insulting you're being right now."

"What do you mean, insulting!?" Heat crept up Gabby's neck, and her head pounded.

"You're saying that the only way I could have possibly won was by default."

"That *is* what happened last year." Gabby flinched and took another swig of whiskey. Even she knew that was a low blow.

Olive stepped back. "I don't want to fight with you. You're obviously upset and taking it out on me. After a good night's sleep, you'll feel better."

Gabby huffed and took another drink. "You don't understand anything. This was my ticket out of Mamma Pacelli's Pizza. It was proof to my family that I have talent. Now they'll just see me as a second-rate photographer."

"You're making some pretty broad assumptions. And I'm your ticket out of the family business. Nothing changes just because I won. We're still going away together."

Gabby stared into her drink. She hadn't even thought about the possibility of losing and what it'd mean to their relationship. She was fine with Olive following her around the world, but Gabby following Olive? That wasn't part of the plan. Gabby's heart constricted, and tears threatened. Were they breaking up right now? Parting ways with Olive would be ten times worse than losing her dream job, but she wasn't sure what else to do.

"Gabby? Nothing changes. Right?"

"Everything changes." Gabby forced her eyes to meet Olive. "I can't go with you. I've spent my entire life trailing behind my family. I'm not going to traipse across the country following you like a little lost puppy."

Olive looked like Gabby had just ripped her heart out, devastated and surprised all at once. "Oh, but it's okay if I follow you? When it comes to the future, me winning shouldn't change our plans." Olive's voice sounded strained. Maybe she was holding back tears as well.

"I need to make my own way. I can't do that shadowing someone else."

"You can work on your photography wherever we are. I won't hold you back."

Gabby shook her head and pulled away when Olive reached out to her.

Olive's expression hardened, her green eyes blazing. "You're seriously going to let your ego stand in the way of us being together?"

"Ego!? What the hell does that mean?" Gabby balanced her drink on the railing. She needed to use both hands for this conversation.

"Your head is so big I'm surprised it fits through the door. You're going to let your damned pride get in the way of our happiness."

Gabby's pulse raced. That was completely uncalled for. "I just lost the competition of a lifetime, and now you expect me to follow the winner around?! I've heard enough." Gabby grabbed her shot glass and took a swig. "I'd say congratulations, but I think we both know who the real winner should have been tonight."

"Oh my God! I can't believe I even wanted you to go with me. You are the most arrogant, stubborn person I've ever met."

"Fine. Then you'll be happy to get rid of me." Gabby stormed past Olive, through the ballroom, and directly to Mrs. Albright.

"Do you have a second?" Gabby pulled Mrs. Albright into a corner before she could respond. "I was wondering if you had the card with the results. I'm sure Olive would love it for a souvenir."

"Actually, I do." Mrs. Albright pulled the envelope out of her purse.

Gabby snatched it, fully expecting to see her name. Instead, Olive's name was printed as the winner. *Damn.* They couldn't possibly have made a new card so quickly. Could they? Gabby had to find out if Carmen had said something about her.

"I know it's none of my business, but I was wondering what the holdup was with the senior editor before the results were announced."

Mrs. Albright cocked her head and stared into space. After a few moments she said, "Oh. She was telling me she had to skedaddle right after the announcement and wouldn't be at the banquet."

"That was all?"

"Yes. Is something wrong?"

"No. Just…no. Sorry to bother you."

Gabby handed the envelope back to Mrs. Albright and exited the Casino. She stood on the steps, closed her eyes, and filled her lungs with the cool night air. Carmen probably hadn't said anything for fear of losing her job for associating with a contestant. Gabby had run out of excuses. She could no longer deny that she was the loser, fair and square.

CHAPTER TWENTY-SEVEN

LAST WORDS

M r. Finkelmeier stared at Olive's resignation letter. "Is this some kind of joke?"

"I'm leaving for Australia in two weeks. I was awarded the travel-photographer position for *Journeys*."

Saying that should have filled Olive with exuberance. Instead, it just made her sad. Damn Gabby for being so prideful. Olive could understand being upset about losing, but parting ways was pointless. Olive would have followed Gabby anywhere, but then again that's what love did to a person. Maybe Gabby didn't feel the same way. Olive's heart ached. The last thing she wanted to do was break up, and she hated the way they'd left things.

Mr. Finkelmeier stared at Olive. "But...who is going to..."

Do your dirty work? Not me anymore!

"I really appreciate the opportunity you've given me here, Mr. Finkelmeier. It's been a pleasure working for you." Olive inwardly grimaced at that last part, but she didn't want to leave on a bad note.

Mr. Finkelmeier silently shuffled into his office, seemingly still in shock. Olive sulked at her desk the rest of the morning, glad there were no appointments. She really needed to organize her life pronto in order to leave the country in two weeks. She had to get a passport, make travel arrangements, and figure out what to do with her condo. She'd probably rent it, maybe to Nicki, and then sell later. Olive couldn't concentrate on any of that, though, because she couldn't get Gabby out of her mind. She was still angry, but she hoped Gabby regretted what she'd said and felt differently today...and there was only one way to find out.

Olive opened Mr. Finkelmeier's door. "I'm taking an early lunch."

"It's not even eleven."

"I'll be back later." Olive closed the door and darted out of Say Cheeze. Normally, she wouldn't be so brazen, but what could he do? Fire her?

Olive walked down the sidewalk to the Pacellis' rented house and rang the doorbell. She waited a few moments before pressing it again. When no one answered she peeked through the window. The place looked dark, abandoned. Olive's stomach quivered, and a chill ran down her spine. Maybe Gabby had left with her Mamma and Nonna. Olive walked around the house and opened the gate to the backyard. She peered around the corner but didn't see anyone. Dread washed over Olive at the thought of never seeing Gabby again. She wouldn't leave without saying good-bye, would she? Considering how livid Gabby had been last night, that was a real possibility.

It was too early for lunch, but Olive walked to Nicki's snorkeling shop by the marina. She entered and tapped her friend on the shoulder from behind, which caused Nicki to jump two feet in the air.

"You scared the crap outta me!"

"Sorry. I thought you heard me come in. You wanna grab an early lunch?"

Nicki looked at her watch. "Since when do we eat at eleven fifteen? Hand me those, would you?" Nicki pointed to a stack of scuba masks.

Olive grabbed a few and watched Nicki place price tags on them.

"Hey. We should go scuba diving before you leave," Nicki said. "You can do that now. Which, by the way, in case I didn't tell you enough times at the reception last night, I'm sooo proud of you for conquering your fear and winning."

Olive sighed and fingered a pair of fins. "Thanks."

Nicki stopped and faced Olive. "Okay. What's wrong? You should be jumping for joy. You're not having a water-phobia relapse, are you?"

"No. It's not that." Olive walked to the cash register and leaned against the counter. "It's Gabby."

"I shoulda known. The way she stormed out last night, I figured something was up. Is she being a sore loser?"

"Yes. And she's letting her big, fat ego get in the way. She isn't coming with me."

Nicki shook her head. "What a dick."

"Hey! You're talking about the woman I love."

Nicki's expression softened. She approached Olive and put her arm around her. "You're in love with Gabby? Did you tell her that?"

"No. But she should know. How could she not? We'd gotten so close."

"I'm no relationship expert, but I'm pretty sure making assumptions isn't the smartest move. What would Harmony say about this?"

Olive felt suddenly hot and itchy. She knew exactly what Harmony would say, which wasn't what Olive wanted to hear. "I really hate when you do that."

"Do what?" Nicki genuinely looked baffled.

"Throw Harmony's words back at me."

"Don't jump down my throat. She's your almighty self-help guru. Not mine."

"Sorry. I'm just a little testy today." Olive took a deep breath and let it out slowly. "Harmony would say to be honest and speak what's in my heart. Otherwise I might regret it for the rest of my life. And who needs that shit?" Okay. That last part was Olive's, but the rest was out of Harmony's relationship book.

"Then that's what you need to do."

Easier said than done.

"Gabby was the one who was mean, not me. I'm not about to tell her how I feel until she apologizes first."

"You do know you sound about five years old right now. Right?"

Olive clinched her teeth. She was about to strike back, except Nicki was right. "Can we just go eat? I don't want to think or talk about Gabby anymore."

They exited the shop and walked down the sidewalk to Mr. Sanchez's hot-dog stand. Olive admired the clear, turquoise water and hundreds of sailboats lined up in the marina. No matter how eager she was to get off the island, she'd miss Catalina. It was a beautiful place to live and had been the only home she'd ever known. Without a doubt, she'd come back and visit as often as she could, even if just to see Nicki and Mr. Piccolo.

When they turned the corner, Olive stopped, confused as to what she was seeing. Barreling straight toward her were the five Pacelli sisters, with Gina leading the pack. They were marching with purpose and determination, like a military troop going to battle. Gabby hadn't said anything about her sisters coming to the island. Why would they be there if everyone had gone back to LA?

If Olive hadn't yelled Gina's name several times and grabbed her arm, they probably would have blindly rushed past her.

"What are you all doing here?" Olive asked.

"Oh, hi. We have to get going." Gina took off in a blur.

"Is something wrong?" Olive asked Isabella, who trailed her sisters.

"Nonna's in the hospital."

"Oh, no." Olive put a hand over her heart. Gabby must be so distraught. She was closer to her grandmother than anyone. "Please tell Gabby…tell her I'm thinking about her."

"I will." From Isabella's compassionate expression, Gabby must have confided in her what had happened between them last night.

Olive watched the Pacelli sisters hurry down the street.

"Are you okay?" Nicki placed a hand on Olive's arm.

"I feel like I should go, too, but…" Olive bit her lower lip, deep in thought. After a few moments she said, "I'm sorry, but I need to take a rain check on lunch."

Olive was probably the last person Gabby wanted to see, but she couldn't sit still. She had to go to the hospital for Nonna and to show her support to the Pacellis, whether Gabby liked it or not.

❖

What an awful day. Early that morning, Mamma Pacelli had awoken Gabby, saying that something was wrong with Nonna and they needed to get her to the emergency room. Despite a ghastly headache from too much whiskey the night before, Gabby had bolted out of bed, thrown on some clothes, and driven them to the hospital. As she sat in the waiting room, a sickening dread washed over her.

She'd had the feeling for months that Nonna's time on earth was nearing an end. Letting her grandmother go would be one of the hardest things she'd ever have to do. If that wasn't bad enough, Gabby felt horrible about her fight with Olive, and she was pretty sure they'd broken up for good. Gabby lowered her head, eyes filling with tears at the thought of never seeing Olive again.

"Oh no! Nonna died." Gina's voice echoed through the waiting room.

Gabby looked up to see her sisters surrounding her in a semicircle.

"She's in intensive care. I'm waiting on Mamma for some news."

"Then why are you crying?"

Gabby hurriedly wiped her eyes. "Just...it's nothing."

Her sisters didn't need to know she was blubbering over a lost love. Gabby wasn't sure when it'd happened, but she was undeniably, completely in love with Olive, which made it all the more heart wrenching that they'd parted.

All eyes turned to Mamma Pacelli when she entered the waiting room. Her complexion was as pale as chalk, and she looked like she was about to collapse.

"How's Nonna?" Isabella asked.

"They said she had a stroke. Her brain is bleeding." Mamma Pacelli collapsed into a chair.

"Will she be okay?" Gabby asked.

"They're doing all they can. It doesn't look good."

"Nonna is strong. She'll pull through," Gina said resolutely.

Everyone nodded, but from the concerned expressions they were probably all thinking the same thing: they might lose their grandmother. Gabby closed her eyes and pressed a finger against her temple, hoping to ease the pounding in her head. She felt nauseous, like she could retch at any moment. When she heard a familiar voice, her eyes popped open, and she stared into Olive's beautiful face.

"What are you doing here?" Gabby asked, more sternly than she'd intended. So much so that it produced a nasty look from her mamma.

Olive ignored Gabby but instead focused on Mamma Pacelli. "I wanted to check on Nonna."

"That's sweet," Mamma Pacelli said. "Nonna had a stroke, and the doctors are doing what they can."

"Oh. I'm so sorry. I hope she's okay. Can I do anything?"

"Some coffee would be lovely. Gabby will help you."

Gabby shot her mamma a no-way-in-hell look. "I have a headache. Someone else can do it."

Mamma Pacelli's gaze bounced from Olive to Gabby. After a few moments she asked, "What's going on?"

"Nothing," Gabby said, much too quickly.

"Olive?" Mamma Pacelli asked.

Olive bit her lower lip. After a few moments she said, "Your stubborn daughter broke up with me last night." Olive's voice quivered.

"You did what?!" Mamma Pacelli glared at Gabby.

"This isn't the time or place to discuss this," Gabby said.

Mamma Pacelli jumped up. "Nonna would be heartbroken if she knew you two had separated."

Mamma Pacelli bolted down the hall to the nurses' station. Olive and Gabby watched as she conversed with a nurse before heading back to the waiting room. She grabbed both their hands and practically dragged them with her.

"Where are you taking us?" Gabby asked and unsuccessfully tried to shake free.

"I'm not sure what's going on, but I have to get back to work," Olive said.

Mamma Pacelli ignored them both. When they reached a door, she opened it and shoved them into an office.

"I'm locking the door, and I'll let you out in thirty minutes. When I come back I want this nonsense settled." Mamma Pacelli slammed the door.

Gabby lunged forward and turned the knob. "What the hell! She actually locked us in here."

"Let me see." Olive tried to open the door.

"You didn't believe me? You had to try it yourself? Great. Now what are we supposed to do?" Gabby glanced around the tiny office. It contained a desk, two visitor chairs, a bookcase, and a window. She walked to the glass and peered outside.

"Are you going to jump?" Olive asked.

"I would if we weren't four stories high. I can't believe she did this." Gabby put her hands on her hips and glared at Olive, who was jiggling the doorknob. "I'm pretty sure it's still locked."

"At least I'm trying to do something constructive." Olive sneered.

Gabby cursed under her breath and slouched in a chair.

Olive crossed her arms and glared at Gabby. "Why do you get to sit behind the desk like you're the big boss?"

"What difference does it make?"

"You always have to be in control, don't you?"

"No, I don't!" Gabby's head throbbed, and her stomach soured even more. She bent over a trash can by the desk.

"Are you sick?" Olive sounded halfway concerned.

"Can you just stop hounding me for a second?"

What Gabby wouldn't give for a gentle back rub from Olive, not that she'd ever admit it. In fact, she wanted nothing more than to hold Olive in her arms. Just the thought of doing so warmed her heart. She hated that they were arguing, especially at a time like this.

"Nonna is a strong woman, and she's getting the best care possible," Olive said. "Try not to worry."

Gabby sat upright and attempted to steady her spinning head.

"Are you feeling better?" Olive asked.

"A little." Gabby rubbed her forehead. "Listen...I...uhh...I want to apologize for last night."

"You were right before. This isn't the time or place to—"

"No. It's the perfect time."

Saying this wouldn't be easy. Gabby wasn't used to being vulnerable and opening up to someone. But then again, this wasn't just someone. It was Olive, the most understanding, kindest woman she'd ever met.

"When your photo was unveiled," Gabby said, "I instinctively knew you'd win. It's amazing, Olive. You deserve the *Journeys* position, and I'm sorry I said otherwise. I'm sorry if I hurt you."

The corners of Olive's mouth curled upward. Gabby hadn't seen that beautiful smile and those cute dimples in much too long.

"Thank you. And I'm sorry for the things I said."

Gabby held up a hand. "You were right. I can be stubborn and controlling. But there's something you need to understand." Gabby stood and walked to the window.

She gazed outside. "For as long as I can remember, someone made all my decisions for me. I never had a say in where I lived, went to college, and especially where I worked. My family has controlled me my entire life." Gabby glanced at Olive. "I'm not saying I was a victim. I let it happen. I didn't stand up for myself. Until now. If I come on strong, it's because I'm tired of being told what to do, but maybe I go overboard sometimes."

Olive sat on the edge of the chair, listening intently. "Balance is a good thing. Particularly in relationships. I know your mamma can be bossy, but I'm not her. I don't want to put you on a leash. I want you to feel free."

Olive glanced down at her hands. "I was really hurt and angry last night, but I understand where you're coming from. I'll support whatever decision you make, even if it means losing you."

Gabby shriveled to the size of a bread crumb. Olive was Mother Teresa compared to her. Talk about selfless. She was willing to let Gabby go if that's what she wanted.

Olive looked at Gabby, tears in her eyes. "I love you, Gabby. All I want is your happiness."

Gabby's heart jumped into her throat. Olive was in love with her? She never thought three words could cause such a rush of warmth through her entire body. They both flinched when Mamma Pacelli opened the door. It couldn't have been thirty minutes already.

"It's time."

"What do you mean?" Gabby asked, but she already knew from the look on her mamma's face.

"Nonna's last words."

Shivers ran down Gabby's spine. Her grandmother was dying. This would be the last time she'd get to talk to her, see her. Tears threatened, but she had to be strong for Nonna. Gabby locked eyes with Olive, who gave her a sympathetic, reassuring nod. Gabby rushed out the door and to her grandmother's room.

Gabby approached the bed slowly, shocked by how small and fragile Nonna appeared. When Gabby touched her grandmother's hand, her eyes fluttered open, thin lips parted, but no sound came out. Gabby hoped the stroke wouldn't prevent her from speaking. Nonna had always said that a person's last words were the most important. She wanted her grandmother to have an opportunity to express her wishes, just as Gabby's father had.

Nonna raised a shaky hand and motioned for Gabby to come closer. She placed an ear next to Nonna's mouth as she whispered a phrase. Had Gabby heard correctly? As though reading her granddaughter's mind, Nonna repeated the words. Gabby straightened and gazed into her grandmother's dark eyes. She hadn't made a statement but instead asked a question. The corners of Nonna's lips quirked upward, and she closed her eyes.

Gabby rang the nurses' station and asked that they send in her mamma and sisters. Everyone gathered around the bed and held hands. No more than fifteen minutes later, Nonna took several shallow breaths before becoming completely still. Maybe Gabby was going crazy, but she could have sworn she saw a flash of sparkling white light after Nonna's last breath. It hovered for a few seconds over her grandmother's body before rising upward and dissolving into the air. Goose bumps appeared on Gabby's arms and the back of her neck. Instinctively, she knew it hadn't been her imagination. Nonna's spirit had left her tired, aged body and was now free to soar with the angels. For some reason, this thought helped ease her sadness. At that moment, Gabby made a decision to celebrate her grandmother's spirit instead of mourn the loss of her physical body.

Mamma Pacelli fingered rosary beads and recited prayers. A few of her sisters sniffled and dabbed tears, while others embraced. Gabby leaned down and kissed Nonna's forehead, mentally thanking her for the love and support she'd given. Gabby scanned the room and realized Olive was missing. She deserved to be there as much as anyone. Not wanting to disrupt her mamma's prayers, Gabby exited the room and went in search of Olive. She needed to say something important.

❖

Dread washed over Gabby when she found the waiting room empty. Maybe Olive had left. She grabbed a nurse who was passing by.

"You know the strawberry blonde who was with my family? Did you happen to see where she went?"

The nurse stared blankly until finally a light flashed across her eyes. "Oh yes. She asked for directions to the chapel. It's down the hall on the left."

Gabby practically sprinted and eagerly opened the door, scanning the room. She didn't care for churches, but this place had a nice feel to it. The room glowed in a golden light and had porcelain, life-like painted cherubs in every corner. One of them even looked like a young Nonna, with smiling ebony eyes and puffy cheeks. Gabby spotted Olive sitting in a pew, glad that she was alone.

Olive's head jerked toward Gabby when she sat beside her. "How's Nonna?"

"She didn't make it." Gabby allowed the tears to flow. Something about verbalizing it made her suddenly very sad.

"I'm so sorry." Olive threw her arms around Gabby's neck.

Gabby closed her eyes and basked in the closeness of the woman who had stolen her heart. As though realizing they were hugging, Olive quickly backed away.

"Are you okay?" Olive asked.

Gabby wiped her eyes. "I will be. I'll miss Nonna terribly, but I think she was ready to leave. She lived a long life." Gabby resisted the urge to tell Olive about seeing the light after her passing. They had plenty of time for that later. Right now, they had a more pressing topic to discuss.

"Nonna whispered her last words to me. Actually, she asked me a question. She said, 'Would you rather be right or would you rather be happy?'"

"Nonna was very wise. What was your answer?" Olive's eyes filled with apprehension.

Gabby faced Olive directly and took her hand. "I want to be happy. I want freedom. I want to pursue my dreams. And most of all, I want you." Gabby kissed the back of Olive's hand. "I'm sorry it's taken my stubborn mind time to accept it, but there's no reason we can't both be winners. I don't want to live my life without you. I want to go with you, Olive. If you'll still have me."

"Yes! I want that with all my heart." Olive cupped Gabby's face and kissed her.

Olive's emerald eyes sparkled like a jewel, love and bliss radiating from her. Gabby had always thought Olive was beautiful, but in that moment she was breathtaking, lovelier than any photo Gabby had ever taken.

The End

About the Author

Lisa Moreau is a 2017 Golden Crown Literary Society Debut Author award winner. She's an ultimate romantic and loves creating lighthearted, witty, happily-ever-after romances. When Lisa isn't writing, her favorite pastimes include perusing bookstores and hanging out at the beach.

Lisa has a bachelor's degree in journalism from Midwestern State University, TX, and has completed an indefinitely large number of creative writing courses at Santa Monica College, CA. She lives in Los Angeles for the ocean, mountains, totally awesome weather, and only occasionally thinks about moving when she feels an earthquake tremble.

Lisa can be reached at www.LisaMoreauWriter.com

Books Available from Bold Strokes Books

Change in Time by Robyn Nyx. Working in the past is hell on your future. The Extractor series: Book Two. (978-1-62639-880-1)

Love After Hours by Radclyffe. When Gina Antonelli agrees to renovate Carrie Longmire's new house, she doesn't welcome Carrie's overtures at friendship or her own unexpected attraction. A Rivers Community Novel. (978-1-63555-090-0)

Nantucket Rose by CF Frizzell. Maggie Jordan can't wait to convert an historic Nantucket home into a B&B, but doesn't expect to fall for mariner Ellis Chilton, who has more claim to the house than Maggie realizes. (978-1-63555-056-6)

Picture Perfect by Lisa Moreau. Falling in love wasn't supposed to be part of the stakes for Olive and Gabby, rival photographers in the competition of a lifetime. (978-1-62639-975-4)

Set the Stage by Karis Walsh. Actress Emilie Danvers takes the stage again in Ashland, Oregon, little realizing that landscaper Arden Philips is about to offer her a very personal romantic lead role. (978-1-63555-087-0)

Strike a Match by Fiona Riley. When their attempts at matchmaking fizzle out, firefighter Sasha and reluctant millionairess Abby find themselves turning to each other to strike a perfect match. (978-1-62639-999-0)

The Price of Cash by Ashley Bartlett. Cash Braddock is doing her best to keep her business afloat, stay out of jail, and avoid Detective Kallen. It's not working. (978-1-62639-708-8)

Under Her Wing by Ronica Black. At Angel's Wings Rescue, dogs are usually the ones saved, but when quiet Kassandra Haden meets outspoken owner Jayden Beaumont, the two stubborn women just might end up saving each other. (978-1-63555-077-1)

Underwater Vibes by Mickey Brent. When Hélène, a translator in Brussels, Belgium, meets Sylvie, a young Greek photographer and swim coach, unsettling feelings hijack Hélène's mind and body—even her poems. (978-1-63555-002-3)

A More Perfect Union by Carsen Taite. Major Zoey Granger and DC fixer Rook Daniels risk their reputations for a chance at true love while dealing with a scandal that threatens to rock the military. (978-1-62639-754-5)

Arrival by Gun Brooke. The spaceship *Pathfinder* reaches its passengers' new homeworld where danger lurks in the shadows while Pamas Seclan disembarks and finds unexpected love in young science genius Darmiya Do Voy. (978-1-62639-859-7)

Captain's Choice by VK Powell. Architect Kerstin Anthony's life is going to plan until Bennett Carlyle, the first girl she ever kissed, is assigned to her latest and most important project, a police district substation. (978-1-62639-997-6)

Falling Into Her by Erin Zak. Pam Phillips, widow at the age of forty, meets Kathryn Hawthorne, local Chicago celebrity, and it changes her life forever—in ways she hadn't even considered possible. (978-1-63555-092-4)

Hookin' Up by MJ Williamz. Will Leah get what she needs from casual hookups or will she see the love she desires right in front of her? (978-1-63555-051-1)

King of Thieves by Shea Godfrey. When art thief Casey Marinos meets bounty hunter Finnegan Starkweather, the crimes of the past just might set the stage for a payoff worth more than she ever dreamed possible. (978-1-63555-007-8)

Lucy's Chance by Jackie D. As a serial killer haunts the streets, Lucy tries to stitch up old wounds with her first love in the wake of a small town's rapid descent into chaos. (978-1-63555-027-6)

Right Here, Right Now by Georgia Beers. When Alicia Wright moves into the office next door to Lacey Chamberlain's accounting firm, Lacey is about to find out that sometimes the last person you want is exactly the person you need. (978-1-63555-154-9)

Strictly Need to Know by MB Austin. Covert operator Maji Rios will do whatever she must to complete her mission, but saving a gorgeous stranger from Russian mobsters was not in her plans. (978-1-63555-114-3)

Tailor-Made by Yolanda Wallace. Tailor Grace Henderson doesn't date clients, but when she meets gender-bending model Dakota Lane, she's tempted to throw all the rules out the window. (978-1-63555-081-8)

Time Will Tell by M. Ullrich. With the ability to time travel, Eva Caldwell will have to decide between having it all and erasing it all. (978-1-63555-088-7)

A Date to Die by Anne Laughlin. Someone is killing people close to Detective Kay Adler, who must look to her own troubled past for a suspect. There she finds more than one person seeking revenge against her. (978-1-63555-023-8)

Captured Soul by Laydin Michaels. Can Kadence Munroe save the woman she loves from a twisted killer, or will she lose her to a collector of souls? (978-1-62639-915-0)

Dawn's New Day by TJ Thomas. Can Dawn Oliver and Cam Cooper, two women who have loved and lost, open their hearts to love again? (978-1-63555-072-6)

Definite Possibility by Maggie Cummings. Sam Miller is just out for good times, but Lucy Weston makes her realize happily ever after is a definite possibility. (978-1-62639-909-9)

Eyes Like Those by Melissa Brayden. Isabel Chase and Taylor Andrews struggle between love and ambition from the writers' room on one of Hollywood's hottest TV shows. (978-1-63555-012-2)

Heart's Orders by Jaycie Morrison. Helen Tucker and Tee Owens escape hardscrabble lives to careers in the Women's Army Corps, but more than their hearts are at risk as friendship blossoms into love. (978-1-63555-073-3)

Hiding Out by Kay Bigelow. Treat Dandridge is unaware that her life is in danger from the murderer who is hunting the woman she's falling in love with, Mickey Heiden. (978-1-62639-983-9)

Omnipotence Enough by Sophia Kell Hagin. Can the tiny tool that abducted war veteran Jamie Gwynmorgan accidentally acquires help her escape an unknown enemy to reclaim her stolen life and the woman she deeply loves? (978-1-63555-037-5)

Summer's Cove by Aurora Rey. Emerson Lange moved to Provincetown to live in the moment, but when she meets Darcy Belo and her son Liam, her quest for summer romance becomes a family affair. (978-1-62639-971-6)

The Road to Wings by Julie Tizard. Lieutenant Casey Tompkins, air force student pilot, has to fly with the toughest instructor, Captain Kathryn "Hard Ass" Hardesty, fly a supersonic jet, and deal with a growing forbidden attraction. (978-1-62639-988-4)

Beauty and the Boss by Ali Vali. Ellis Renois is at the top of the fashion world, but she never expects her summer assistant Charlotte Hamner to tear her heart and her business apart like sharp scissors through cheap material. (978-1-62639-919-8)

Fury's Choice by Brey Willows. When gods walk amongst humans, can two women find a balance between love and faith? (978-1-62639-869-6)

Lessons in Desire by MJ Williamz. Can a summer love stand a four-month hiatus and still burn hot? (978-1-63555-019-1)

Lightning Chasers by Cass Sellars. For Sydney and Parker, being a couple was never what they had planned. Now they have to fight corruption, murder, and enemies hiding in plain sight just to hold on to each other. Lightning Series, Book Two. (978-1-62639-965-5)

Summer Fling by Jean Copeland. Still jaded from a breakup years earlier, Kate struggles to trust falling in love again when a summer fling with sexy young singer Jordan rocks her off her feet. (978-1-62639-981-5)

Take Me There by Julie Cannon. Adrienne and Sloan know it would be career suicide to mix business with pleasure, however tempting it is. But what's the harm? They're both consenting adults. Who would know? (978-1-62639-917-4)

The Girl Who Wasn't Dead by Samantha Boyette. A year ago, someone tried to kill Jenny Lewis. Tonight she's ready to find out who it was. (978-1-62639-950-1)

Unchained Memories by Dena Blake. Can a woman give herself completely when she's left a piece of herself behind? (978-1-62639-993-8)

Walking Through Shadows by Sheri Lewis Wohl. All Molly wanted to do was go backpacking…in her own century. (978-1-62639-968-6)

A Lamentation of Swans by Valerie Bronwen. Ariel Montgomery returns to Sea Oats to try to save her broken marriage but soon finds herself also fighting to save her own life and catch a murderer. (978-1-62639-828-3)

Freedom to Love by Ronica Black. What happens when the woman who spent her lifetime worrying about caring for her family, finally finds the freedom to love without borders? (978-1-63555-001-6)

House of Fate by Barbara Ann Wright. Two women must throw off the lives they've known as a guardian and an assassin and save two rival houses before their secrets tear the galaxy apart. (978-1-62639-780-4)

Planning for Love by Erin Dutton. Could true love be the one thing that wedding coordinator Faith McKenna didn't plan for? (978-1-62639-954-9)

Sidebar by Carsen Taite. Judge Camille Avery and her clerk, attorney West Fallon, agree on little except their mutual attraction, but can their relationship and their careers survive a headline-grabbing case? (978-1-62639-752-1)

Sweet Boy and Wild One by T. L. Hayes. When Rachel Cole meets soulful singer Bobby Layton at an open mic, she is immediately in thrall. What she soon discovers will rock her world in ways she never imagined. (978-1-62639-963-1)

To Be Determined by Mardi Alexander and Laurie Eichler. Charlie Dickerson escapes her life in the US to rescue Australian wildlife with Pip Atkins, but can they save each other? (978-1-62639-946-4)

True Colors by Yolanda Wallace. Blogger Robby Rawlins plans to use First Daughter Taylor Crenshaw to get ahead, but she never planned on falling in love with her in the process. (978-1-62639-927-3)

Unexpected by Jenny Frame. When Dale McGuire falls for Rebecca Harper, the mother of the son she never knew she had, will Rebecca's troubled past stop them from making the family they both truly crave? (978-1-62639-942-6)